LA

They murdered for money, they killed for love, and sometimes wantonly butchered for reasons no other human mind will ever understand. A sisterhood of mayhem, a sorority of murder, they are the women who now wait on the death rows of state prisons across America. They wait for the hour they will face the terror of a final walk to their doom and pay the awesome penalty their crimes have earned—death.

LADIES WHO KILL

Tom Kuncl and Paul Einstein

PINNACLE BOOKS
WINDSOR PUBLISHING CORP.

PINNACLE BOOKS

are published by

Windsor Publishing Corp.
475 Park Avenue South
New York, NY 10016

Second printing: June 1989

Printed in the United States of America

Acknowledgments

THE AUTHORS WISH to gratefully acknowledge the assistance provided by the following newspapers, their publishers, editorial management, staff reporters, photographers, and librarians, who so generously assisted us in the preliminary research and subsequent development of the materials contained in this book. The quality and thoroughness of the coverage these publications provided their readers as the drama of the cases presented in this book unfolded in their individual communities reminded us once more of what F. B. Sanborn said about the great newspaper tradition of our nation: "The careful reader of a few good newspapers can learn more in a year than most scholars do in their great libraries." Our thanks go to the *Florida Times-Union* and the *Jacksonville Journal* of Jacksonville, Florida; the *Charlotte News and Observer* of Charlotte, North Carolina; the *Tuscaloosa News* of Tuscaloosa, Alabama; the *Tulsa World* of Tulsa, Oklahoma; the *Sun* and the *Daily Herald* of Biloxi, Mississippi; the *Cincinnati Enquirer* of Cincinnati, Ohio; the *Nevada State Journal* and the *Reno Evening Gazette* of Reno, Nevada; the *Idaho Press-Tribune* of Nampa, Idaho; the *Vindicator* of Youngstown, Ohio; the *Rome News-Tribune* of Rome, Georgia; the *Dalton Daily Citizen-News* of Dalton, Georgia, and the editors of *True Detective* magazine. Our very special thanks to Pat Vail, chief of research, Worldcom News Group, for her invaluable assistance.

LADIES WHO KILL

Chapter 1

Janice Buttrum

MOODY CONNELL KEPT HOPING someone would cover the girl up with a blanket, a bed sheet, anything that might offer her some small, final dignity.

He had been to more than his share of crime scenes in Whitfield County over the years and had grown that extra layer of skin that God is sometimes good enough to give newsmen, cops, and coroners; that thin and fragile wall that helps you on the days when your job makes you stare straight into the cold, wide eyes of madness.

But there was no shield impregnable enough to protect Moody Connell from the horror that waited that morning inside room 254 at the Country Boy Inn, just south of Dalton, Georgia, near the Carbondale exit, off I-75.

The pretty teenaged girl lay spread-eagled on her back on the dingy green carpet. A wide pool of her congealing blood screamed up like an obscenity. The light blue fabric of her pajama top was gathered up about her neck and shoulders. Her slim arms spread out at angles of unanswered supplication. A light, still burning in the small bathroom near which she lay, threw a grotesque, votive flicker on the nakedness of her slashed torso and legs.

Connell stepped out of the room and braced himself against the cold aluminum railing of the seedy motel's second-floor cement walkway. He tried to clear his mind with deep drafts of the September morning air, but even the sweet scent of Georgia pine didn't help on that late summer

1980 morning. The carnage he'd seen behind the door
would never leave his mind.

Inside, the crime-lab crew had nearly finished taking the
exact measurements and cruel photos that would become
the official diary of the young girl's brutal murder. An inch-
by-inch search for latent fingerprints had already begun in
the room. Connell could hear the soft, red-clay voice of
Whitfield County Coroner Leon Helton apprising Sheriff
Jack Davis of what little could be determined just then.

"Doc Metcalf will have to tell you for certain, but I'd say
there are close to a hundred stab wounds. They're all over
the body. I never saw anything like it," Helton told Jack
Davis.

"From the lividity, my guess would be that she's been
dead six hours or so, but don't hold me to that exactly."

Sheriff Jack Davis felt the muscles in his jaw tightening
and a film of ice gathering near his heart. He looked again at
the wide-open eyes of the pretty teenager and shuddered at
the thought of what they must have seen until, mercifully,
their power to see anything had dimmed and died.

"The thing between her legs—do we know what that is?"
Davis asked, almost hesitantly, of Helton.

"Plastic . . . cylindrical . . . forced into the vagina
with a great deal of thrust. I can't tell exactly what it
is as yet," Helton answered haltingly. "The autopsy
should. . . ."

Chief Deputy Ray Swanson entered room 254 in time to
help the coroner's crew gently pick up the body of the young
girl from the floor and place it on the crisp white sheets of
the ambulance gurney. Now they reached over to fold her
arms. Leon Helton felt the glacial coldness of the girl's
hands. Jack Davis saw the slim bands of pale skin on her
fingers. She had been wearing rings. He made a mental
note.

They covered the girl with several sheets before the body
was taken from the room to the ambulance waiting below.
Moody Connell's vigil was over for now. There was a story

to be written for the next edition of the *Dalton Daily Citizen-News*. It would be unusual for the city editor of the newspaper to be filing the copy. It was only by accident that Moody Connell had been at the sheriff's office when the first report of the murder came in. But Moody Connell was certain of one thing. He was staying with this story, no matter what. Some kind of hound from hell had visited Dalton, Georgia, the night before and had wreaked the bloody nightmare in room 254. Moody Connell wanted to know the name of that beast and to see it caged like the wild animal it was.

Deputy Ray Swanson handed the small motel registration card to Sheriff Jack Davis. The handwriting was girlish, sweetly feminine, but the strokes were strong and bold and filled with young life. Davis read the information aloud.

"Demetra Faye Parker . . . 704 Maple Heights . . . Kenton, Tennessee."

Davis' eye quickly took in the rest of the information on the registration card. It indicated that her mother, Barbara Parker, of the same address, was the person to be notified in the event of an emergency. It also noted the guest was the owner of a 1964 Buick, and gave the Tennessee license plate numbers.

"Check the parking area real quick and see if that Buick is parked down there someplace," Jack Davis ordered deputies.

Davis copied down the phone number in Kenton and felt himself let go of a long sigh. "I'd better call the girl's momma," he said softly. "Lord, I wish I didn't have to."

Jack Davis checked his watch as he stepped outside the room. It was nearly noon. Below, small knots of people had gathered in the parking lot of the Country Boy Inn, drawn by the unusual hubbub of ambulances and Whitfield County sheriff's cruisers summoned to the crime scene. Davis watched as his investigators worked their way through the small groups, taking time to question everyone. Word had reached down to the deputies about what had taken place in

the motel room upstairs. Davis felt a taut satisfaction at the
way the deputies were checking everyone out. That was the
approach he wanted for his investigation. No detail was
going to be too small, no effort too large until whoever had
done that to the girl in room 254 was behind bars.

As Davis made his way down the motel stairs toward his
own cruiser, two deputies flagged him down. They had in
tow the manager of the motel, a Mr. Chandrankant Patel.

The deputies were Captain Don Gribble and David
Gordon, two of the investigators around which Davis had
built the sheriff's detective unit. They were a pair of
Georgia-born bloodhounds, and in the hour that had passed
since the discovery of the body of Demetra Parker, they had
already given the impression they were ten men, not two. It
had seemed to onlookers as though the two investigators
had been everywhere at once, swarming over the rundown
transient motel at the edge of town like men possessed.
Each had a sheaf of notes in his hands. Davis could sense
their determination as they led the motel manager toward
his squad car.

Gordon introduced the nervous motel manager to Davis.
At the same time he handed the sheriff another room
registration card he had picked up from the manager only
minutes before.

"It looks like we might have something here, Jack,"
Gordon said. "This pair sneaked out of here early this
morning without saying a word. Just left the key behind.

"Several witnesses said they'd seen the man hanging
around outside the victim's room, and we've got another
one says he thinks he saw them tear off outa here this
morning in her car."

Davis quickly scanned the information on the card.

"Mr. & Mrs. Danny Buttrum," it read.

The address given was in Adairsville, Georgia, a town
not too far from Dalton.

"Get hold of somebody at the Bartow County Sheriff's

office," Jack Davis snapped tersely. "See if they can give us a line on these people.

"Then get a pickup out on that Buick. Maybe they still got it," he added.

"The woman's name is Janice," Captain Don Gribble added, glancing down at the notes he had taken. "She's apparently his wife. People say she looked pretty young. They had a kid with them also. Probably not more than a two-year-old."

"What room were they in, Don?" Jack Davis queried.

"Two forty-three. Just a couple doors down from the girl's room," Gribble replied.

"And here's something that'll break your heart," Gribble added sadly. "The young Parker girl was going to check out this morning. She was apparently going to stay with relatives of her boyfriend."

The manager of the motel broke into the conversation.

"That's why I went down to her room about eleven to check," the manager said. "She hadn't come by the office. That wasn't like her. When I went up to the room, I found her . . . like that. . . ."

Jack Davis headed back to the Whitfield County Sheriff's office. He picked up the telephone and made the call he had dreaded making.

Cigarette butts and half-filled cups of tasteless coffee had started to pile up in Jack Davis' office. It was nearly midnight now. Gribble and Gordon looked bushed. They hadn't let up for a minute since the body of nineteen-year-old Demetra Parker had been discovered. Now they both had folders in front of them, filled with the efforts of their relentless investigation. Jack Davis had pages of his own notes he'd been making all through the day. It was time to take a look at the pieces of the puzzle. They poured themselves cups of fresh-brewed coffee. It still tasted bitter.

Whitfield County Prosecutor Steve Williams had stopped by to check on developments in the case. Moody Connell had commandeered a typewriter at a desk outside Jack Davis' office, adding new leads and revised paragraphs to the main body of the story he had earlier hammered out for the *Citizen-News*.

Piece by piece, the investigators now reviewed what was known about the death of Demetra Parker and what was known about her life before it was so brutally snuffed out by a murdering sex maniac. A growing file of data had accumulated on the man the investigators were now almost certain had something to do with that sickening and senseless death. Danny Buttrum had come to the attention of Georgia law enforcement before, but not in any spectacular way. His prior conviction record lay on the table with the other information now flowing into the sheriff's investigation division. It was strange. You wouldn't have guessed him for a killing like this.

"Buttrum's about twenty-eight years old," Captain Don Gribble said.

"He's a walkaway from the Cobb County Work Farm. There's a warrant out on him. They'd given him a term as a habitual offender. Seems as though he's had three drunk driving charges in a pretty short patch of time.

"We don't exactly know what he was doing up here staying at the Country Boy, but someone says they thought he may have been working up at the truck stop, changing tires. We're checking that out.

"He's been a pill popper. Uses speed, when he can get it. Apparently he's not real bright. Word is that his wife runs his head. Don't know much about her just yet, except that she's some younger than him. Best guess is she's only about eighteen.

"The baby's pretty young, about nineteen months. We've got a witness who says the Parker girl met the Buttrums a week or so back when they moved into the motel.

"She was real fond of youngsters and made a real fuss over the baby. She gave the mother and father a few rides around town on errands because they didn't have a car to go pick up food and such for the baby," Deputy Dave Gordon added.

Steve Williams asked if the autopsy report had come in yet. Sheriff Jack Davis nodded grimly and pushed it across the table to the county prosecutor.

"It'll make you want to upchuck, what he did to that girl," Davis said. "I don't think there's ever been a murder like this in Whitfield County. Not ever."

Williams read through the pages written by County Medical Examiner Dr. James Metcalf. He wondered if his face looked as ashen as it felt as he read the examiner's report.

There were ninety-seven separate stab wounds, the report said. Repeated patterns of wounds were clustered in the area of the face, neck, breasts, abdomen, and legs. Another savage group of wounds surrounded the vaginal area. Stab wounds to the hands indicated the victim had tried to ward off her attacker. A deep slash of almost eight inches crossed the abdomen area sharply. It had almost laid open the intestines. She had been struck in the nose and other areas of the face by what appeared to be blows from a hand. Her lips were bruised.

The victim had been raped. Trauma to the rectal tissue indicated she had also been sodomized. The plastic object that had been rammed into the vagina proved, upon removal, to be the base part or holding stand of an electric toothbrush, probably belonging to the victim. It measured approximately eight inches in length. The object had probably been introduced into the rectum also before being lodged in the vagina.

Zipper burns on the upper torso were probably the result of the victim's attempting to free herself from the strong grip the assailant had on the fabric of the loose-fitting pajama tops. The bottoms of the pajamas had been found thrown on the floor of the room. It did not appear the victim had been wearing underclothing beneath the nightwear. Bruises to the lips indicated the assailant may have clamped his hand over the victim's mouth to prevent any outcry, but the repeated stab wounds to the neck area may also have rendered the victim unable to cry out for help, the report theorized. Several of the stabs had reached the heart. The weapon was probably small-bladed—perhaps a pocket knife.

Williams felt his hands trembling in horror and outrage as he placed the medical examiner's report back on the sheriff's desk.

"It took that poor child a long time to die," Jack Davis said. "It could have been as much as an hour. What kind of animal you suppose did something like that?"

"A kind we can't have on the loose," Steve Williams answered, sharing a thought that had haunted the veteran lawmen all through that day.

While the lights burned through the night in Sheriff Jack Davis' office, investigators from his department checked out every lead that turned up in their search for Danny Buttrum and his young wife.

One team of investigators had been assigned to visit Buttrum's mother in adjacent Bartow County. She had proved uncooperative. Why were they hounding Danny? When they told her, the woman's face registered honest disbelief. "Danny would never do anything like that," she said, "unless . . . unless Janice had talked him into it."

Within a few hours of that visit to her home by Whitfield deputies, the saddened mother of Danny Buttrum reached for a telephone and called the office of Jack Davis.

She had just heard from Danny, she said. He had called from Pensacola, Florida. He wouldn't tell her what he was doing there. He wanted her to wire him some money, in care of Western Union. He needed it badly and he would pay her back, the way he always had. No, he wasn't in any kind of trouble, he told her. But the mother knew better. She knew her son. He was in trouble.

The FBI agents who placed Danny and Janice Buttrum under arrest in Pensacola several hours later were prepared for anything. The violence of the young girl's death in Georgia was keenly in their minds. They would take no chances. The Buick bearing the Tennessee plates was found in a restaurant parking lot near the Pensacola Western Union office. In the back seat, Danny Buttrum slept soundly, his nineteen-month-old baby daughter cuddled up at his side. The agents waited until Janice Buttrum had finished her sandwich and exited the small café. She struggled furiously to free herself from the handcuffs the agents clamped firmly on her wrists. She screamed at them that they were making some terrible kind of mistake.

Danny and Janice told the FBI agents a farfetched story about how they came to be driving the dead girl's car.

Agent Fred Faul asked Janice to explain why a driver's license and credit cards in the name of Demetra Parker had been found in her purse.

Then Janice Buttrum began to tell the story of how the pretty teenager from Tennessee had died. In another room, Danny Buttrum offered his own version.

The FBI men sat in shocked silence as Janice described in sickening detail the death of Demetra Parker.

"Here. You might as well take this too," Janice said as stenographers wrote down the details of her confession. Janice slipped off a ring she admitted having taken from the dead girl's hand. She threw it on the table as though it was of no further concern to her. The sound it made falling on the table echoed through the hushed room.

Sheriff Jack Davis and two investigators had driven with their feet all the way down to the floor on their way to Pensacola once the news of the successful capture had been relayed to them.

The Buttrums were brought back separately. Florida officials had taken into court-approved foster care the child Janice had admitted had been with them in the victim's room as a mute and uncomprehending witness on the night Demetra Parker was raped, tortured, and murdered. Jack Davis remembers today the almost unreal lack of emotion shown by Janice Buttrum on the long ride back to Dalton.

"She said she wasn't sorry about anything much," Davis recalled. "She said it sure had taken that girl a long time to die. She was talking about the death of that young woman with no more emotion than you'd use to order your morning breakfast. She was evil. I don't think I'd ever met anyone that evil before."

The arrest of Danny and Janice Buttrum nearly turned the small town of Dalton upside down.

"There were death threats made against him," Moody Connell remembers. "At that time no one knew how much of a role she had played in the murder or there probably would have been more threats against her," Connell recalled.

"They had extra guards on them every time they moved them for a hearing or an examination. Feelings were definitely running high in the area. There really was a chance that something could have happened to them. People were riled. They were plenty angry," he added.

Dalton is a small town, but a busy one. While only 17,000 people live in the bustling little city, workers from all over a several-county area commute into the town and its outskirts every day to work at one of many carpet mills. There are a half dozen places like the Country Boy Inn, sagging old motels past their prime, that rent out rooms by the week and month to newly employed mill hands who stay in the places only long enough to find a small apartment or a house to rent in a better part of town.

Demetra Parker had moved into her room at the Country Boy Inn only a short time before her death. She had found work on the third shift at one of the mills, in the bindery of the sample room.

She was a beautiful girl. No doubt about that. But she was nice as could be too. She'd made a lot of friends at the mill. Demetra had a steady boyfriend. That was one of the reasons she had moved up to Dalton in the first place. She wanted to be near him, and she wanted to work for a year before enrolling in college the following autumn.

Demetra's bubbling personality and her lithe good looks made her more noticeable than the average tenant at the Country Boy Inn. And now, as sheriff's detectives continued their quizzing of every guest in the motel to complete their case against Danny Buttrum and his wife, bizarre stories began to be told. Many of those stories were also being circulated in the town, and with each new revelation, anger against the pair in custody mounted.

A young man named Leon Busby recalled that on the night of the murder he had taken Danny and Janice Buttrum for a ride. They drank a few beers and then, strangely, Danny asked Busby if he knew where they could find a girl who wanted a little loving.

"What would your wife think about that?" Busby asked Danny, trying to speak softly so that Janice, in the back seat with the baby, would not hear.

"She wouldn't give a damn—just as long as she could have the girl first," Danny answered with a laugh.

Another story made the rounds of Dalton. Janet had run across Demetra Parker a few days before the murder in a laundromat near the motel. Janice asked the surprised girl if she would be interested in having sex with her. The story went that Janice exploded in anger when the shocked girl brusquely turned her down.

Others had heard Janice complain that Danny had been wildly smitten when he first saw Demetra Parker and that he was following the girl around like some lovesick puppy. The way Janice had told the story, the pretty young girl was encouraging Danny. The mere thought would have been funny if it hadn't been for the hate that filled Janice Buttrum's eyes when she told the story.

Janice had an angry fight with Danny over the foolish way he was acting about the girl in the room down the hall. The dowdy-looking Janice was now pregnant with the couple's second child, and the thought of Danny mooning over that other girl made Janice lash out cruelly about how ridiculous it was of him to think Demetra Parker would have anything to do with an illiterate loser like him.

"Danny smacked me around pretty bad the other night," Janice had told the few other guests in the motel who were willing to listen to her problems.

On the night of Tuesday, September 3, 1980, after the ride with Leon Busby, Danny Buttrum had managed to get his hands on some speed. He was washing them down with beer in the dingy room at the Country Boy Inn. Janice had joined him in the impromptu bash, matching him drink for drink, but she stayed away from the amphetamines because of the baby she was carrying. Before long they were both pretty stoned. Danny started talking again about the girl in the room down the hall. Janice felt her anger starting to mount once more, but kept her silence. She didn't want another beating from Danny. It may have been three o'clock in the morning, or maybe it was four. Neither Danny nor Janice could remember exactly when deputies interrogated them later. But one thing was certain. Now both Danny and Janice had Demetra Parker on their minds.

"They would both tell different stories, later, about who did exactly what," Steve Williams, the county prosecutor, would recall. "But as we finally put it all together it became clear they had both been involved in the very savage murder of the girl."

It was Janice who knocked on the door of room 254 in the middle of the night. She carried the baby, Marlena, lightly on her hip. It took several minutes to rouse the sleeping girl inside, and before she opened the door she wanted to know who was there.

"I just need a cigarette," Janice answered. "We're all out. Can you let me in for a minute? I've got the baby with me. It's cold out here."

Demetra Parker smiled when she saw the baby. She put her arms out as if to take it from the mother when Danny Buttrum propelled himself through the now open door, grabbing hold of the startled victim, throwing her to the floor in his drugged frenzy.

"Demetra was fighting very hard to get herself out of

Danny's grasp," Steve Williams recounted. "Janice put the baby down on the bed and rushed to help Danny subdue the terrified girl.

"Together, they ripped the bottom of her pajamas off and Danny raped the girl while Janice helped hold her down, holding a knife to her throat. He told her to stop kicking and fighting, but she wouldn't. They used the pocket knife and began stabbing her in the face and neck."

Janice was angered by the fight the wounded girl was putting up. She took the knife back from Danny and began stabbing the girl more fiercely. Danny turned the bleeding girl over then and sodomized her while Janice continued to make stabbing cuts in the weakened body of Demetra Parker.

"Even after all that, the victim was still alive," Steve Williams said.

Danny Buttrum staggered back onto his feet. He went into the small bathroom of room 254. He picked up a pale lemon washcloth that belonged to the girl he had just savaged. He washed the blood from his hands.

"He said he could see back into the room from the mirror," Williams added.

Janice was still stabbing at the breasts of the girl with the knife. At the same time her head was between the victim's legs. She was performing oral sex as the girl lay dying.

"Danny said he saw her make a long, deep cut across the girl's stomach. When she lifted her face up from between the girl's legs, it was covered with blood."

Danny would tell deputies he was frightened when Janice came into the small bathroom and rummaged through Demetra's belongings, before her eyes fell on an electric toothbrush standing on the counter near the sink.

"She went back to the dying girl and abused her with the toothbrush holder. Desecration is too pale a word. The things she was doing were just plain perverted and sadistic," Williams said.

Death finally came for Demetra Parker. Danny Buttrum

remembered hearing Janice laugh as she slipped the ring from the dead girl's hand. "She doesn't look so pretty now, does she?" Janice said.

Now Janice made a methodical inventory of the room. She poked through Demetra's possessions. She was particularly fascinated by the girl's large wardrobe. She picked up numerous items of the slain girl's apparel. Not many of them would properly fit her, but Janice took them anyway.

By the time the Buttrums were ready to be arraigned for the brutal murder of the pretty young woman from Tennessee, some of those details of the girl's cruel death had also made the rounds as gossip in small-town Dalton.

Moody Connell wrote a tender page-one profile about Demetra Parker for the September 9 edition of the *Daily Citizen-News*.

"Murder Victim Was Quiet, Friendly Girl," the main headline read. A one-column picture of the dead girl leaped out from the front page. Her eyes were wide and down-home friendly. Her smile was genuine. A cascade of lush auburn hair framed her slim face. The photo was taken for the 1979 Kenton High School yearbook, and the story that went with it would have summoned tears from a stone.

Demetra had been a contestant in a recent beauty pageant, Connell's story said. On the night before her murder, she had spent a half hour on the phone with her mother up in Tennessee. She had planned to drive home for a brief visit that weekend. She had just turned nineteen in July, and as her half brother, Ewell Anderson, told the newspaper's city editor, "She was just a normal teenager. She wanted to get out of the atmosphere of a small farming community for a while.

"She was raised in a Christian atmosphere and sang in the choir at the Second Baptist Church," Anderson was quoted as saying. She had never so much as received a traffic ticket in the small west Tennessee town where she had grown up. If she had any shortcomings at all, it was that she tended to be too naive sometimes, too trusting of strangers. Hundreds of people had attended the somber last rites for the fun-loving youngster, crowding the funeral home beyond capacity. Her mother recalled Demetra mentioning she had met a young couple, somewhat down on their luck, who had the most adorable baby. She had told her mom she had tried to help the young couple. That was the kind of person she was, the mother told the newspaper man.

To the two attorneys who had been appointed to represent the Buttrums, the Connell story was just one more example of the inflamed public opinion in Whitfield County which they believed would make a fair trial impossible for their clients.

Greg Melton and Steve Fain did what they knew they had to do. They petitioned the court first for a gag order that would prevent further leaks and disclosure of evidence in the case. At the same time, they filed a unique civil motion that would ban news reporters from gathering further information and disseminating it until calm was restored to the community.

The lawyers for the defense then demanded that they be permitted to employ psychiatric experts to determine the competency of Danny and Janice to assist in their own defense.

Melton and Fain fired off a flurry of other motions that seemed alien to small-town, Deep South Dalton, but among community leaders there were expressions of quiet satisfaction that the Buttrums were being given a first-rate defense against the background of noisy threats aimed at the couple. The case had begun to attract national attention, and Dalton did not want to present some distorted, red-neck image to the rest of the nation.

The motions that Fain and Melton raised were patiently heard in the courts. The gag order was not issued, but some parts of the testimony in early proceedings were held behind closed doors, with edited versions of the testimony released by the presiding judges to insure that an unbiased panel of

jurors might be found. The motions to obtain independent
psychiatric evaluations of the Buttrums at public expense
were denied, but an appeal by the attorneys for help brought
forward mental health experts who offered their services
without cost.

The crucial issue of the Buttrums' mental competency
was hard fought. The courts had ruled that examinations
conducted by doctors at the Central State Mental Hospital in
Milledgeville would produce impartial findings regarding
the competency question.

The psychiatric tests were conducted by Dr. Timothy
Bullard and Dr. Juan Perez. Their findings were then
reviewed by Dr. Henry Adams, a research professor of
psychology at the University of Georgia in Athens.

The testimony given by the doctors concluded that the
Buttrums were competent to stand trial for the murder of
Demetra Parker.

"They knew what they were doing when they killed that
girl and then tried to run away," Prosecutor Williams
thundered during the competency hearing. "They remembered every sickening, graphic detail."

The issue of competency had been one thing, but as the
psychiatrists probed the minds of Danny and Janice Buttrum, a painting on a larger canvas appeared. When the
charges of murder were finally presented to two separate
juries, after nearly a year of legal wrangling, the psychiatric
experts would play an even larger role as the small-town
men and women empaneled to weigh the fate of the couple
wrestled with the question of whether they were dealing
with people who really *did* understand the difference
between right and wrong.

A parade of experts who had encountered Danny and
Janice on their troubled road to adulthood now testified that
both of them had been children with little going for them in
life. Danny's IQ tested at about 70. His was a borderline
intelligence at best. He developed alcohol problems while
still a boy. He was easily led, easily duped, and often

victimized by people who would pay him almost nothing to do a man's job, then laugh behind his back. When he combined the alcohol with amphetamines, Danny Buttrum sometimes didn't know if he was on planet Earth, or somewhere else. He'd been charged three times with driving while intoxicated, but he'd probably driven a car, stoned out of his mind, more times than anyone could count.

Parts of Janice's history were vague. Social workers thought she may have been bartered away, or if not, given away shortly after her birth by an alcoholic, unwed mother. The couple who took the child in were little better, according to those same workers. She grew up in an alcoholic atmosphere, and there were undocumented allegations of early sexual abuse.

Concerned agency officials had taken charge of Janice on different occasions and in several instances kept her in their own homes. They wanted Janice to be exposed to a normal environment for at least a brief period, to help her resist the wallow of despair they feared she was sinking into.

Janice had told the psychiatrists of her early years. The woman who raised her reminded her continually that her own mother had been a no-good and that Janice was certain to grow up to be just like her. She was an awkward kid and not very pretty at all. She could never remember being invited to go to a birthday party. She had no friends. Janice remembered particularly a day on which her foster parents had taken her to a landfill where old clothes had been thrown away. They rummaged through the heaps until they found several items of clothing they said would be okay for her to wear when school opened a few days later.

At fourteen, Janice went to bed with two roustabouts from a nearby town. Both were in their late twenties, and they used the girl badly. She didn't care, Janice had said. At least they pretended they loved her, even if it was just for one night.

Janice was fifteen when she met Danny Buttrum. He

offered to take her away from the home she hated so much. She didn't think twice. They were married by an obliging justice of the peace outside Adairsville. The little girl was born the next year.

As Dr. Henry Adams pored over the thick sheaf of reports compiled by Drs. Bullard and Perez, prior to offering his opinions in the courtroom, he was struck again and again by the sharp contrast between Janice Buttrum and her victim, Demetra Parker.

"When you looked at it in that light, you began to understand where the savagery came from on the night of the murder," Dr. Adams remembers. "She was so full of anger. Demetra Parker was every beautiful thing that Janice Buttrum never was, and never would be.

"The murdered girl had a warm and loving family. She was exceptionally pretty. She had friends, a steady job, a car, and money to buy clothes with. When she put on nice clothes, people gave her admiring glances. No matter what Janice Buttrum wore, no one would take a second notice.

"Janice Buttrum took one look at Demetra Parker and wanted her to die. And she wanted to be the person that did it. She egged Danny Buttrum on.

"The sexually sadistic things she did to her victim had a very real purpose in her mind, even though she might not have been able to articulate them," Dr. Adams continued.

"She wanted to humiliate that girl, to degrade her in the most vile ways imaginable. That's what the brutal sex was about, that's why she forced the object into the victim's vagina. She wanted to desecrate that girl. She wanted to destroy something she could never be.

"Janice Buttrum is an extremely rare creature. She is a genuine sexual sadist. I believe her primary mode of obtaining sexual gratification had become acts of perversion committed on an unwilling female victim.

"Taking the dead girl's ring and wearing it and stealing articles of her clothing and wearing them were acts filled with symbolism as well," Dr. Adams stated.

"She was taking on the characteristics of a beautiful woman, in her mind, by wearing those objects."

Dr. Bullard did not believe a diagnosis of sexual sadism was completely justified.

"She had been involved in some rough sexual play with Danny on occasion, but in my judgment, she was still essentially heterosexual," Bullard says.

"But somewhere in her mind a connection between sex and violence had been growing. Janice had told of some sexual encounters with women in her past, but they had not focused on violence.

"My hunch is that the alcohol she was drinking that night loosened her inhibitions. Once the attack began on the girl, perhaps some fantasies she'd had in the past came to the foreground.

"What was happening in that room may have taken on a life of its own. Later, she could tell me with complete clarity what she had done to the girl, but she couldn't tell me why," Bullard remembers.

"Janice admitted her role in the killing. She never admitted that she was the instigator, or that it was she, in fact, who first stabbed the victim, but my hunch was that she had been.

"I asked Janice why she had stabbed the girl so many times. We were exploring a little-understood theory that the actual act of stabbing may have been a form of sexual relief.

"Her answer was that the knife had just been too small, and that the girl just wouldn't die."

Bullard remembers a long conversation with Janice in which he tried to gauge her emotional response to the death of the Parker girl now that some time had passed.

"She had no feelings at all for the victim. There was no indication of remorse. My judgment is that part of that lack of feeling was a simple denial that anything had ever happened. She couldn't show remorse for something she wasn't ready to face as a real thing that happened."

Dr. Bullard agreed that Janice's theft of the victim's ring

and clothing were part of some warped transference of qualities taking place in the murderer's mind.

"She came from a very poor background. Those little trinkets wouldn't have meant much to anyone else, but they conveyed special meanings to Janice," Dr. Bullard said.

The state psychologist said he came away from his hours of interviews with Janice feeling sad about her fate.

"You couldn't say that Janice Buttrum wasn't legally responsible for her crime, because she was. But you also could see how she got there. In many ways Janice Buttrum had been a victim too," Bullard said.

On one aspect of Janice Buttrum's mental state, the experts were in complete accord. If Janice had not been apprehended so swiftly, there was an almost certain chance she would have killed again in a sexually sadistic assault.

"She said her attack on the Parker girl had really turned her on," Dr. Adams recounted. "It scared me to death.

"I don't believe there is a doubt in the world she would have done it again. She had begun to find her real sexual self in the violence and the blood. There was no way she could easily have turned that off. It's possible she might have responded to treatment, but it would have been a long road," the psychology professor added.

It was Danny Buttrum who went on trial for his life first in the slaying case that had so stirred Whitfield County.

The defense battled without ceasing to save Danny Buttrum's life. At one point it dropped a bombshell by introducing a letter the attorneys said had been written by Janice.

In the letter Janice claimed it had been she who goaded Danny into the murder because of her jealousy of the Parker girl.

The lawyers argued that Danny Buttrum had a mind that on the best of days couldn't fully cope with the world around him, and when it was fueled by drugs he was not responsible for what happened.

Prosecutor Steve Williams answered that no one had

poured alcohol down Danny's throat and that the slaying had been "a cold, methodical, and torturous act." The jury returned in only thirty minutes with a verdict of guilty in the case of Danny Buttrum. Later, it would recommend his death in the electric chair, a sentence the judge imposed on him.

Demetra Parker had been in her grave almost a year to the day when Janice Buttrum was brought to the Whitfield County Courthouse to stand trial for her role in the murder.

Prosecutor Steve Williams had already determined he would seek the death penalty for Janice Buttrum.

"She was cold. She was calculating. She was mean and perverted. In my mind she was a butcher and a murderer who didn't have the slightest regret about what she had done," Williams says.

"I believe it was she who put Danny Buttrum up to helping her kill that girl, and as far as this community was concerned, she deserved to die for her crime every bit as much as her husband did."

Steve Fain threw every ounce of his energy and legal skills into the task of saving Janice Buttrum from the electric chair.

Fain pointed the blame at Danny, arguing that Janice had lived in fear of his beatings. He told the jury that a sentence of death would mean that Janice could never again see and hug her two little children. The second child, also a girl, had been born while Janice was held in custody. Both children had been placed in the homes of Danny's relatives.

But the letter that Janice had earlier written, taking the blame in hopes that it might mean life for Danny, now came home to roost.

Fain argued that she had only written it to save the life of a man she still loved, but the jury seemed unswayed.

Williams was relentless in his summation to the jury. If Janice Buttrum had shown no mercy for Demetra Parker, Steve Williams would show her no mercy now.

"Many criminals escape punishment. None of their victims ever do," Williams said.

He quoted at length from former U.S. Attorney General Griffin Bell.

"We're just not tough enough or strong enough to have a safe society.

"We're constantly wringing our hands about what we can do to rehabilitate people and place them on probation and worry very little about the victims of crime."

Some people deserve to die, he charged. Janice Buttrum was one of them.

The jury that found Janice Buttrum guilty had deliberated slightly less than forty-five minutes.

While Janice had not taken the stand on her own behalf, Fain now brought her to the witness chair as the jury reconvened to consider its recommendation of life or death.

Janice remained emotionless as Fain gently led her through a recitation of her unhappy life. She said she was now sorry about the death of Demetra Parker.

Steve Williams then had a chance to cross-examine Janice Buttrum on oath. Janice Buttrum did not fare well under the lash of his angry questions.

"Didn't you hear her screams as you were killing her?" Williams demanded.

"Yes, sir," Janice answered softly.

"Didn't you think she was hurt when she was screaming?" Williams demanded again.

"I don't know," Janice answered.

"At one point she started talking baby talk on the stand. I still don't know what the point of that was. I don't think it fooled the jury," Williams recalls today.

The jury that had heard the pleas for Janice Buttrum's life returned in two hours with a recommendation to the judge that she be sentenced to death.

Superior Court Judge Charles Pannel paused several times as he set the date of execution. The sound of Janice Buttrum's sobbing keened loudly in the packed courtroom.

At the back of the room, Barbara and Ray Parker lowered their heads as they heard the verdict pronounced.

Outside, Moody Connell approached the parents of the victim and asked their reaction to the verdicts against the Buttrums.

"I prayed immediately for the souls of Janice and Danny Buttrum," Mrs. Parker said. She recounted to Connell that when she had checked into the Passport Inn Motel several days earlier, she had found the motel room Bible on a nightstand opened to the thirty-seventh chapter of Psalms.

"The wicked should not be envied their position in life," one of the verses read. "They will fade away like grass and disappear."

It was prison chaplain Billy Joe Gibson who found Danny Buttrum hanging in his cell a week later.

Danny had used a sheet to hang himself. Gibson noted the time at 1:04 A.M., as he helped another jailer cut Danny down. Sheriff Jack Davis awakened Janice in her cell in the women's section at the other end of the Community Correctional Center. He told her that Danny was dead.

Danny had asked Gibson to deliver a note to Janice just the day before. It had contained no hint that he planned to take his own life. On the Sunday prior to his death, Evelyn Buttrum, Danny's mom, had brought the couple's two children to the center for a visit with Danny and Janice. She thought her son had been in good spirits, all things considered.

Deputies Roy Lee Wells and Charles Nix escorted Janice to the Barton Funeral Home in Adairsville to say a final good-bye to Danny. She hugged her two little girls, Marlena and Marie, and laid a rose near Danny's cold hands.

Chapter 2

Rosalie Grant

LEN DENICLO TRIED DESPERATELY to calm the woman down.

It sounded as though she was saying the fire was on Orange Avenue, but that didn't make sense. He kept his own voice even, cool, and asked the woman to try to spell the name of the street slowly.

Her answer was a haunting shriek that made the blood pound in DeNiclo's temples:

"My kids are burning up, my babies are on fire. Please . . . please, help me," the woman's voice, now hysterical, pleaded as DeNiclo fought to break in again, hoping to help her regain control of her terrified mind long enough to tell him where the fire was taking place.

Now she was stammering the name of the street again, and this time DeNiclo caught enough to swing into action. He triggered a claxon that would roll Engine Company Twelve and Squad Thirty-three, the rescue unit.

"You're saying Orin Avenue? O-R-I-N?" DeNiclo queried the distraught woman.

"Yes . . . yes . . . three one two seven. Tell them to hurry, my babies are on fire, my babies are on fire."

Now DeNiclo moved in a blinding flurry to dispatch other units to the burning house in Youngstown, Óhio's Sharon Line District. In seconds, the thirty-three-year fire department veteran had also activated the downtown ladder company, number Twenty-two, and Engine Company Seven. He knew that Thirty-one, carrying the assistant chief, was already tearing through the early morning streets in response to the call. DeNiclo instantly coded the alarm to advise the units that children were in the house. He knew the drivers of the big red pumpers had their feet down on the gas pedals. They all had kids too.

Len DeNiclo paused long enough to exhale a long pent-up breath. He allowed himself a small smile of satisfaction. Help was on the way. He logged the time of the call at 6:11 A.M. on the call sheet bearing the date April 1, 1983. He would pick up the other details he needed from the tape recording that had begun rolling the instant he picked up the Youngstown Fire Department's central emergency line. DeNiclo heard the sirens knifing the cool silence outside. He knew that Engine Twelve's boys would be on Orin Avenue in no more than two and one-half minutes. He hoped the kids would be okay.

Captain Dominic Barber and his brother Ron Barber looked away. Ron felt the contents of his stomach try to heave their way up. It hadn't taken the two firemen more than minutes to crash through the tiny bedroom's door and knock down the fire.

"Nothing could have saved them," Captain Dom Barber heard himself say. "This place must have been a furnace."

Ron Barber reckoned that the oldest boy couldn't have been much more than two. The little one, maybe not even a year old. They were burned so badly they couldn't bear to look. It appeared as though the older one had tried to crawl toward the door. The baby must have been thrown to the charred floor when the crib burned and collapsed. The instense heat had literally exploded their small skulls.

Dom Barber had remembered seeing the mother as he and Ron fought their way into the small house behind the heavy spray of the number-six hose nozzle. People had reached out to hold her back. She was trying to claw her way into the house, screaming and sobbing for her children.

Ron Barber had seen her too. Jesus, how she must have

felt. He was glad he didn't have to tell her. Ron Barber had four kids of his own.

The stench in the room was wrenching, but the two career firefighters had smelled death before. It went with the territory. But now that the fire was knocked down and the adrenaline had slowed, their trained senses swept across the room.

"Do you smell it?" Dominic Barber said softly to his brother."

"Damn straight," Ron Barber answered. Their faces had turned to hard, grim masks.

"Charcoal lighter, maybe. Some kind of accelerant."

"Yeah," they agreed. They took another look at the two small corpses on the floor. How tiny they were. How helpless.

Saturday afternoon's newspaper told the rest of Youngstown what was then known of the details of the fire on Orin Avenue that morning.

Tim Yovich got the front-page by-line under a banner head, along with four-column art that showed firemen bringing out the bodies of the two little victims.

"Two small boys died in their bedroom this morning as their mother tried desperately to put out a fire and save them," the lead of Tim Yovich's story read.

"Firefighters rushed to the house after their mother, Rosalie Grant, gave up the fight and called the fire department screaming for help.

"Two firemen entered the bedroom of the East Side house, at 3127 Orin Ave., as others beat back the flames with sprays of water.

"But it was too late. The youngsters, Joseph Clinkscale, Jr., 2, and his brother, Donovan Grant, who would have been a year old tomorrow, were both dead."

The story in the *Youngstown Vindicator* graphically told how Rosalie Grant had to be restrained from entering the house to reach her children.

But Tim Yovich was the kind of reporter who asked a lot

of questions. He saw Fire Chief Charles O'Nesti and wondered what had brought him out. Yovich asked.

"So far, we have no belief that anything looks suspicious," O'Nesti was quoted as saying. But Yovich hunted down the department's chief arson investigator too before he wrote the final paragraph of his story. Captain John Zamary had been investigating suspicious fires for a lot of years. Yovich wrote the last paragraph carefully.

"Zamary said that there was only one electrical outlet in the room and it appeared to be OK. He said he was having trouble figuring out how everything in the room burned, including a mattress, while the rest of the house incurred little flame damage."

John Zamary was not the only person having problems making the still-hot pieces of the puzzling fire come together. Down in the basement of the tiny house, beneath the small room where Rosalie lived alone with her three children, arson-investigation-trained firemen had made a chilling discovery: fires had been started in three different areas of the basement, from the look of things, at the same time as the fire broke out upstairs. One of the fires had been set by pouring a flammable substance on the outer case of a fuse box but had quickly burned itself out. So had the other basement fires, each located directly below one of the main rooms of the house upstairs.

One of the investigators noticed the strong odor of fuel on scorched wires leading to the electrical panel. He carefully snipped a piece of wire and placed it in an evidence tube and sealed it.

"Somebody was trying to torch this whole damn house," he said to one of the other firemen. "They were trying to make it look like an electrical short that took off and spread."

"We better get hold of the chief," the investigator added. "Somebody should get the cops down here too."

Youngstown Police Department Detective Michael Landers and his partner, Cosmo Santillo drew the call. Mike

Landers had trouble finding Rosalie. Her grandmother thought other relatives had driven her over to St. Elizabeth Hospital Medical Center, where they had taken her young sons for autopsy.

As it turned out, someone had. The nurses who filled out the forms that had to be filled out felt their hearts go out to Rosalie. She was so tiny. She couldn't have been more than five feet tall, and couldn't have weighed more then ninety pounds. But she was being incredibly brave.

Coroner's investigator Angelo Kissos found her that way too. She seemed calm. Maybe she was holding it all in. Kissos didn't identify himself to Rosalie as a member of the Youngstown Police detective bureau as well as a coroner's office investigator. He quietly asked her to tell him all the details she could remember about the fire. There were these forms that had to be filled out, he said kindly, before the bodies could be released to the funeral home.

No one had yet told Angelo Kissos that the question of foul play had come up back at the scene of the fire. But Kissos was thorough anyway. He'd been a cop for a lot of years.

Rosalie Grant told the investigator she had put the two boys to bed a little later than usual. The following day was Donovan's first birthday and there was the expected excitement in the air about that. Their older sister, Sheylene Grant, three, had been allowed to spend the night with her grandmother. She wasn't expecting any company that night. She was just going to watch TV. She bagged up the garbage, she said, maybe at about 1 A.M., because she had forgotten to do it earlier, and put it on the front porch. There was a late movie on TV and she settled back down to watch it on the couch. It hadn't held her attention, though, and she must have dozed off. The next thing she knew, she woke up sharply. There was a strong smell of smoke in the room. She ran through the house, saw the black smoke pouring under the crack of the closed door that led to the children's bedroom. She froze for a second in terror as she heard the sounds of her children screaming. She pulled open the bedroom door, Rosalie told Kissos, and was nearly thrown to the floor by the blast of heat and choking smoke. She tried repeatedly to enter the bedroom, but couldn't. She didn't care if she died. She tried again. But her body simply could not move through the wall of flames. It was then that Leonard DeNiclo received the hysterical call. Rosalie fled outside then, ran next door, pounded on the windows of her cousin's house until Loretta Charity and her husband came sleepily to the door. They had to pin her to the ground to keep her from reentering the house. Then the fire trucks arrived.

The rest of Kissos' questions were routine as well: Could one of the kids have gotten up and played with matches? Had she left the house, even for only a minute, before the fire had started? Had she seen anyone suspicious in the neighborhood? "No," Rosalie said. "Absolutely no." Kissos closed his small notebook and went on his way. The report could be filed tomorrow.

When Detective Mike Landers finally tracked Rosalie down a few hours later, he got much the same story. Landers didn't tell Rosalie what the investigation of her home was starting to turn up. He needed more time to evaluate that himself. He didn't know, just then, there was a great deal more grist for his mill still to come.

Captain John Zamary was now almost positive that the fire that roared through the bedroom and killed the children had been deliberately set, as had the abortive blazes in the basement. Zamary wanted another opinion, and Chief O'Nesti called in Chief Donald Cover of nearby Boardman, Ohio, to make an independent survey of the evidence in the house. Cover probed the ruins with a fresh eye. It had been several days now since the fire, but he had no trouble coming to exactly the same conclusion as the Youngstown arson probers had reached. The investigators fanned out for an inch-by-inch search of the area. Maybe the killer had dropped the can that had held the accelerant. Landers wanted to lend a hand. He paired off with a fire department lieutenant and scoured an area directly behind Rosalie Grant's home on which an abandoned shed had stood for some years. They pushed open the rusty hinged door and threw the beam of flashlight inside.

The floor was littered with empty beer cans, old garden hoses, thrown-away sneakers, and God knew what else. All of it was covered with a patina of dust that indicated neighbors had been using it to get rid of trash for a long time. Then the beam of the light threw back a surprising glitter. Landers held the light steady. He whistled softly under his breath and reached for an evidence baggie and hunted up a piece of broken stick to ease the object inside.

"A can of charcoal lighter fluid, and there isn't a speck of dust on it," he said to the grinning lieutenant.

"What do you make of that?" he asked, a smile of his own starting to form.

"I'd say someone did something dumber than hell," the fireman answered.

"I'd say you're right," Landers replied.

While Landers sweated out the report on the can from the state crime lab boys, he hit the street again with an icy resolve in his heart. "I kept thinking of those two little kids," Landers would say later. "I couldn't get it out of my head, the terrible way they died."

Landers and Santillo made a routine stop at the McCullough-Williams Funeral Home from where little Joseph and Donovan had been buried. The undertakers checked their records and told the detectives that Kathylene Carson had made the funeral arrangements on behalf of her sister, Rosalie Grant. Miss Carson had assigned the value of two insurance policies covering the children over to the funeral home to guarantee payment of the approximate $1,800 the two burial services had cost.

The policies had been in the amount of $5,000 each and so the funeral home was not concerned about receiving its money. It would all be quite routine. Even though the insurance company might not be terribly happy, the undertaker added with a small chuckle, the policies had been issued only two weeks before the children had died!

Mike Landers felt a knot being tied by two sailors in his guts. He called the crime-lab crew and told them he needed that print from the can, and he needed it right goddamn now.

"Keep your shirt on, Sherlock," the man on the other end of the phone answered. "We did manage to pull a print. Would you like a little hint?"

"You don't even have to tell me," Landers heard himself say. "But go ahead. Tell me anyway."

Mike Landers felt his hand shaking as he placed the call to the office of Jim Coyle, Mahoning County Prosecutor. They were already good friends, and Landers had been talking to Coyle for the past several days about the direction the investigation was taking. Together, they had read the grim autopsy report that County Coroner Dr. Nathan Belinky had sent over. Coyle had slid across the desk the colored photographs the technicians had taken of the fire-ravaged bodies of the two toddlers. Mike Landers said he didn't want to look at them unless Coyle had some reason why he absolutely should. "I don't need anything else to wake me up sweating in the middle of the night," he told Coyle, and pushed the pictures back.

Now he asked to be put straight through to Jim Coyle, even though he knew he was in conference on another murder-one case.

"Jim? This is Mike," Landers said when Coyle came on the line.

"They got a print off the can of charcoal lighter. It was Rosalie Grant's."

"Haul yourself over here," Coyle said tersely. "We'd better talk right now."

County Prosecutor James Coyle and Detective Michael Landers settled down for the rest of the night to play a game they had played before. Landers laid out his case against

Rosalie Grant. Jim Coyle tore the hell out of it, never yielding Landers an inch.

"Why shouldn't you find an old can of lighter fluid in a trash heap with Rosalie's prints on it," Coyle demanded. "Look around my house and you'll probably find a couple."

"Rosalie Grant doesn't have a barbecue grill. She's never had one as far as any neighbor can remember," Landers shot back.

"So she took out life insurance policies on the boys. All that proves is that she loved them," Coyle snapped back.

"Then why didn't she take one out on the girl?" Landers replied.

"For God's sake," Coyle snapped, "she tried to pull those kids out of the fire and could have killed herself. They had to hold her down."

"Then how come no one smelled a bit of smoke on her clothes when everything calmed down. How come her eyes weren't watering like hell and glued shut from the heat. They should have been and I'll tell you why they weren't. She was on her way out the door, not in, right after she set the fire," Landers shot back.

Now Coyle played a heavier card: "Give me the name of one eyewitness who saw Rosalie Grant set fire to her own house. At least give me the names of some neighbors who said they always knew she was going to hurt those kids someday."

"I can't," Landers said softly. "You know I don't have anything like that yet."

Both of the men slumped back in their chairs.

"Jesus, Mike. What you got here is a piece of Swiss cheese, it has so many holes in it. Every damn thing you're telling me is circumstantial. To tell you the truth, I think you're absolutely on the money, but you tell me where I'm going to find a jury that will buy what you're showing me."

"I'll be back to see you later," Landers said. "Have

another read of the file in the meantime. Especially the part where Belinky talks about how the kids died."

"They didn't suffocate, you know. They were burned alive. Don Cover says the heat probably got up to fifteen hundred degrees in that room. The lighter fluid was sprinkled on the mattress and the bed sheets and under the bed and under the crib before she threw the match in there."

Jim Coyle held his head in his hands for a minute before he looked back up at Landers. "Call me again in the morning," he said. "I feel the same way you do about this. We'll do something. We'll give it a shot."

It had been more than a week since the fire now. Landers and Santillo continued the painstaking gumshoe work of checking every detail of Rosalie Grant's story. They talked to dozens of neighbors, friends, relatives, boyfriends, and ex-boyfriends; anyone and everyone they thought might be able to tell them the smallest fact about the mother they now believed to be a cold-blooded murderer.

Rosalie Grant was a street-wise young woman, they learned soon enough. She had come from a shaky home. Her family had move around a lot before coming to rest more or less permanently in the Sharon Line neighborhood on Youngstown's mostly black east side. The area had taken its name from an old trolley line that once connected to the hub of the city, but it was no ghetto. The homes were modest but pleasant and most of the families who lived there were average hard-working, Bible-believing people. The neighborhood was proud of North High School, where a black child could get as good an education as any kid in Ohio. Rosalie Grant hadn't made it through high school, but that didn't mean she wasn't smart. Behind her jive-talking street manners, people who knew her believed there was a basically good, if lonely and sometimes aggressive, woman. There were no loud parties at her home at night. No stream of boyfriends to attract neighborhood disapproval. She had become pregnant while still a teenager and the little girl that was born to her was given the name Sheylene.

Later, she would have two sons by her steadiest boyfriend, Joseph Clinkscale. They were living together when Joseph, Jr., was born, and Rosalie gave the child the father's name. But there had been some angry scenes since that time, and Joseph Clinkscale had moved out. When little Donovan had been born, Rosalie spitefully insisted that his last name would be Grant, the same as her own.

There had been one or two comments from neighbors that Rosalie had beaten the boys more than once, and had to take them to the hospital because she was frightened by the injuries she had inflicted. But the records Landers and Santillo checked couldn't back that gossip up. Other neighbors said she loved the kids and was a very good mother. There was another rumor that Rosalie had angrily demanded that Joseph Clinkscale take the two boys to raise. Some who knew the young mother said she was furious that Clinkscale was living a good life, driving around in a nice car, seeing other women whenever he wanted, and leaving Rosalie alone to raise the kids as best she could on welfare payments. That was a story the investigators heard more than once, and it came from sources the two cops had no reason to doubt.

For much of her life, Rosalie and her sisters had been under the gentle wing of their grandmother, Rosa Carson, who lived nearby on Fairview Avenue. In fact, the small homes in which Rosalie and her cousin lived, side by side, on Orin Avenue, belonged to Mrs. Carson. Landers and Santillo had already heard a great deal about Mrs. Carson, and when they met her they understood why people in the neighborhood revered her.

"She was a wonderful, hard-working woman. Everyone liked her," Mike Landers remembers. "She had done a lot for Rosalie and for a lot of other people too. Once I met her, I liked her too."

As his investigation progressed, Landers began to hear another story on the street. He didn't know exactly where to file it.

"Rosalie once saw her mother stab a man to death," a source told Landers and Santillo. "In fact, she was standing right in between them and was all splattered with the blood. She saw the man die. She was only a little kid. It had happened down south someplace, when the family lived down there. Her mother had been a streetwalker. Rosalie used to have terrible dreams about it, watching her mother stab the man."

Landers kept trying to sit down for an hour with Rosalie, to put some of his suspicions to her, to see how she would react to the evidence that now clearly showed the fire had been deliberately set and that the finger of suspicion was pointing directly at her.

But Rosalie's family was being unusually protective. Each time Landers phoned and asked to speak to her, Mrs. Carson, or a sister, or a cousin, would tell Landers it wasn't possible to talk to Rosalie just then. She's still in mourning, they would say, or she has a doctor's appointment, or she's laying down right now, trying to get some rest.

But Landers was persistent, and had managed to grab the woman briefly on several occasions. During one such meeting, Rosalie Grant dropped a bombshell on the veteran detective.

"She told me someone had made a threatening call to her house the day before the fire," Landers recalls.

The caller had been a woman, Rosalie said, and the message was this: "You're a dead bitch. I'm going to burn your ass."

Why hadn't she told the police? Why hadn't she reported it at once? Landers demanded to know.

"I did," Rosalie shot back angrily. "I called the police department and made a report. For all the damn good that did."

Landers and Santillo headed back to the department and began a time-consuming check of all emergency calls that had been placed to the Youngstown police department in the days preceding the fire. Routinely, all such calls were taped,

but in the event phone traffic was more than the four
emergency lines could handle, a call could have come in
and not have been recorded. But the procedure then would
have been to make a written record of the complaint, and if
the call had been made, either the tape or the complaint
form had to be somewhere in department files.

No record of any such call could be found. Landers came
to his own conclusion: "She had seen all the activity going
on at the fire scene and she must have figured out that we
were suspicious. No one would be tearing that place apart
the way we were for an ordinary house fire, and she must
have figured she was going to need some kind of story
before long."

Landers was called to a meeting that week by the fire
investigators to lay out the results of their investigation.
Most of the reports were in now. Samples of flooring and
wiring had been sent off for analysis and hundreds of
pictures and diagrams of the house had been reviewed.
Based on all the evidence, the coroner's office was ready to
rule the death of the two boys as homicides. City Prosecutor
William Marshall reviewed the legal grounds for the case.
He authorized the arrest of Rosalie Grant on two counts of
aggravated murder. They were convinced the case was
strong enough to at least get Rosalie Grant bound over to a
county grand jury. After that it was up to Jim Coyle to make
the case.

Mike Landers was taking no chances with his suspect.
With the warrant issued, he called to find if Rosalie was still
at the home of her grandmother. Up the street, out of sight,
Landers had dispatched a police cruiser with two officers
under special instructions from him.

The woman who answered Landers' phone call was
reluctant to say whether Rosalie Grant was at home. Finally
she admitted she was, but said she was unable to come to
the telephone just then.

Landers had a message relayed immediately to the
waiting cruiser.

"Go grab her!"

"I jumped straight into her face the minute they brought her through the door," Landers remembers.

"She'd had her rights, and I figured the whole thing was going to take about five minutes."

"You killed your babies," Landers thundered at Rosalie Grant. "We know it, and you know it. Now I'll tell you how you did it, and why you did it. Then you can tell me."

Rosalie Grant met Landers' icy stare with one of her own. Landers felt his five-minutes-to-crack notion fly out the window.

"I'll tell you what, Rosalie," he said, trying a gentler tack. "You go on the lie box. We're all set up. And if you're telling the truth you can take a walk, and you won't ever see me again."

Rosalie Grant told Mike Landers to go fuck himself. She wasn't saying another word until there was a lawyer in the room with her.

Jack Ausnehmer and Howard Zlotnick were appointed by the court to defend Rosalie Grant in the arraignment and bind-over procedures. She was without funds to obtain counsel, but even if Rosalie had been a wealthy woman, she couldn't have done better than the pair of scrappy young attorneys assigned to her case.

Ausnehmer was a pro at criminal law. Zlotnick could convince you the sun rose in the west. They took a look at the evidence that had brought Rosalie Grant before the courts and had a hard time believing what they saw.

"We thought the cops, the fire department, and the county prosecutor had all lost their minds," Ausnehmer remembers today.

"It was one of the poorest jobs of investigation we'd ever seen. They had done things that were simply incredible.

"No one had cordoned off the investigation scene. They were wandering all over the place without a search warrant, investigating a so-called murder case. They had a can of lighter fluid they said was used to start the fire, but their own lab reports couldn't identify it positively as the same fluid they said was used to start the fires.

"The woman they had under arrest had reported threats on her life from someone who said they were going to burn her. Other people in the neighborhood had been in her home when similar threats were made, but the only person they focused their investigation on was Rosalie Grant.

"They didn't have a single witness who saw Rosalie Grant try to burn her house. They couldn't find anyone who they could get to say she'd ever even thought of it, or that she was the kind of person who might do it.

"They took a sample of electrical wire and sent it to a crime lab. When the report came back, it indicated two pieces of wire had been sent. Somebody was playing games," Ausnehmer continued.

"They had been wildly overzealous. They started out with the premise that Rosalie Grant had killed her children and then built a circumstantial case that was nothing more than a castle of sand to try to prove it.

"We couldn't believe that Jim Coyle was going to take this to a grand jury."

There was another reason that Ausnehmer and Zlotnick felt confident the charges against the petite black woman would never stick. They had listened to her story themselves, then checked it out. They believed she was telling them the truth.

"I practice criminal law. I don't believe a lot of things that people tell me. When I first listened to Rosalie Grant, I have to admit I thought she was lying through her teeth. But the more we checked, the more it proved she was being truthful. We believed her," Ausnehmer says today.

Zlotnick and Ausnehmer weren't the only ones who had reservations about the solidity of the evidence a jury would be asked to weigh to determine if Rosalie Grant had killed her innocent children in such a hideous and cruel way.

Jim Coyle had reviewed the evidence with several

colleagues whose opinions he respected. Their reactions had been almost unanimous.

"They all said they agreed with me that she did it, but they all said I'd have a hell of a time proving it," Coyle recalls.

"Beyond a reasonable doubt means just that in a courtroom. Most of the people I asked for advice said I'd be lucky to keep a jury out for twenty minutes with the case we had."

But Coyle wasn't ready to let go that easily. He *had* looked at the pictures of the two little boys, and saw the two half-column pictures of them grinning, full of mischief, still alive, which had run with their newspaper obituary.

"I asked myself a thousand times who else could have committed this crime. Who hated Rosalie Grant so much that they went into her house while she was sleeping and could have been an easy victim, but instead went into the bedroom where the children were asleep, poured lighter fluid all over them, and set the room on fire?

"Why was there this spanking new can of charcoal lighter, with her fingerprint on it, in an abandoned shed out behind her house? She had just put the garbage out that night, the way she always did. What was she using lighter fluid for? She didn't have a grill.

"Why were the life insurance policies taken out only two weeks earlier? Why was the little girl staying with her grandmother that night?

"Why wasn't she burned from trying to get into that room? Why wasn't she singed or smell badly of smoke? Most people would have put up a better try than that to save a dog in a house that was burning. She ran over to a neighbor's and stood on the porch until the newspaper photographer arrived and then she went screaming over. She knew no one would let her in that house by then," Coyle said.

"I finally came to the place in my mind where I knew it

would have been criminal of me not to take this case to a jury," Coyle said.

"I knew she was guilty, and I knew what my duty required."

Ausnehmer and Zlotnick hammered away at the state's case like men possessed.

"This isn't a prosecution, it's a persecution," Zlotnick thundered before the jury. About the only thing the prosecution had proved conclusively, he argued, was that a fire had taken place in the house on Orin Avenue and that two children had tragically died. The rest of it was an investigation filled with such basic errors and faulty conclusions that the jury could reach no other verdict but innocent.

A defense witness testified he had seen the charcoal can lying out in the shed a month earlier. Several witnesses told of being present when threatening calls had been made to Rosalie. One witness was a woman now dating a former boyfriend of Rosalie's. She was suspicious that Rosalie was still seeing the man who now belonged to her. Why hadn't the police checked that out? Testimony from another person alleged there was evidence of a fire having taken place in the basement of the Grant home months before. Was the fire department able to determine that? The rest of their evidence about the fire having been deliberately set was all based on observation, arrived at by their training and experience. Where were the samples that named the brand of lighter fluid they said was used on the floor of the bedroom and in the fuse box? The fact was there wasn't any such evidence. The lab couldn't present those findings with scientific certainty. And the insurance. Let's talk about the insurance, Zlotnick demanded. The man who came and sold Rosalie the policy had been sent there by a friend who had just taken similar coverage out on her own children. He had sold dozens of policies just like it to black families in Sharon Line. He clinched the sale with Rosalie when he told her that the policies would continue to build a cash value and that someday Joseph Junior and baby Donovan could cash them in for $10,000 each. He had offered her a double-indemnity rider to the policies, and explained to her that for only thirty-seven cents extra each month, the policies would pay double the $5,000 face amount if, God forbid, anything should ever accidentally take the lives of the kids. Rosalie had declined that waiver, which she could have had for pennies, the defense told the jury. Why would a woman who was going to kill her children to collect insurance money do a stupid thing like that?

The defense and the prosecution argued hotly about whether the photos of the children's bodies should be shown to the jury. Mahoning County Common Pleas Judge Peter Economous ruled that a carefully selected group of the photos would be given to the jury, who could view them if they wished. Ausnehmer and Zlotnick hoped they wouldn't.

Dr. Belinky's testimony left no doubt in the jurors' minds that the children were burned alive in the inferno created in the tiny bedroom. Soot was found in the larynxes of both bodies. The level of carbon monoxide in the bloodstreams had been established at between twenty and twenty-five percent. A more merciful death by smoke inhalation would have left traces of forty percent or more. But a defense pathology expert, brought in from the Walter Reed Army Medical Center, rebutted the findings of the crusty county coroner. The children could have died of asphyxiation much before the flames reached them, that expert testified.

With the case almost ready to go to the jury, Jack Ausnehmer and Howard Zlotnick were satisfied they had done their job. No jury was going to convict a woman of murder on the totally circumstantial evidence the jury had presented.

"It was my decision not to put Rosalie on the stand in her own behalf," Ausnehmer remembers today.

"Even an innocent person can be made to look bad by a skillful cross-examination, and there wasn't any need in my mind to take that chance. Rosalie was willing to testify, but I didn't think she should."

"Hindsight is a hell of a wonderful thing," Jack Ausnehmer would say ruefully a day later, after the jury had returned a verdict of guilty.

James Coyle admits he didn't know for sure which way the jury was going to go.

"I think they read that jury wrong," Coyle said. "I don't think she helped herself by her demeanor in the court. She sat there every day, wearing that same blank stare. She sat there as calmly as could be when the jury listened to the tape of the call she had made to the fire department the morning of the fire. The jury was watching her very intently, but I don't think she changed her expression an inch when she heard her own voice shouting that her children were on fire."

When Coyle made his closing arguments to the jury, he asked them to consider what he called the fatal flaw in the defense of Rosalie Grant.

Coyle picked up the copy of that tape recording and held it in plain view before the jurors.

"She says she couldn't get into that room that night, because the smoke was so thick and the heat was so great, but then she screams for the firemen to hurry because her children were on fire.

"How could she know that?" Coyle softly demanded.

"I'll tell you how.

"She was the one that set the fire, and closed the door behind her."

Jack Ausnehmer said he believed another factor had worked against his client.

"There is no worse nightmare for a defense attorney than a case built on circumstantial evidence," Ausnehmer lamented.

"It allows the members of the jury to play detective. It invites them to solve a mystery. They forget about facts and rules of evidence; they get caught up in an Agatha Christie plot and believe the final chapter has to end with an answer—any kind of answer.

"I don't think the pictures of the children helped her either. I saw them myself and you can't imagine how horrifying they were.

"When a jury takes a look at something like that you can just hear them saying to themselves somebody is going to pay for this."

Now the jury convened again. It was a pleasant late October day, but the task they faced was grim. Under Ohio law it was now their duty to determine if Rosalie Grant should, on their recommendation to the judge, be sentenced to death for her crime.

The jury would be given the results of presentencing investigations conducted by both the prosecution and defense. The story of Rosalie's troubled childhood would be put before them by Zlotnick and Ausnehmer. Jim Coyle had decided that he would mount no extraordinary demand for the death penalty. This was the jury who had found her guilty. They now had the duty to decide her fate.

Zlotnick asked the jurors to consider her tender age, her troubled family background, that she had no prior criminal record and posed no danger to the citizens of Youngstown. He told them she was a good candidate for rehabilitation, and pleaded that they consider the impact of her execution on the surviving child, little three-year-old Sheylene.

"I'm asking you to heal the wounds of her family by showing mercy. All life is worth saving," Zlotnick said.

Ausnehmer asked the jury to think of how that child would be taunted for life by other children because her mother had been put to death in the electric chair. He told the jury how he and Zlotnick personally dreaded their required attendance in the death chamber, as witnesses, if the jury demanded that she die in the chair.

But it was Rosalie Grant who sealed her own fate that day before the jury of nine men and three women who had, up until then, never heard the sound of her voice except on the tape-recorded call to the fire department.

"She told us, this time, she wanted to talk to the jury herself," Jack Ausnehmer recalled.

"What could I really say? I was the guy who had decided she didn't need to take the stand before.

"She stayed up half the night in her cell. She made a bunch of notes on sheets of yellow legal pad, but she wouldn't tell us what she was going to say to the jury.

"We had a terrible feeling, but we both told her to just remember one thing. We told her to ask the jury not to sentence her to die, to thank them, and sit down.

"We didn't know she was going to do what she did," Ausnehmer said.

Her testimony was unsworn. There would be no cross-examination.

The defense attorneys felt a terrible apprehension as Judge Economous motioned her toward the witness chair. They didn't want her to settle down for a long diatribe. They tried to catch her eye. She ignored them.

"For the first ten minutes, some of the members of the jury had tears in their eyes," Jim Coyle remembers. "If she had stopped there things might have been all right."

Rosalie wept as she talked. Her voice was low. The jury strained forward.

"I didn't come before you today for sympathy or to make you feel sorry for me. I came here to tell you I did not kill my kids. I am not guilty.

"I don't want my daughter to hear that her mother died in the electric chair for a crime she didn't commit," Rosalie said in a whisper.

But then her voice became harsh, angry, whining, and accusative.

"It reminded me of someone scratching their fingernails on a blackboard," Coyle would remember.

"I feel I've been wronged. I'm not going to be put down

for something I didn't do. You were the ones that made the mistake," she angrily spat out at the jury.

"You only heard opinions in this case, not the facts.

"I can tell you had doubts about the verdict because none of you could look me in the eye when the judge asked you if these were your verdicts."

Rosalie lunged on. She was becoming incoherent now. Zlotnick and Ausnehmer felt their hearts sink.

Then Rosalie Grant stunned the courtroom into an eerie and frozen silence.

"There was a man came in the house that night. He only had one arm. He was carrying a heavy piece of lead pipe. He wouldn't let me get into the bedroom to get my babies out of the fire."

The voice that interrupted her from the back of the courtroom sounded like a sob.

"That's enough, Rosalie. Get down."

It was Rosalie's father whose emotion-choked voice had rung out.

Rosalie's head fell into her hands. There was only the sound of her soft sobbing. Her testimony was over.

"It was probably the strangest thing I'd ever seen in a court of law," Jim Coyle remembers now.

"We talked to people, of course, after she told the story about the man with the pipe. She had never told the story to anyone before that moment. Not the police, not friends or relatives. Her father said he'd never heard her say anything about it before."

"It surely didn't do her any good," Jack Ausnehmer remembers.

"You could see how the jury took it. It was an insult to their intelligence. You knew they were going to come back with a recommendation that she be executed," Coyle added.

The jury did, in fact, recommend that Rosalie Grant be sentenced to death. Even then, community feeling for Rosalie ran high in the Sharon Line district. A group of black clergymen asked Judge Economous to delay the sentencing while new evidence was obtained. The judge denied their plea. On Friday, October 22, Rosalie appeared before the judge to hear the date of execution set. Judge Economous knew that it would not be carried out on the date he specified, December 21, 1983. The automatic appeal process before the Ohio Supreme Court did require that that date be set aside.

It may be several years before the final fate of Rosalie Grant is determined.

The full impact of the case only began to hit Jim Coyle after his job had been successfully finished. He left the county prosecutor's office and took an offer made by one of the area's most prestigious law firms.

"It wasn't only the case that made me want to practice a different kind of law for a while, but it did enter into my consideration," Jim Coyle says today.

"You can't take pleasure when you know the fruits of your labor will cost someone her life," he said. He remembers losing ten pounds during the trial.

"I found that I didn't like playing God with other people's lives. Don't misunderstand. Rosalie Grant was guilty of murder and it was my duty to see that she was punished for her crime, the same way it was the jury's to convict her and the judge's to sentence her to death."

Coyle believes today it will be a long time, if ever, before Rosalie Grant faces death in the electric chair.

"I'm not certain the sentence will ever be carried out," he said.

If Jack Ausnehmer has his way, it never will.

He is not handling Rosalie's appeal. A firm specializing in that complex area of the law has been assigned. What he hopes is that the efforts made by himself and Zlotnick will result in a new trial for Rosalie.

"I think it is going to come bouncing back for a new trial and I hope I handle it.

"I don't know what made her come up with that story she told the jury. The only thing I could imagine was that it was something similar to what Vietnam veterans experienced. She was under enormous pressure, accused of the most horrible kind of crime you could imagine. I think something inside shouted out and made her believe what she said herself," Ausnehmer said.

There is something else that makes the lawyer want to represent Rosalie Grant again. It isn't the money. That's certain. For the exhausting effort the two young lawyers made on their client's behalf, each was granted payment of $12,500 for their role of defender.

"I still am not willing to believe that Rosalie Grant set that fire. I've seen her with her other child, the little girl, and the love she shows for that girl just isn't something she is capable of faking. I think she loved those little boys in the same way."

Ausnehmer made Rosalie Grant a promise the day she was taken to death row. He said he would see that her daughter was taken care of.

"We've arranged a guardianship for the girl with her aunt. Rosalie is pleased about that," Jack Ausnehmer said.

The words that follow may come as a surprise to Jack Ausnehmer. While he and Detective Michael Landers are friends, Landers has not shared with him a nagging concern he has still not been able to shake long after the case was closed.

"Rosalie Grant is guilty. I don't have the slightest doubt about that," Landers says today, "but I can't get away from the gut feeling she had a helper. I think it was a man.

"I don't think Rosalie would have figured out that the fire could be made to look electrical by starting a fire in the fuse box down in the basement. I have a hunch that was a man doing the thinking down there.

"I have a candidate, but I don't have a case. If I did, I'd snag the bastard and he'd be up there with her."

"It isn't something I'm going to stop thinking about. There's no way you can ever get this case out of your mind.

"Maybe I'm wrong about someone else being involved, but I don't think so. I'm going to keep looking."

Michael Landers has kids too.

Chapter 3

Judith Ann Neelley

SHE CALLED HERSELF "Lady Sundance." "You know, like in Butch Cassidy and the Sundance Kid," she'd say, just in case you hadn't caught the meaning.

He chose "The Nightrider" as his CB radio handle. Down in the parts where he came from you didn't have to explain that one to anybody.

Judith and Alvin Neelley had given a great deal of excited consideration to the names they wanted to be known by when their voices crackled across the citizen-band channels along the narrow miles of pavement and graveled loops of country back roads that crisscross that part of the small-town South where the state lines of Tennessee, Alabama, and Georgia converge like the point of an arrow up near Chattanooga.

Judith and Alvin traversed the back roads of a dozen counties in the three-state area with the practiced skill of old-time moonshine runners. She loved putting the pedal to the metal on the souped-up Dodge Charger she piloted like a Daytona 500 driver and roaring off in clouds of blue smoke, trying to outrun her husband, Alvin, who thought his powerhouse Ford Granada made him look a lot like the Old Bandit when he was behind the wheel.

They chattered back and forth to each other like magpies across the CB radios as they came up on towns like Summerville, LaFayette, Fort Payne, Murfreesboro, Tullahoma, Rome, and Chatoogaville.

They'd exchange coded opinions about whether the

towns looked right for one or the other of the basic, small-time con games that kept them afloat. Most often they'd leave behind a few phony checks. Sometimes an altered money order, all depending on what they had done the last time they'd passed through that neck of the woods.

They each carried a .38 under the seats of their car, but just then, in the early part of September 1982, they weren't as cocky as they once had been about using the weapons for larger enterprises, such as armed robbery.

The last time they had done that, about two years earlier, when Judith had been only sixteen, they found themselves in custody so fast it had made their heads spin. Alvin, who was then twenty-seven, got sent away to do some serious time, and Judith was remanded to the custody of the Youth Development Center in Rome, Georgia, where she was kept long enough to give birth to twins before being sent away to another facility in Macon.

Now they were back on the road together. Just like Bonnie and Clyde, the way they saw it, even though Bonnie and Clyde would have laughed out loud at some of the minor-league gimmicks the Neelleys thought of as big-time capers, not to mention the fact that the Parkers weren't dragging along two kids still in diapers.

Since their reunion, Alvin had taken a job in a small-town Tennessee filling station just long enough to convince the owner he could be trusted to deposit the $1,800 weekend receipts in the bank, a very bad mistake on the owner's part but just what Judith and Alvin needed to put the two sets of wheels under them they now used to prowl the tristate area looking for an illegal livelihood.

Lady Sundance and the Nightrider had been back at their shifty business for several months as September drew to a close.

Chances were good that it wouldn't have been much longer before the pair bungled some petty bunko attempt badly enough to put them back in custody again, but Judith and Alvin Neelley had made a bizarre decision to broaden their repertoire from petty grifting to ruthless, premeditated sexual assault and murder.

Within a month, with no forewarning from their past methods of operation, Judith and Alvin Neelley would become two of the most desperately sought murderers in the memory of the hundreds of law enforcement officers from a dozen separate police agencies that combed the area in hopes of capturing them before they could cruelly rape and kill again.

When they were brought to bay, less than a month after the discovery of their first victim, police authorities were convinced they had run to ground two perverted and savage killers responsible for as many as fifteen slayings.

What had triggered their sudden, bloody spree? Much of that answer, investigators would discover, depended on who you wanted to believe—Judith Neelley or her husband, Alvin. Sometimes you had to flip a coin.

Alvin would confess that he had, for certain, been involved in the sex assaults on a thirteen-year-old girl from a youth home whom Judith had lured into her car from a shopping mall in Rome, Georgia. He had also raped a twenty-seven-year-old woman Judith had enticed into her car from a quiet street in the same town.

But after he had satiated himself with the victims, Alvin said, Judith had taken her turn in sexually abusing them, later driving them to remote areas and killing them, all on her own.

Alvin said he could link Judith to between eight and fifteen similar murders committed by Judith in her roles as a procurer of young girls for a major prostitution ring in the state of Georgia and as a paid enforcer who killed girls who got out of line.

Stunned police heard Alvin offer convincing details of deaths and disappearances of women in all of the states he and Judith traveled. His guarded revelations touched off an intense flurry of renewed investigation into cases that had almost been closed for lack of new leads or developments.

Confronted by a mass of evidence, Judith Neelley also sang under police interrogation, but it was a somewhat different tune.

Yes, she had been involved in the killings of the young girl and the woman abducted from Rome, but she had never attempted to violate them sexually because of her own lusts. What she had done, she had done because Alvin had forced her. In fact, everything she had done had been ordered by Alvin, on pain of severe beatings unless she did exactly as he had ordered.

Alvin had accused her of having sex with a correctional officer during the time they had been apart. She had denied it. Now, to prove her fidelity to him, Alvin demanded that Judith entice young women into her car and drive them to some place where Alvin could be summoned on CB to take part in their kidnapping and sexual assault.

And, Judith said, when she had killed the thirteen-year-old victim, Alvin had been lurking near the scene, armed and holding her two children as hostages to guarantee that Judith did his bidding, even though it had been her, it was true, who killed both the youngster and the woman.

The first victim who fell prey to the blood lusts of Judith and Alvin might never have come to the attention of police if it had not been for an almost unbelievable need by the pair to demonstrate how much smarter they were than the cops.

Judith actually telephoned the police and a Rome radio station to make certain authorities were aware they had committed their first murder.

Lieutenant Ken Kines, a dogged investigator who'd been with the department for more than fifteen years, listened tensely as the radio dispatcher played him the tape of the call Judith had placed minutes earlier to the Rome emergency dispatcher.

"I can tell you where to find the Millican girl. You know, the runaway you're looking for. She's dead. Up in Little River Canyon. That's where I put her."

Kines hastily called up every runaway report that had

been filed in the past month. He quickly sifted out the routine form that noted the disappearance on September 25 of thirteen-year-old Lisa Millican.

The missing persons report had been filed by administrators of the Ethel Harpst Home in nearby Cedartown, a facility for neglected children.

Pretty young Lisa Millican had been a resident of the home for about a month. She was described by counselors at the home as a sad, troubled girl, one with a history of running away.

But Lisa was not at the home because of any trouble with the law. Things were tough for her single mom who was trying to put back together some kind of life for her family. For a while things had gotten so bad Lisa's mom and the rest of the kids were sleeping in their rattletrap auto.

When counselors told the kids at the Ethel Harpst Home they would be permitted to take the trip to Riverbend shopping mall in Rome on Saturday, Lisa was quick to show her enthusiasm for the outing. She was among the seven girls and six boys accompanied by the counselors for the pleasant break from the routine of the home.

Lisa and the other kids were told to stay with their groups as they browsed at the attractive mall. They were to meet at a designated location at 8 P.M. for the trip back to the center.

When Lisa Millican failed to show up at the appointed time, kids and counselors fanned out through the sprawling mall to find her. But Lisa was nowhere to be found.

Jean Jones, the home's assistant administrator, had the feeling that Lisa had decided to run away back home to Walker County to be with her mom and the rest of the family.

"Fall is the time when our children run away sometimes," Jones said. "School scares them," she added. "It happens every year."

"We have no reason to think she has been abducted," Jean Jones told Rome police when she filed the report that Lisa Ann Millican was missing.

The friendly girl who approached Lisa Millican as she wandered through the mall asked her if she wanted to go for a ride around town. She told Lisa she had just moved there and didn't have any friends. Lisa knew all about that. Out on the parking lot, Lisa admiringly appraised the runaway lines of the rakish-looking brown Dodge Charger.

"We'll head out toward the edge of town," Lisa's new friend told her. "If you want to, I'll let you drive for a while."

When they cleared the parking lot of the shopping center, Judith Ann Neelley reached down to set the squelch button on the speaker of her CB radio.

She picked up the mike from its magnetic mount on the dashboard.

"Breaker one nine," she said. "This is Lady Sundance. Do you read me, Nightrider?"

Nightrider replied that he copied, five by five.

"They kept the girl with them for three or four days," Richard Igou, district attorney for De Kalb County, Alabama, says.

"They sexually assaulted her repeatedly. They dragged her from one seedy motel to another in different parts of the area. I hesitate to describe what-all they did to that little girl.

"All the time this was going on, by the way, their own two little children were in the room, seeing the torture and sexual abuse of Lisa Millican," Igou added.

After her capture, Judith Neelley offered a partial account of the savagery Lisa Millican had endured. Dr. Clifford Hardin, a psychiatrist at Bryce Hospital in Tuscaloosa, listened.

"Judith said the little Millican girl was frightened to death. By the time they had finished with her, she was willing to do anything they demanded. Judith thought she was trying to please them in the hope they might spare her life."

For Lisa Millican it was a forlorn hope. "They decided to

kill the girl by injecting a caustic drain cleaner into her veins," District Attorney Igou recounts. "The chemical formulation was later determined to be consistent with commercial products such as Drano or Liquid Plumber."

Judith admitted it was she who injected Lisa with the deadly compounds. Alvin would later deny he had any part in that maniacal torture inflicted on the terrified thirteen-year-old. He said Judith had told him she might use that method to kill the girl because she was curious about what effect the searing acids would have on a person's body.

Investigators theorized that what Judith may have been attempting was a ruse to make it appear that the young girl had died of a drug overdose when her body was found. Judith had obtained several medical syringes in her travels, and it was these into which she loaded the cleaning compound. Police believed that what Judith did not know was how to find a vein on the child's body in which to inject the needle.

"She injected the drain cleaner into the girl intramuscularly, instead of in a vein. She managed to pump the fluid into several muscle areas, such as the victim's buttocks," Prosecutor Igou says.

"A pathologist who autopsied the girl later said the injection had turned tissue in those areas of the body affected into something the consistency of anchovy paste.

"There is no reliable way to calculate how excruciatingly painful that must have been. No one was there who can tell us that now except Judith Neelley," Igou added.

While Lisa was doubtless in agony after the brutal injections, she did not die. Judith bundled her out of the motel room and into the Dodge Charger. She sped off toward Fort Payne, Alabama, through the edge of De Kalb County, toward a remote area near the Little River Canyon, one of the deepest gorge areas east of the Mississippi River. Alvin was following, Judith said, and in touch with her by CB radio.

At the deserted recreation area, Judith dragged Lisa

Millican from the car and led her to a lip of the canyon whose floor lay more than a hundred feet below. It was a rocky slope to the bottom, gouged by rock piles and brush-covered crevasses. She injected the girl again with the caustic compounds and was disappointed when she did not die. The overdose scenario to account for the death of a troubled runaway was not going to work. Judith pushed the trembling girl to within inches of the canyon precipice. She coolly withdrew the .38 she had slipped, Bonny Parker style, into the front of her jeans. She shot Lisa Millican in the back and listened as her body bounced down the canyon wall. She threw the syringes over the cliff too.

Alvin Neelley was watching from behind a tree, Judith would later tell officials. He was masturbating as he watched the scene.

Both police and psychiatrists asked Judith Neelley a series of questions about that moment at the cliff as they later tried to understand why the eighteen-year-old had done what she had done.

"Why did you do that to the girl?" they asked.

"Because Alvin told me to," she would answer.

"But you had a gun," they would insist. "Why didn't you shoot Alvin?"

"Because he never told me to do that," Judith replied.

As Lieutenant Ken Kines and the hasty squad of detectives he assembled listened once more to the tape-recorded message phoned in by the woman describing the whereabouts of Lisa Millican's body, they tried to analyze its total meaning, hoping to draw some useful inferences from the flat, calm, emotionless woman's voice.

"I had the feeling we were going to hear that voice again," Ken Kines remembers. "I had the horrible certainty she hadn't finished with us yet."

When police from Georgia and Alabama converged on the Little River Canyon area that afternoon, a search of the area failed to turn up a body.

The next night the woman called again.

She was disturbed that she had heard no reports on the radio of the girl's body being found. She accused the police of trying to cover up the death of the girl. She gave them another set of explicit directions. They had better look harder, she said. The girl's body was there.

Police and firemen with rappelling gear assembled at the canyon again at sunup the next day. Inch by inch they worked their way down the face of the canyon. This time they found Lisa Millican right where the woman had said. Looking back up, the search team could see how the body had been missed before. The overhang of the canyon shielded from view the place where the girl's body had come to rest.

The medical examination quickly confirmed the grisly details of Lisa Millican's cruel death. The young girl had been a virgin, and the rapes she had endured were particularly painful. Investigators decided not to release just then the fact the child had been sexually abused. The cause of death had been the gunshot wound, although the plunge down the canyon would have been sufficient to cause death. Baffled doctors at first could offer no opinion about the use of the substance that had been injected into the body.

Lieutenant Ken Kines replayed the haunting tape recordings when he returned to the detective bureau in Rome. "I put her there," the terse voice of the woman had said. Ken Kines now knew he was listening to the voice of a murderer.

Several other police agencies were quickly drawn into the net that Kines was throwing out in the rapidly escalating hunt for the young girl's killer.

Lisa had not been in Rome long enough to have any friends outside the home. Had she been out thumbing a ride that night, trying to find her way back to LaFayette where her mom lived? Had she been picked up along the way by someone who then used her murderously and dumped her in Alabama?

"We tried to cover every possibility. We just hit the streets. We talked to everyone we could think of. Nobody was in a mood to stop until we found that woman," Kines remembers.

As the wearying search went on, other strange events happened that would find their way into the growing puzzle.

Ken Kines had walked into the Rome Police Department radio room late one night several days after the first victim had been found.

"I had my mind on something else, but I always half listen to the transmissions in the radio room.

"I happened to hear some traffic coming in from Gordon County, not far from here.

"A man had just been reported shot in the back out in a wooded area by a woman who had offered him and his lady friend a ride.

"Deputies up there believed the weapon had been a .38 caliber.

"I figured we needed to check that one out pronto," Kines said.

The victim had been twenty-six-year-old John Hancock of Rome. With him had been his live-in girlfriend and intended wife, twenty-three-year-old Janice Morrow Chatman. Hancock told Kines's investigators that he and Janice had been taking a walk late that afternoon along Shorter Street. As they strolled, a woman in a brown Dodge Charger with Tennessee license plates had glided up to the curb and asked them if they would like a ride.

The woman had blond, reddish hair, Hancock said. She told them she had just arrived in town, was looking for a place to stay, and was feeling bummed out and lonely because she didn't know anyone in the area. Hancock and Janice weren't doing anything that special and took her up on her offer. The woman told the couple she might be able to contact a friend of hers on the CB who might join them with a cooler full of beer. Sure enough, John Hancock said, the man showed up in a red Ford Granada. They drove along highway 136 for a while, the girls in one car and the men in the other. Then there was some chatter on the CB and both cars pulled down a lane that led to a secluded, wooded spot.

The next thing Hancock knew, he was staring into the business end of a .38, pointed between his eyes by the friendly young woman who'd first offered him and his girlfriend a ride.

Hancock was marched off into the woods by the woman. His terrified girlfriend was ordered by the other man not to attempt to get out of the car.

Hancock assumed he was being robbed. He tried to keep his wits about him. "Listen," he said, "drop my girl off someplace where she can get back into town, will you? This is all scaring her bad."

"Don't worry about your girlfriend, pal," the woman replied. "We'll take care of her."

The next thing Hancock heard was the explosion of the .38. He felt a slug tear through his back. Scared as he was, he believed the shot was not fatal. He did the best job of acting he'd ever tried to do in his life, lying still as death, hoping to convince the woman another blast from the revolver wasn't needed.

He could hear the voice of the man calling down to the woods, yelling for the woman to hurry up. He listened to her footfalls through the leaves as she returned to the road. He took a look at his wounds and decided he could make it back up to the highway for help. Within a short time, Hancock had flagged down a passing vehicle and was being treated in a hospital. He was surprised to see the swarm of police officers suddenly cram themselves into the room. He couldn't believe he was quite that important.

The first thing Lieutenant Ken Kines wanted to do was to play the tape recording of the voice to John Hancock.

"I'd say that's her," Hancock told Kines and his investigators.

"Yes, I surely would."

Now the police pumped Hancock for every possible detail he could remember about the woman who had shot him and the man who had been her accomplice. As quickly as Hancock could get another line of description out of his mouth, deputies in two states were being advised by car radio of the information. The police wanted to get Janice Chatman back alive. Kines knew down deep that they had better hurry.

If Kines and the other growing members of agencies now involved in the investigation thought the case had already taken some strange turns, they didn't know the half of it.

Since the death of Lisa Millican, police in Rome and other towns had begun to receive reports from the mothers of young girls who told of having been approached by a friendly young woman who offered them a ride.

A thirteen-year-old near a playground remembered that the woman had seemed creepy to her. She told her very pointedly she didn't take rides from strangers.

A young woman of about twenty, who looked much younger, was waiting outside a fast-food restaurant where she worked when she was chatted up by a woman who matched the same description. She used the new-lonely-girl-in-town routine, but the intended victim didn't buy it.

Rome Police Chief Joe Cleveland was worried. So far, the kids who had been approached had been savvy enough to say no. But how long would that luck last? How long would it be before some trusting youngster did accept a ride from the sweet-talking woman? A ride that would end in death. Cleveland told his department that all hands would now be on deck. Hang the overtime hours. This woman and her partner had to be found. Ken Kines and his people hadn't needed to hear that. They'd been working virtually around the clock already.

Kines's task force also brought into the station the kids who had been approached by the woman. He played the tape of her voice for them. They were convinced it was the same.

When an employee of the Youth Development Center reported that someone had tried to firebomb his home, and another told police a shot had been fired into his house that week, the investigations were handled routinely. But then an administrator at the center called police to add a new piece of information to those cases. A call had been made to the center by a woman who said people who worked there were going to die. They were going to be paid back for the sexual abuse the caller had suffered there once.

The person who received the call was rushed down to the detective bureau. He listened to the tape recording. It was the same woman, he said.

Kines borrowed investigators from the juvenile division. He wanted the name of every girl who had been housed at the center in the past two years. They were to focus on the ones from out of town and see if any of them had ever complained of sex abuse in their family histories, Kines ordered. By three in the morning, exhausted investigators had winnowed down the list to six possibles. Kines asked for their photographs to be provided along with their case histories. He spent an hour sifting through them himself. From the descriptions provided by the girls who had been approached and from the description provided by John Hancock, he narrowed the files down to three. Judith Neelley was one of them. It wasn't a name Kines remembered hearing before.

Kines showed the photo to Hancock. The girl in the picture looked younger, but he was pretty certain. Then he showed it to the girls. They thought it was close. The thirteen-year-old said it was the same person. She was absolutely certain.

Kines felt his pulse racing when the final identifications had been made. He was now certain he knew his quarry. The net was stretched out farther yet. Authorities in three states were now involved. Hundreds of law enforcement agents searched for Lady Sundance and the Nightrider. John Hancock had overheard their CB monickers as they drove around on the day he was shot. It was another handy piece of information the police would know how to use.

* * *

Judith and Alvin were out of money again. They fell back on one of their favorite old scams. They passed some worthless checks in a town near Murfreesboro, Tennessee. Within a few hours, they found themselves in jail in Murfreesboro, the center of a hurricane of police attention.

It was then that Alvin made his confession, placing most of the blame on Judith and telling the story about the other fifteen of Judith's murders he was willing to assist police in solving.

The stories created a furor in the three-state area. Veteran cops were leery of Alvin's story. They remembered that he had once gotten a sentence reduced for giving evidence in a murder case. There were strong suspicions that Alvin was trying to work his way up to copping a plea now. However, the police had to take Alvin's allegations seriously, no matter what their doubts. He was offering some details that only the killer could know. It would be months before most of the law enforcement agencies were finally able to satisfy themselves that Alvin had been running a scam.

"He was trying to take some heat off his own ass," district attorney's investigator Darryl Collins of Fort Payne would say more than a year after the pair's arrest.

A confession was obtained from Judith as well, but in her version Alvin was the villain, a sexually insatiable monster who demanded that she procure young victims for him, or suffer the brutal consequences.

It was Alvin who rushed to tell Lieutenant Kines where the body of Janice Morrow Chatman could be found. He drew Kines a map of an old trail that led off Haywood Valley Road up in Chattooga County where Judith had marched the dazed woman before shooting her in the back and the head with the .38.

Neelley said that on the day Hancock had been shot by Judith, the pair sped off with Janice still their captive. They took her to a motel, he said, where she was sexually assaulted by both of them and kept handcuffed, naked, to a bed for the remainder of her last night on earth.

With Judith and Alvin Neelley finally in custody in Tennessee, police and prosecutors from Georgia, Alabama, and Tennessee met to determine how, when, and by whom the pair would be charged for the file drawer full of charges pending against them.

While Lisa Millican had been abducted in Rome, Georgia, with some aspects of the events leading to her death taking place there, Judith's confession placed the girl's actual killing across the state line in Georgia, within the jurisdiction of De Kalb County.

Theoretically, Alvin's role in that crime had been limited to the rape of the child, which took place in Floyd County, Georgia. He had not been involved in her murder at Little River Canyon, police finally concluded, despite what Judith said, and would not be extradited to Alabama for trial.

Under Georgia law, however, Alvin was a co-conspirator in the death of Janice Chatman in Chattooga County as well as a participant in her kidnapping.

Judith was also presumably indictable for the murder of Janice Chatman in Chattooga County, but with her life already at stake in an upcoming trial in Alabama, it seemed a redundancy to plan for an immediate Georgia prosecution in that case.

Hanging above that whole skein of legal arrangements was the prospect, shortly after the capture, that yet more jurisdictions might have murder warrants forthcoming on the basis of the revelations Alvin had promised to make.

While Judith would stand trial for the death of Lisa Millican in Alabama, her husband would never face a jury in either of the deaths to which both had confessed their participation.

Alvin pleaded guilty to the murder of Janice Chatman before a judge in Summerville, Georgia, and was given two life sentences, one for the murder, the second for aggravated assault.

Alvin Neelley could be eligible for parole in as little as fifteen years, under Georgia law, but officials doubt that any plea he might make for parole would be sympathetically heard.

Alvin never testified in any of the proceedings against Judith, nor she in any of the plea and sentencing sessions involving him.

Because that was so, some of the central questions raised when each gave their separate versions of what really happened on their crime spree went unanswered.

The inflammatory speculation raised by Alvin's accusation that Judith was a sadist with lesbian tendencies was not crucial to the relatively open-and-shut case that Prosecutor Richard Igou presented on behalf of the people of De Kalb County against Judith Ann Neelley.

As much at issue as anything was the state of Judith Neelley's mind at the time of the brutal crimes, and whether she was mentally competent to assist in her own defense.

In regard to her competency, the answer was clear-cut. A team of four psychiatrists had Judith under observation for thirty days.

"There was no doubt about her competency. She was extremely rational in most ways," Dr. Clifford Hardin remembers.

"What surprised me, I guess, was that she was such a likable person. She helped other patients; she was actually becoming a role model for some of them before her stay ended.

"I kept looking—we all did—hoping to find something that would account for the crimes she had been charged with.

"She had been responsible for her actions. She was aware of what was happening.

"Her answer to most of our questions about the killings was that Alvin had made her do it. But it seemed clear that if she had been under duress, there had been many opportunities for her to get away from Alvin. None of which she took," Dr. Hardin observed.

"As to the notion that she had been brainwashed by Alvin

to such a degree that she could only do his bidding, she presented none of the symptoms one might have expected to find in that condition.

"I have treated numerous battered-wife cases, and Judith was not presenting reactions or mind states that are common in those kinds of situations. Frankly, there was much about her that was inexplicable."

Dr. Hardin said that when Judith spoke of her early life, she told a story of frequent sexual abuse following the death of her father in a motorcycle accident and the arrival on the home scene of new boyfriends paying court to her mother.

She ran off to marry Alvin when she was only fifteen to escape sexual abuse from boyfriends of her mother and felt that Alvin would protect her from that sort of thing.

"She had always considered herself a very plain looking girl and had a general lack of self-esteem," Dr. Hardin noted. She had superior intelligence, with an IQ testing at about 110, but failed to give herself much credit for that intelligence.

During her stay at the mental facility, Judith frequently wore a T-shirt that bore the legend: "Eat Your Heart Out. I'm Married." The psychiatrists concluded she felt it conferred some self-satisfying status of normalcy for herself.

While in incarceration, Judith Neelley gave birth to a third child. Dr. Hardin said she seemed to express the normal amount of mother love for her children and reasoned that one of the motives behind the puzzling telephone calls she made to police may have had some of its origin in maternal concern.

"She said she was thinking about that little girl lying up in the canyon and wanted her to be found and given a Christian burial. That's what prompted her to make the calls," Hardin said.

Police officials believed otherwise. Alvin wanted her to make the calls, they theorized, as a way to thumb his nose at police, to show them that they were so dumb they couldn't even catch a person who was calling them up and giving clues.

Those differing opinions about Judith and Alvin still crop up today when people they had encountered on their trek through the justice system remember them.

Attorney Floyd Farless of Rome represented Alvin during one of his earlier brushes with the law. "Alvin was a poor slob in love. I don't think he could ever have been the brains behind the things they did. Shooting people with a gun wasn't part of his thing."

Ralph Van Pelt, the Chattooga County D.A. who worked out Alvin's sentencing in the Chatman murder, remembers him as a chameleon. "He wanted to please whoever it was he was talking to at the time, whatever he had to say to do it," Van Pelt says.

"Alvin was a bad guy, but I don't think he had the ability to turn her into a robot. He did get ahold of her at a very young age, and no doubt he had his influence on her, but she was smart. Smarter than him.

"In my mind she was the boss, the dominant part of the pair. I believe she did take part in the sex assaults, although she denied any willing participation. She was a hard lady and a killer," Darryl Collins of the De Kalb County D.A.'s office still believes today.

"There wasn't one manly thing about Alvin Neelley's makeup," Lieutenant Ken Kines says. "He was a slob, easily dominated by her. She was a cold-blooded killer and a good little actress."

"There are some things regarding both of them that we're just not ever going to know," Prosecutor Richard Igou says.

"There are some things we have no way of establishing in a court of law. What could be proven was that Judith Neelley had wantonly and in cold blood murdered an innocent child in De Kalb County, Alabama.

"I've been a prosecutor for thirteen years and I never met a more cold-hearted and unnatural person than Judith

Neelley. Based on the evidence we had, I had no qualms at all about asking for the death penalty.

"She was a sociopath. She was in control of herself at all times. What was in my mind was the lives of the others she had taken. Were we sure we even knew that these were the only victims?

"I think the only sorrow she ever exhibited was for herself. For the fix she was in because she had been caught.

"All during the trial she broke down in what sounded like sobs. Her body was racking. Her head was in her hands. I went over at one point and lifted her chin so the jury could get a look at her face. Her eyes were dry. There wasn't a tear there," Igou recalled.

Attorney Robert French handled Judith Neelley's defense and is still, today, involved in her appeal before higher Alabama courts.

French says his efforts on behalf of the young woman have cost him enormously.

"I have become one of the most hated men in this part of the country," French said. "I've lost business, my life has been threatened, and I still get ugly letters and phone calls."

French said Judith Neelley was found guilty and sentenced to death because she had been brutalized, brainwashed, and beaten into a kind of submission difficult for the average person to understand. Her tormenter was her husband, Alvin Neelley.

"He is the Marquis de Sade, Svengali, and Jim Jones all wrapped up in one," French said. "And Judith Neelley isn't the only woman he's beaten into submission. He's brutalized every woman who has ever been a part of his life."

French recalled tracking down a woman to whom Neelley had been married for six years. He once shot her in the back with a pistol, but she had been so desensitized to pain that she was not immediately aware she had been struck by a bullet, French said.

It was not until Judith heard that former wife's story of suffering at the hands of Alvin that French was able to elicit any degree of cooperation from Judith Neelley in her own defense.

"She was still trying to protect him. She still loved him. She was writing poetry to him, after all he'd done to her," French said.

"He never told Judith about any of that. He's a great actor. He puts on a convincing show.

"All through her trial I was without a client who was capable of cooperating. I didn't know why until I got to the bottom of Alvin. Now I know.

"I'm going to get Judith Neelley a new trial, and when I do she is going to walk," French said.

The Fort Payne, Alabama, defense attorney says Polaroid pictures of Judith taken by Alvin show her to be the victim of savage beatings by her husband.

"There were color pictures of her in which it looked as though her breasts had almost been torn off. Her eyes were beaten shut. He made her stand there naked while he took them. He would show them to her later in order to terrorize her," French said.

Investigator Darryl Collins says the only pictures he can remember being recovered when the pair were arrested had been given to the defense in response to a discovery motion, but that they did not show Judith's condition to be as her attorney described.

"I've had bigger bruises on my body from bumping into a coffee table," Collins says.

When Igou addressed the defense contention about the brutalization of Judith Neelley, he posed the question that continued to cast doubt in the minds of police and prosecutors. "Why hadn't she fled? Why hadn't she driven off in some other direction in her own car? Why, if she feared for her life, hadn't she aimed the gun at Alvin and pulled the trigger?"

In the end, it was an Alabama jury who weighed the contradictory claims put forward by the prosecution and the defense as they tried to make sense out of the life and crimes of Judith and Alvin Neelley.

The jury found Judith guilty as charged, but recommended not the death sentence, but life in prison for her crime.

Richard Igou believed it was her youth that made the jury recommend to the judge that her life be spared.

Under Alabama law, however, the judge is not bound by the jury's recommendation and in this case, the court ordered the sentence of death for Judith Neelley.

While Judith and Alvin Neelley have been removed from society for the foreseeable future, the end of their saga has not meant the end to haunting suspicions still left in the minds of police who mounted the manhunt that brought the Nightrider and Lady Sundance to justice.

"I think they killed some others we've yet to know about," Lieutenant Kines believes.

"It was too smooth an act. She had gotten too good at it to have only done it a couple of times. I think there are some other kids out there someplace, lying in shallow graves, who were also the victims of these two.

"I'm glad they're off the streets, but my mind still doesn't set easy when I think about what else they might have done.

"There are still far too many little girls out there who don't know better than to take a ride from a stranger."

Chapter 4

Priscilla Ford

OFFICER PAM ENGLE NUDGED the sleeping man on the bus-stop bench gently, but firmly enough to rouse him from what she guessed might be a wino's muscatel-induced dream state.

It wouldn't do the glamorous image of Reno's glittering Casino Row any good to have vagrants snoozing on benches in the middle of the afternoon at the corner of North Virginia and Second streets, the most trafficked intersection in town. Thousands of tourists a day walked by that corner on their way to the gaming rooms at Harrah's, the Nevada Club, Harolds Club, and the Club Cal Nevada.

Even more disconcerting, today was Thanksgiving Day 1980, and throngs of visitors who had just finished a hearty holiday meal were now heading back out onto the pedestrian-packed streets to stretch their legs a bit before getting down to the carefree business that had brought them to Reno, Nevada, the exciting blur of the roulette wheel, the enticing chant of the blackjack dealers, and the silvery clang of the slots paying off another big winner.

Downtown beat officer Pam Engle gave the sleeping man another nudge to get him on his way. People out for a good time on Thanksgiving Day didn't need to see someone homeless to turn their minds toward more somber concerns.

Suddenly behind her, the policewoman heard a rush of heart-stopping sounds. Screams, shrieks, moans of pain, cries of alarm rushed toward her like the first cold waves of an avalanche. Preceding the mind-numbing wails, Officer

Pam Engle saw in stunned disbelief what seemed literally an explosion of human bodies hurtling toward the corner where she stood. Behind that screaming litany of horror, she heard the sound of an auto engine accelerating and the blue-black shimmer of a large car smashing its way through still-frozen crowds of pedestrians like some deadly machine of harvest, carrying on its hood the broken forms of two humans, then spilling them off, careening into yet more victims and throwing them at all angles like the horns of some maddened bull.

In less than a heartbeat, while her reeling mind tried to take in the bloody tableau unfolding before her, the car was bearing down on the spot where Officer Pan Engle stood, her admonishment to the sleeping vagrant still frozen on her lips. By instinct, she pulled back, but it was only a hairsbreadth from the juggernaut of death. She heard the roar of the engine and felt its barreling heat as the car passed within inches of her and continued to stalk down the sidewalk on North Virginia Street, churning yet more victims beneath its wheels and cascading still more bodies headlong from its path in grotesque somersaults of agony and death.

Pam Engle's head swiveled back to the path of carnage through which the car had hurtled toward her, then ahead to where more bleeding, dying, horribly injured victims had just been scythed down. She regained control of her shattered senses and pursued the car to the intersection where it had paused, shouting at the top of her lungs for the driver to stop.

In the same instant, Officer Engle's hours of police training screamed at her to reach for her portable police radio and get help on the way for the victims of the nightmare she had just witnessed.

Her voice was breathless, tinged with the hard colors of shock as it reached the central dispatch room at Reno P.D.

"It's a runaway vehicle! I've got about ten casualties," policewoman Engle shouted into the hand-held radio she was carrying. "Send everything you've got—send everything."

The black auto had sped from her view. Pam Engle whirled again to look southward down Virginia Street. She knew at once she had been wrong about the number of victims. It looked more like twenty. The street was littered with dead and dying. Cries of pain reached out to her from both sides of the broad avenue. Their voices of agony were mixed with the shouts of panic of those who had escaped but witnessed the two minutes of terror that had just knifed through the street.

She saw a severed leg, still trembling from nerve excitation, a blond wig now dyed crimson with human blood as it lay cockeyed on the pavement. Single shoes, a dental plate. Human forms that had been flung into unyielding building walls lay crumpled like shattered dolls.

"My God, it's like a battlefield," Officer Engle heard herself think. She raced toward one of the injured, to do whatever she could until help arrived.

From the rear-view mirror of his car, which was approaching the intersection of North Virginia and Third, Tom Jaffe could scarcely credit what he had just seen.

The black 1974 Lincoln approaching his auto from the rear had just struck a pedestrian and the blur that arched across Jaffe's rear-view mirror had been a human body! Jaffe was unaware of the rampage that had just occurred a block behind him, and thought he had just witnessed a single hit-and-run accident. He saw the Lincoln veer into the right-hand lane behind him and pass around him at a fast clip.

"That woman just hit someone back there, and she isn't even stopping," the sixty-four-year-old Jaffe said to his wife, Ethel, who sat beside him on the front seat of the car.

"I'm going to stop her," Tom Jaffe said. Mrs. Jaffe worried. Tom had a heart condition, but she knew there was no use arguing with him just then. Tom Jaffe wasn't going to sit idly by.

Jaffe pulled through the intersection and stepped on the accelerator. He pulled even with the Lincoln and looked over to see the face of the small black woman behind the wheel. She seemed oblivious to the world. Her hands were gripped firmly, almost comically, to the big steering wheel of the car. He accelerated again, got ahead of the Lincoln, and began to slow sharply to block the woman's flight. He saw her come to a stop. Both he and his wife jumped from their car and dashed over to the driver's side of the Lincoln. He rapped sharply against the driver's window, demanding that she roll it down. Slowly, the woman complied, but she never turned to look at Jaffe or his wife. "Do you know you just hit someone back there?" he shouted. The woman still stared out through the front windshield as though she had not heard his angry voice.

Tom Jaffe looked up then as he heard the thunder of dozens of pounding feet approaching the car he had just halted.

At the front of the grim-jawed group was a man wearing a Reno police officer's uniform. It was patrolman Steve Baring. He took over. Baring placed the tight-lipped fiftyish black woman behind the wheel of the car under arrest. He summoned a unit to help him take her away.

Stunned Reno emergency authorities now had some beginnings of an idea of the horror that had happened on North Virginia Street. Baring heard some of that information crackling over his police monitor. As many as five dead, maybe six. Twenty or more injured, many critically. Baring looked uncomprehendingly at the small black woman in the back of the squad car. She was smiling. He asked her again what her name was. "Priscilla Joyce Ford," she replied. "Sometimes I am called Jesus Christ."

At Reno police headquarters, senior officers who briefly tried to speak to the woman confirmed Baring's observation that her breath smelled of alcohol. She had been read her constitutional rights before being placed in the squad car, but just to be sure, she was read them again. Baring was given special instructions regarding the prisoner. He was to take her at once to Washoe Medical Center and remain with her as blood alcohol tests were administered. He was not to attempt an interrogation until representatives from the Washoe County District Attorney's office arrived on the scene along with detective department investigators. He was, however, to write down anything the woman said voluntarily.

The car in which Baring drove Priscilla Ford to Washoe Medical Center was passed more than once by wailing ambulances heading to the emergency entrance with more of the victims of her deadly ride through the town. At St. Mary's Hospital, additional doctors and nurses were quickly summoned away from family Thanksgiving dinners to handle the dead, the dying, and the injured.

Officer Steve Baring made notes of what Priscilla Ford said as technicians took the required three blood samples at half-hour intervals. He tried to keep his hands steady on the small notebook as the woman talked in eerie, disjointed phrases. His notations were methodically precise.

"I'm a New York teacher, tired of life. I want attention. I'm sick of trouble," the woman said.

"I deliberately planned to get as many as possible. A Lincoln Continental can do a lot of damage, can't it?

"In June I was in Boston. A voice told me to drive through a crowd at a theater and kill as many as possible, but another voice said she's too much of a lady to do that.

"I had wine today specifically to blame it on the accident.

"The more dead the better. That will keep the mortuaries busy. That's the American way.

"Did I get fifty? How many did I get? I hope I got seventy-five."

By now, Detective Sergeant Duane Isenberg had arrived to take over a more formal interrogation. Along with him was John Oakes, a deputy district attorney, carrying with him a special set of orders from his boss, Cal Dunlap, the D.A. of Washoe County.

Dunlap too had been taken away from a family dinner by the tragedy. He immediately dispatched key staff members off on assignments while he and other city and county officials tried to pull together the threads of the madness that had just struck downtown Reno.

Dunlap told John Oakes to be certain that Priscilla Ford was given both a complete physical exam and a mental-status evaluation at the medical center before she was booked and returned to the Reno city jail. Dunlap said he wanted to be certain the woman now in custody was not suffering from any organic problem that could have led her to the rampage she had unleashed that afternoon, and wanted the mental exam to forestall the possibility of confusion later should a plea of insanity be entered on her behalf. "I don't want any phony insanity argument coming up when this thing goes to trial," Dunlap told John Oakes.

Analysis of the blood drawn from Priscilla Ford quickly established a blood-alcohol level above the norm used in Nevada to conclude that a suspect is intoxicated. The reading of .162 was considerably above the .10 level established for drunkenness.

The doctor assigned to the examination of the prisoner was Craig Trigueiro. He found no brain tumors, abnormalities, or other organic types of dysfunction that could account for the crime with which the woman was charged. During the conversation he conducted with Priscilla Ford to determine her mental status, Dr. Trigueiro turned on a tape recorder so his report would be indisputably accurate.

Priscilla Ford began to tell the examining physician an incoherent tale about the disappearance of her eleven-year-old daughter in 1973. The child had been kidnapped, Priscilla said, and Reno authorities had refused to help her get the child back. The drive that ended in death for the victims was her vengeance against Reno, the woman said.

What had the people who were walking down the street in Reno that afternoon had to do with the disappearance of her child? Dr. Trigueiro asked softly. Nothing, the woman replied.

"They were just pigs, animals let out wild in a place," the woman said of her victims.

Had she felt nothing as she mowed them down?

"No, I could care less. They were like pigs to me," Priscilla Ford answered as the tape rolled on.

The doctor asked if she thought it was wrong to kill.

"It's not wrong for me to kill because I deserve vengeance. Vengeance is mine."

Now Priscilla offered another reason why the tourists on North Virginia Street were destined to be her victims:

"I heard the voice of Joan Kennedy telling me to find a crowd of people and run them down," she said.

She told the doctor that she had heard the voice of the then wife of Senator Edward Kennedy instruct her to "run through a whole bunch of people and kill everybody."

But Priscilla Ford said it would not be right for the police to blame Mrs. Kennedy for what had happened.

"She's not implicated because she does not have to admit it was her—and it might not have been," Priscilla added.

She had planned to have Thanksgiving dinner that day at a restaurant in her neighborhood near South Virginia Street, but had found it closed. She had to settle for cheese and crackers and a half gallon of wine from a convenience store she had finally managed to find open on the holiday.

"I ate some of the cheese and crackers and had some wine. Then I sat there and finally said the hell with it. I got in the Lincoln and went looking for a crowd of people."

In a conversation filled with bizarre twists and turns, Dr. Trigueiro nearly missed the significance of the woman's next remark.

"I had the instrument, which I had control over—the wheel and gas pedal. As far as I'm concerned that Lincoln Continental did it. I only steered toward them."

Deputy D.A. Oakes and Detective Isenberg came away from their interview almost unable to believe the prisoner's callous curiosity about the trail of blood she had hacked through the city that day.

Priscilla Ford demanded of Oakes to know exactly how many people she had killed. Oakes said he did not know, but would check with doctors. He returned later to tell her that at least five were dead and that a sixth would probably be dead before long.

"Well, at least I made the funeral homes happy today," she said.

John Oakes asked the woman how she felt. "I feel good," she answered, "just like I felt yesterday, and tomorrow."

Priscilla Ford was taken to the Reno city jail. She was held under five murder charges and twenty-three counts of attempted murder. She quarreled briefly with jailer Sylvia Gray when Gray refused to drop everything to find her some cigarettes.

"You just don't want to give me any cigarettes because of what I did," she shouted angrily at the retreating back of the jailer.

"I just did what I had to do."

At Washoe Medical Center, Dr. Craig Trigueiro listened again to the tape. He made notes on a legal pad from which he would have a diagnosis typed up later. "Actively psychotic," he noted to himself. "Schizophrenic with paranoid overtone."

If Priscilla Ford had wanted attention, she had undeniably gotten her wish. All three major television networks carried the bloody details of her revenge on Reno as Americans still basking in the warm glow of Thanksgiving turned to the evening news that night. Reporters from all over the country were on their way to Reno to see what could be learned firsthand about the fifty-one-year-old woman who had decided to wreak an awful vengeance on a town that lived in the shadow of legalized sin.

In Reno, police shifts were held over to push ahead through the night in search of what might be known about Priscilla Ford. Reno wanted a quick answer to the damage that had been done to its good name as a place where tourists could have a fine time without the fear of big-city crime or problems.

Bail for the prisoner was set at $500,000. It seemed quite unlikely it would be met. The Washoe County Public Defender's office had already been notified the woman would require representation.

Public Defender William Dunseath spoke to Priscilla Ford. "She talks well and was pleasant enough to me," Dunseath told reporters. He said it was too early to decide how she would plead to the numerous counts. Dunseath ran a mental inventory of cases assigned to the defenders in his office—who was working on what—but even more importantly, who would offer the best defense for a woman charged with the most nightmarish crime in Reno history. He thought Lew Carnahan might be the right person. Lew was a fighter, not to mention a damn good lawyer.

If Priscilla Ford thought she might somehow benefit from the spotlight of attention that now focused on her across the nation, she would in no way be as big a beneficiary as the toiling staff of the Reno Police Department's overloaded detective bureau.

All over America, people were remembering that they had once encountered Priscilla Ford. Calls were now pouring into the grateful detectives who desperately wanted to know everything they could about her.

Within a matter of days, probing reporters would wrest those details from the police, along with the fruits of their own investigations, and the final product would be a chilling portrait of a woman who seemed to have been well set along a path that would lead to the Reno disaster as far back as ten years before the anger exploded on the city's downtown streets.

Priscilla Ford had only arrived in Reno a few weeks before that Thanksgiving. But it had not been the first time she had lived in the city. She had come there in early 1973, down on her luck, out of work, hoping things might change in upbeat Reno. She had with her the only person left in the world whom she loved, her eleven-year-old daughter, Wynter Scott, a pretty child born of her second of four marriages. Her bad luck continued. There were three quick brushes with the law. In each instance, Wynter was taken temporarily to a juvenile home until her mother was freed. On the third occasion, Priscilla claimed the welfare department would not give Wynter back to her. They had kidnapped her, were holding her illegally. It was the rage over the abduction of her child, she would later say, that determined her to take the bloody revenge against Reno.

Priscilla Ford had told the story to co-workers in the gift-wrapping department of Macy's where she had found a job shortly after her return to Reno in early November 1980. To anyone who would listen, she would rail against snot-nosed young white women whom states gave the authority to take children away from their mothers without due process of law.

So there it was, reporters poring over the details of Priscilla Ford's life surmised. Her child caught up in some bureaucratic shuffle, her helpless rage finally reaching the boiling point after seven years of unsuccessfully trying to find the youngster. Was that the key to Priscilla Ford's killing hatred of Reno?

Not quite, investigators following the trail of her troubled life even more intensely would discover.

The theory had a few major holes. Yes, it was true that the county welfare department had taken the child into custody those three times when Priscilla had run afoul of the law. But the first two times the child had been returned to her custody. On the third occurrence, concerned case-workers said the child would not be returned until there was satisfactory evidence that Priscilla was working and could provide shelter for the child. Priscilla stormed off, threatening dire legal consequences. In a note to the child, she said she was heading for Chicago where she would find a lawyer who would make the county reunite them. More than a year passed before caseworkers would hear from Priscilla again.

This time an angry letter warned caseworker Susan Nelson that if Wynter were not returned immediately Priscilla would "take the law into my own hands and dispose of you."

Ironically, Susan Nelson had tried for more than a year to locate Priscilla Ford to determine if the mother's situation was now such that she could resume custody of the child. She had written to relatives and friends in every place Priscilla had listed having kinfolk. Her search had been fruitless. Priscilla Ford was never in touch with Reno welfare workers again.

And by now, detectives following the trail that led further into the past of Priscilla Ford had satisfied themselves that her problems were older and deeper than just her anger about her daughter.

Priscilla had been born and raised in Berrien Springs, Michigan, growing up in a hardworking black family of nine girls and two boys. Her mother, Lucille Lawrence, and her father were devout members of the Seventh Day Adventist Church, and raised up all their children in the sight of the Lord. Priscilla was generally acknowledged to be the pride of the whole family. She was smart and a go-getter. She earned a degree and a teacher's certificate. Her parents weren't exactly happy about an early marriage that resulted in two sons. She married again soon after that unhappy first attempt, this time to William Scott, by whom she had her only daughter. That relationship was troubled too, however, and it was in this period that Priscilla first came to the notice of the police. During a quarrel, she had shot Scott, then turned the gun on herself. Both recovered, and charges were dropped. But that marriage too collapsed, and people who knew her up around Berrien Springs say that's when Priscilla Ford's problems may really have begun.

Priscilla had been an excellent schoolteacher in the area's system. She was highly thought of and at one point even ran for a seat on a district education board. While she did not win, many believed it was only because whe was a black living in rural Michigan at a time when black citizens were not really enfranchised. She had earned the respect of those who knew how good an educator she was and how unfair small-town politics could be.

It was about 1966 when she packed up herself and her young daughter and left Michigan. Priscilla told well-wishing friends she was heading for Buffalo, New York. She told some that she had been offered an excellent job there. She told others she was going back to school to work on advanced degrees.

What really happened was that Priscilla Ford began to drift aimlessly around the country with her child in tow, taking meaningless jobs far beneath her abilities, moving from town to town and state to state in a baffling pattern, often returning to one or another after a year or two of living somewhere else. Authorities believed she married at least twice more. One of those marriages was to a white man, and it apparently degenerated quickly into a bitter and furious wrangle that left Priscilla scarred with a new kind of hatred, and back on the road again.

Wynter Scott loved her mom. But even she realized that her mother wasn't always in control of herself. By the time Wynter was nine, her mom frequently shared marijuana with her as a mind-opening religious sacrament. Her mother was using a lot of pot, Wynter was old enough to know, and her behavior was definitely changing more with each passing day.

Priscilla told Wynter that she had been receiving a series of revelations from Ellen G. White, a Seventh Day Adventist prophetess who had caused a firestorm of controversy in the church in the nineteenth century.

Before long, Priscilla told her daughter that she had been visited by a vision of the prophetess and told that she was now the reincarnation of the holy woman. Within a few months, Priscilla believed she had transcended even that status and had, in fact, become Jesus Christ herself.

She had a plan for Wynter too, Priscilla told the girl one night as she rolled another joint. "We are going to find someone who can artificially inseminate you," she told the child, explaining to her what that meant. "The child you shall bear will be Jesus Christ, even as I am Jesus Christ," the mother told the bewildered child.

Her mother had business cards printed that described herself as being divine. She signed letters as the Rev. Dr. Priscilla Ford. By the time they had reached Reno for the first time in 1973, Wynter was eleven years old. She no longer had any doubts in her mind. Her mother was a sick person. The first encounter they had with police that time came when her mom passed out in a restaurant and couldn't be wakened. Police who were summoned shook her rudely to get her out of the booth. They couldn't understand when Wynter fought furiously to prevent them from waking her mother. They didn't know, as she did, that her mother was involved in out-of-body travel, attending to the needs of suffering humanity, and that to be awakened from such a trance could mean serious problems. The police just thought she was drunk.

Others too were becoming concerned with the state of Priscilla Ford's mind. Shortly before the 1973 trip to Reno, Priscilla and Wynter had moved in with her son Franklin Scott and his wife in Illinois. Ford had just been discharged from the army. It had been quite a few years since he had seen his mother. He was shocked by the way she had changed. He remembered his mother as a woman who followed her demanding faith, who pounded into her two sons the value of an education. She believed in hard work and sacrifice to get ahead.

Now Franklin met an eerie woman he could hardly recall. She was intoxicated most of the time. She smoked more dope than anyone he had ever met and gave the stuff to his little half sister. Once she had locked herself in the house, turned on the gas from the oven, and methodically broken every piece of crockery in the house while waiting to die.

Her son had to summon police to rescue her from the house. She demanded that her son accompany her and Wynter to the 1972 Republican Convention in Miami where, she said, she had been invited to speak on the revelations of Ellen G. White. Of course, she had not, and when security officials rudely threw them all out of the convention center, Priscilla said it was the devil who had prevented her from getting her message to the convention delegates.

Old friends in Michigan had begun to receive troubling letters from Priscilla. They were querulous, argumentative, accusing, rambling, and confused. Her messages were filled with impossible metaphysical jargon and discourses that made absolutely no sense at all.

Her sister, Myrna McClain, received incomprehensible notes in which Priscilla called herself a doctor, a healer, a minister. She knew Priscilla was none of these.

After her mother's third arrest in Reno in 1973, Wynter did not hear from her again right away, other than the note saying that she was off to Chicago to find a lawyer. The girl was at first unconcerned. She was certain her mom would do exactly as she had said and that soon they would be reunited. Wynter couldn't imagine that her mom would leave her behind, but that was exactly what happened. It wouldn't be until several years later that Wynter would find her first real home, with a half brother in Los Angeles. When, in 1980, she finally received a letter from her mother asking her how she was, just as though none of those years had passed in between, Wynter wasn't exactly in a charitable frame of mind. She wrote back to her mother, and the words she wrote rang with anger.

"You should be proud of the way I grew up," Wynter's letter read, "even though you let that responsibility go years ago."

All through the years that Priscilla had turned her back on the child's fate, she nonetheless continued to tell almost everyone she met the heart-wrenching story about how the child had been ruthlessly kidnapped by Nevada authorities, and though she had moved heaven and earth she had never had enough clout to win back the child's freedom.

It was true that Priscilla had written to relatives in Michigan asking them to try to intercede to win the release of Wynter, and once, when committed to a psychiatric facility in New York state, she agreed to cooperate with treatment if the staff would try to establish the whereabouts of her daughter.

But the conclusion authorities finally reached was that Priscilla had abandoned Wynter, refusing to meet the modest demands the Nevada agency had set as a precondition for returning the child. Instead, investigators believed, she had turned that incident into a smoldering bed of hatred and begun concocting in her own troubled mind a tortured scenario that blamed nearly everyone else in the world but herself for the misfortune that had separated her from her child.

In the seven years that followed her separation from Wynter, Priscilla became a wanderer again. She retraced some of the routes she and her daughter had earlier traveled. In 1978 she had more or less settled down in Boise, Idaho, and was working steadily. Then, in U.S. District Court, using the name Rev. Dr. Priscilla Ford, she sued astonished officials of the Mormon Church, leaders of her own church, and an even more astonished Joseph Califano, the Secretary of the Department of Health, Education, and Welfare.

Priscilla was demanding $500 million in compensation from the trio on the basis they had caused her to suffer mental and physical agony, not to mention "the keenest anguish and a sense of God's displeasure and discrimination."

Ford accused them of waging war against her and "ignoring the fact that God gave testimony of Jesus to the church in the body of the Holy Spirit, the plaintiff, who receives divine visions."

A federal judge who reviewed the pleadings dismissed them, stating that the court had no jurisdiction over the matters she had raised, assuming that he could even understand what they were.

In less than a year, in early 1979, Priscilla had moved to Buffalo, New York. Within weeks she was facing eight petty criminal charges that included bad checks, theft of services, and possession of marijuana. Her odd behavior earned her a trip to the Buffalo Psychiatric Center. Under observation there, Priscilla said she sometimes thought about people being decapitated. She told them of a fantasy she had in which she was the driver of a car that drove through a crowd of people, killing many of them. Priscilla was diagnosed by the staff as a paranoid schizophrenic. She refused any medication, a note penciled on her release chart noted.

Shortly after her problems in Buffalo, Priscilla loaded her belongings into the 1974 Lincoln Continental she had purchased in better times. She drove to Jackman, Maine, and introduced herself as a successful author who was looking for some tranquil place to settle down to work on her next project. Within a month she had moved to Bangor, renting a tiny apartment, once again saying she was a writer seeking a peaceful place to create.

In Jackman, Irene Gagne, who ran a local motel where Priscilla stayed, would recall her as constantly depressed. She gave Mrs. Gagne a bundle that contained nearly three hundred handwritten pages. "It was the story of her whole life," Mrs. Gagne would recall. Her marriages, her stays in mental institutions, the story about how her daughter had been taken away. It was sad.

"I told her she should erase the past and start all over again," Mrs. Gagne said.

In Portland, Maine, at about the same time, U.S. Attorney Thomas Delahanaty, Jr., received an alarming phone call. It was Priscilla Ford, who demanded that he immediately bring civil and criminal actions against individuals who had kidnapped the caller's daughter seven years earlier. The caller also added a threat that would later prove prophetic.

"She said if I wasn't going to help her, she would get in her car and drive from Jackman to Portland and kill everybody she saw along the way," Delahanaty remembered.

Priscilla actually did show up at the attorney's office several days later, but she was subdued and did not create a disturbance when he explained he had no jurisdiction outside of Maine.

It was in early November 1980 when Priscilla Ford's big Lincoln pulled up again in Reno. She managed to find the job as gift wrapper in Macy's in Meadowland mall and co-workers found her likable, if a bit obsessed with the story of her kidnapped daughter. They didn't know that the "kidnapped" little girl was now a young woman of nineteen, living happily in California and that the mother knew perfectly well where she was, having just recently received a stinging letter of rebuke from the daughter she had abandoned so many years before.

By the time District Attorney Cal Dunlap was ready to ask a Washoe County grand jury to indict Ford on six counts of murder and twenty-three counts of attempted murder, police detectives had gathered still more evidence of her troubled life and clouded state of mind.

Reno Police Detective Phil Galeoto had taken a search warrant to the small rented home where Priscilla had been living briefly before the Thanksgiving Day massacre.

Among the curiosities Galeoto found were copies of a scathing, if illogical, letter that Ford had written to lonely-hearts columnist Abigail Van Buren, disputing advice Dear Abby had given in a recent syndicated column. Priscilla had said she felt it her responsibility to correct Dear Abby because it was "my duty as America's only authorized divinity to make the truth known."

The detective also found a handwritten grant application prepared for submission to the U.S. Department of Education. In it, Priscilla Ford asked for $3 million to conduct research into the anatomy and physiology of the soul. She set her own salary for serving as director of the project at $60,000 per year.

A grand jury seemed unhesitant about indicting Ford on all the counts and specifications asked for by the prosecutor. By the end of December, at a formal arraignment in Washoe County District Court, Dunlap did not object when Lew Carnahan, the public defender assigned to Ford's case, asked for a complete psychiatric examination of his client to determine her competency to stand trial. While the request seemed routine enough, and was approved without fanfare by the presiding judge, the decision to determine Ford's competency would quickly break out into a lengthy furor that would require consideration by the Nevada Supreme Court to put back on the legal rails. At the confusing heart of the legal free-for-all that ensued were the actions of two court-appointed psychiatrists who reported back to the court that in their opinion the defendant was not then competent to stand trial for her crimes. Very well, the judge said, then she'll be sent to an institution where she can receive treatment. Not so fast, the defense argued, the court can't order treatment unless it rules the defendant is insane. If the defendant is insane and was at the time of the incident, the court cannot now permit the use of antipsychotic drugs to make her sane again and face the consequences of a crime for which she should properly be tried and acquitted by reason of insanity. To use the drugs could alter the fabric of the defendant's mind, changing it from the condition it was in at the time of the crime, rendering it impossible for the victim to assist in defense or offer testimony in a mind state similar to that which preceded the alleged offenses. "Hogwash," "fraud," and "sham" were some of the milder words used by D.A. Cal Dunlap in response. He argued that Nevada law required medical experts to use every tool at their command to improve the mental condition of persons ordered into their custody by the courts, and that included the use of whatever drugs that might assist in rendering her once more competent to stand trial. He blasted as nonsense the defense contention that Priscilla Ford, as a patient, had the right to refuse medication, which, in fact, she had announced through her lawyers she would do.

More than three months passed before the judge ruled that Priscilla Ford was required to take drugs prescribed by physicians directing her treatment, using force if need be. The judge based his ruling on evidence offered by psychiatrists who informed him that the use of antipsychotic drugs would likely be successful in aiding Priscilla Ford reach a state of mental competency sufficient to assist in her own defense.

In late July, two of the three psychiatrists treating Ford reported to the court they believed she was competent now to stand trial. Their opinions, they noted, did not go to the state of her mind at the time of the crime—whether she was sane or not in that hour. That would be for a jury to decide, should the defendant's plea be one of not guilty by reason of insanity.

It was now August 1981, and during a hearing in which Ford's now established competency was formalized, yet another brush fire blazed up between the defense and the prosecution. Carnahan asked that the trial be delayed to January 1982. If it were not, he argued, the trial would be conducted during some part of the Thanksgiving holiday of 1981, renewing in the minds of the jury hostile feelings toward his client.

D.A. Dunlap demanded in angry exasperation that the trial go forward in October as the judge had earlier indicated. The victims had waited long enough to see jusitce done, he argued, and it would be a worse tragedy to delay any further.

Carnahan was not happy, but he pleaded his client not guilty by reason of insanity and accepted the October court date.

"I think it is clear she was insane at the time," he told reporters. "It is only a matter of whether the jury will follow the law and find her insane."

In the furiously fought five-month trial that followed, a jury of seven men and five women would often wonder how Carnahan could ever have been quite so optimistic. They would learn, to their wonder and grief, that it is no easy thing to determine the state of a person's mind at the moment when a crime is committed, and that for every positive statement put forward by experts trained in the study of human emotion, an observation that seemed the exact opposite could be heard from yet another such expert an hour later. The jury would hear one of the most exhaustive arguments about the potential for forensic psychiatry to guide the law in reaching a decision ever made in an American courtroom. They would hear it explained to them under the direction of two skilled and determined lawyers who stood at opposite poles on the question of whether it is humane to take the life of a person who clearly is afflicted by some degree of mental incapacity, and they would come finally to understand the agony that our system forces upon twelve ordinary persons when it expects of them a rendering of justice in a matter so complex that even the experts cannot agree. The weight of their decision was burdened by the prosecution's determination to ask that the death penalty be imposed on the defendant, if found guilty.

District Attorney Cal Dunlap was as suspicious on the day the trial opened as he had been on the night of the crimes that an unwarranted plea of insanity would be put forward on the behalf of Priscilla Ford.

Dunlap knew from the reports of the earlier psychiatric exams to determine Ford's competency that at least several eminent defense psychiatrists would testify, with complete honesty, that they believed she was suffering from paranoid schizophrenia, one of the most severe forms of insanity by both clinical and legal definitions.

But Dunlap had a strong belief of his own, one that he held with the same honest conviction as the psychiatrists had. He believed that what the woman had said on the night of the massacre, only hours after she had set it in motion, was a much more accurate reflection of the true state of her mind than the stories she would later offer to psychiatrists as clever rationales for them to further embroider upon. Dunlap's view of Ford's history was that she was a highly intelligent, even if disturbed woman, who had spent many years manipulating sympathetic social workers, mental health experts, and others with alternating exhibitions of irrational behavior and flashes of keen intelligence in order to use them toward her own ends.

Dunlap intended to attack current psychiatric opinions as what he firmly believed them to be, a highly subjective art, not a verifiably agreed upon and uniformly applied science. He believed that too much emphasis was being placed on this highly vulnerable craft in the courtroom.

As the trial wore on, it became exactly what Dunlap had anticipated, a grueling war of words between himself and three defense psychiatrists who testified that from their observations and from careful scrutiny of her extensive notebooks, letters, and other writings, it was clear that she suffered from the kind of schizophrenia accompanied by delusional states which rendered it impossible for her to know the difference between right and wrong as related to her actions. Her chief delusion, they asserted confidently, was that she had been granted a godlike authority to kill with impunity.

Dunlap grilled the experts relentlessly. He reduced each complex line of theory to language he hoped the jury would understand. He played before them the tape that Dr. Craig Trigueiro had made of his conversations on the night he interviewed Ford at the Washoe Medical Center.

Dr. Trigueiro recounted again the final conversation he had with Ford in which he asked her if she knew what would now happen to her because of the charges under which she was being held:

"First they'll examine me to see if I'm crazy; they always examine me to see if I'm crazy," she told the doctor.

"Then they'll take me to jail. Then maybe I'll get a

lawyer. What happens depends on the end of all that," she said.

She had foreseen the consequences of her act in a way that met the legal standard for knowing the nature and quality of an action used as a test for sanity under Nevada law as well as in other states.

Did she not know she was doing something that would result in the death of others—a companion aspect of the sanity determination? She had gone looking for a crowd of people in order to drive into them and kill them. She had told the doctor that in her own words.

But the defense psychiatrists reasoned that that was exactly one of the symptoms of her insanity. She would rather face punishment than admit that she was mentally unbalanced. Dunlap could barely conceal his scorn.

What followed next may have rendered much of the painstaking testimony and rebuttal on insanity a total exercise in frustration.

Priscilla Ford insisted on taking the stand in her own behalf. She was upset by the impressions being given that she was insane, she notified the judge in a note she had delivered from her cell. She demanded the right to speak to the jury herself, through testimony, to set that matter straight.

A distraught defender, Lew Carnahan argued passionately that the judge deny her request on the basis that her testimony would be tantamount to "committing public suicide."

While Judge John Barrett seemed understanding, he ruled that the constitution and recent decisions obliged him to permit the defendant to take the stand under pain of committing irreversible error by denying her a clear legal right.

Reporters broke from the courtroom to inform editors to hold open spots on page one and major segments for the six o'clock news. They knew that the testimony of Priscilla Ford had to be dynamite. No one was disappointed.

Under a cross-examination that lasted for more than three days, Dunlap read to Priscilla Ford key passages from the testimony of the psychiatrists which supported the plea of insanity by offering variations of the basic diagnosis of paranoid or psychotic schizophrenia.

"I would disagree with that," she responded as Dunlap paused for her reaction.

She said she didn't think the doctors who testified really believed she was a paranoid schizophrenic.

"No one really thinks I've been sick. And I haven't been. They wanted me to be," she said.

Carnahan faced the agonizing need to examine his client on the stand as well, to show through her bizarre ramblings that she was, indeed, the desperately ill woman the experts had found her to be.

He asked her why she had written the name of Barbara Walters frequently in the margins of passages of the Bible that had to do with prophecies depicting the end of the world. "Because she is a wild, fierce beast," Priscilla explained.

"Why were so many books about Hitler and the Nazis found in her room?" Carnahan wanted to know.

"Because I've always had a soft spot in my heart for Hitler."

She explained that her battle against the Mormon Church was based on their teaching of a heresy—that founder Joseph Smith had spoken to God and Jesus. "Joseph Smith did not see Jesus. I was Jesus," she answered.

At present, she said, she was the Holy Spirit. She had been Adam and other souls thoughout many lifetimes, but it would be wrong to confuse what she was saying with the false doctrine of reincarnation. Her soul had continued to live on, she said, because she had never sinned, and therefore never died.

Dunlap asked her repeatedly about the day she drove the car that spread death and injury down the streets of Reno.

Priscilla Ford answered that she had no recollection of

ever running down anyone. Her car was not steering well, she said, and she was driving around to find a service station to have it checked. The car must have gone out of control and rammed into the crowd. When it was over, she was once again in control of the car, and of her mind. But no one was hit by the car that she could recall.

"I am human and I am divine," she said on her last day of testimony. "I don't like it any more than anyone else does. I don't want to be divine," she said, looking down toward the floor.

"I'm tired. Very tired."

The district attorney was filled with righteous fire as he made his closing arguments to the jury.

"She is a black widow full of venom," he thundered, "and what she did on Thanksgiving Day was filled with premeditated hatred and malice.

"Without question, without doubt, she is guilty. She said what she was going to do, and she did it and afterward she said why she did it.

"We are not here to argue whether she is mentally ill. I'll concede that," Dunlap said, but he would not concede that her illness made her incapable of knowing the difference between right and wrong.

"She went out there to kill as many people as possible. She was only sorry she hadn't killed more."

Lew Carnahan had mounted a defense on behalf of Priscilla Ford that won him wide praise. If ever a defendant in Nevada had been given every benefit of the law that a skilled lawyer could conceivably put forward, it had been Priscilla Ford.

He argued now that the jury need not be sympathetic to his client in order to find her not guilty. They needed only to look to the law that made the insane, sick through no fault of their own, not guilty of crimes, no matter how tragic, no matter how offensive to the public conscience.

Priscilla Ford was insane, he told the jury. They had seen and heard that for themselves.

The courtroom was packed when the jury returned with its findings in thirteen hours. The verdict was guilty on all counts of the indictment. Lew Carnahan asked that the jury be polled individually. Was it the verdict of each? "Yes," each juror answered softly in reply.

Priscilla Ford sat expressionless, as she had through every hour of the trial.

Now the jury faced the final phase of the somber duty for which they had been empaneled months before. Once more they heard arguments, this time about what their hearts and minds should tell them about the life or death of the woman they had found guilty.

Carnahan now argued that even though the jury had rejected the insanity plea, it must still be clear to them that Priscilla Ford was mentally ill, and that illness mitigated her guilt. They should not sentence her to death in the gas chamber.

"Every human life has dignity. We don't establish that principle if we sink to the level of the people we are punishing," Carnahan pleaded.

"You have fulfilled your obligation to society. You have made sure Mrs. Ford will not have the opportunity to do such a thing again," he reasoned, telling them that a sentence of life in prison was the only verdict that would permit them peace of mind.

Dunlap did not yield the advantage the guilty verdict had won him. Dozens of doctors and institutions in the past had the opportunity to confine and cure Priscilla Ford, but they had not, he insisted.

"Now Mr. Carnahan stands up and suggests you make the same kind of mistake again," Dunlap said.

Dunlap said the death penalty was "the only one sure way to solve the problem of Priscilla Ford."

"Ladies and gentlemen, there is no cure for evil," he said.

This time the jury remained out for an unprecedented five

days. At several junctures they called for the transcripts of the complicated psychiatric testimony.

While reporters sweated out the jury's return, they filed sidebar pieces about the fact that Nevada had never sentenced a woman to death for a capital crime. Some speculated the jury might be hopelessly deadlocked. But even if they were, it was not necessarily good news for the defendant. Nevada law provided for the judge to dismiss the jury, with the judge and two other judges appointed by the Supreme Court to then rehear the sentencing evidence and arrive at a decision.

Later, it would be learned the jury spent much of its time determining whether justice would be better served by a sentence of life imprisonment. In the end, however, the jury concluded that death was the fit punishment for the lives Ford had taken and the others she had interrupted so savagely.

Lew Carnahan expressed bitter disappointment at the verdict, and Dunlap was candid enough to admit some surprise.

It may be several more years before the appeals in Priscilla Ford's case have all been heard, but if the voices of the survivors of Reno are heard, she will meet death in the gas chamber someday.

Bob and Shirley Haun of Idaho were among the visitors to Casino Row so mercilessly struck down that day. Shirley suffered a shattered knee and a broken back and has had four operations.

"I have no mercy for her at all," Shirley said when reporters asked for her reaction. "It wouldn't even bother me to witness the execution."

Bob Haun was no less unforgiving. He feels he has a right to be. His spleen was removed after the injuries he suffered. He has not felt well since.

"I think they should string her up from the closest tree myself—that's the way I feel."

Chapter 5

Sharon Faye Young

"CALL ME T.C.," Sharon Faye Young sometimes told a new friend she might make while prowling the homosexual bars of Cincinnati, Ohio.

The initials stood for a particularly vulgar obscenity, and when Sharon told the person she had met just what it meant, she would fill the air with a burst of lewd and raucous laughter at the sight of the embarrassment that often crept over their faces.

"Well, okay—call me Casey, then. Just don't call me Sharon."

Sharon Faye Young didn't try too hard to mask her lesbian life-style. She fancied herself a tough cookie; the equal of any man as a lover, or as a barroom brawler.

Sharon Young was decidedly unwelcome in many of the city's bars. There was a hard, unpleasant glint in her ferret eyes and a raw edge of anger in the jutted way she shoved out her chin when an argument started. She was big—nearly five-foot nine. She weighed 160 pounds. She could look mean as hell when she wanted.

Sharon Young liked her reputation as a hard character. She found it attracted to her a certain kind of docile lesbian lover that allowed her to release oceans of pent-up anger and frustration that had often caused trouble during her twenty-six years.

Sometimes during lovemaking, Sharon would tell her partner how she had been beaten and sexually abused by her own stepfather while she was only a tiny girl and how it still gave her nightmares, reliving the things he had done to her.

"Maybe that's why I sometimes drink more than I should," Sharon would say. "To get rid of the memories of his hands on me, under my nightgown. God, it would make me sick."

And maybe there was another reason that Sharon Young was so unhappy, those who got as close to her as anyone could, would speculate. The little son she had to give up for adoption when she was only seventeen. In her mind she had named him Gary Christopher. She did not know what his adoptive parents had named him or where he was now. She only knew she loved him with all her empty heart and that someday, when she was able to get her life together, she'd hire someone to find the child, just so she could see him.

Maybe Gary Christopher would love her. Really love her, Sharon would dream. It was pretty certain that not many other people cared.

Sharon had started drinking early on the sultry afternoon of June 12, 1984. She had been staying on Handman Avenue, in one of Cincinnati's sprawling neighborhoods known as Columbia-Tusculum. She was sharing a small apartment with two lesbian friends who knew that Sharon could sometimes be troublesome, but who were still willing to lend her a hand because she could be such a good friend too.

Her roomates knew that there was a warrant out for Casey for walking away recently from a halfway house where she was finishing out a sentence for writing bad checks. They also knew why Casey had taken the walk.

"While Sharon was doing time for the check charge, she got a Dear Jane letter from another lesbian to whom she considered herself married. They had exchanged rings and the whole works. It apparently really hit her hard. She walked away so she could find the woman and try to patch things up," Sergeant Dennis Lantry, an investigator for the Hamilton County Sheriff's office, would later recall.

But when Casey tracked down her former lover, it became apparent that no reconciliation would be made. Sharon was hurt, bitter, confused, and angry. She sat around the apartment on Handman and filled notebooks with poetry, remembering the love she and her former friend had shared, brooding because that love now seemed hopelessly lost.

Sharon had taken the time to roll a drunk after her walkaway from the corrections house. She used a tried and true scam that almost always worked. She went to a straight bar, settled down on a stool, and ordered a bourbon double. She had dressed just mannishly enough to convey the impression that she might be a lesbian, but she had combed her autumn-touched blond hair very prettily, and with her freckled face and cute smile, she knew it wouldn't be long before one of the macho patrons of the bar would take up the challenge she posed.

"She would indicate to a man over a few drinks that she was a lesbian, but that it was probably because she had never been made love to by a real man," Sergeant Lantry says.

"She would let on that the guy buying the drinks might just be the fellow who could do it, and there would always be some sucker who would believe he was the guy to convert her back to men.

"What the man usually got for his trouble was a knock on the head in some alley and getting himself rolled. Sharon made her living that way fairly often.

"Between pulling that trick and being a petty thief, she made a small living," Lantry said.

At about 4 P.M. on June 12, Sharon had finished most of a pint of bourbon at the apartment house. The money she had picked up from the last obliging drunk was almost gone. Sharon knew she would need to work some scam before the day was over, if there was going to be enough money to treat her roommates to dinner as she had promised.

Sharon lurched in and out of several neighborhood bars

that afternoon, but business was slow. The afternoon wore on into evening and before Sharon knew it, her wanderings had taken her to a gay bar in Madisonville known as Patches Café.

Sharon had been nursing her drinks for a while. Her money was running out. Her mind was alert as she surveyed the patrons and the layout of the bar.

She remembered having been in the place once or twice. It had, until recently, been a saloon frequented by bikers, but the new owner, sixty-one-year-old Elefterios "Larry" Smyrlakis, had prudently put the run on the motorcycle crowd, opting instead to make the bar an attractive place for neighborhood homosexuals who spent more and didn't pose the problems that followed in the wake of the noisy and tough-looking bikers.

Smyrlakis was a robust and darkly handsome man for his age. He was a friend to many of the gay patrons of his club. He was far too virile to understand their sexual preferences, but he was Greek, and understood that passions were a puzzling thing. He was not offended by the mild petting and displays of affection that went on at the crowded tables in the dimly lighted bar between people of the same sex. "It is their own business," he would tell his two young sons and his wife. "Our business is to run a decent place."

Vice squad cops who occasionally shopped Patches Café, just to keep an eye on things, were not troubled by the way Smyrlakis ran his place. He was the kind of bar owner who kept a sharp eye on things and weeded out undesirable customers by showing them the door if they went beyond the quiet ground rules he had established for the club.

To regular patrons of Patches Café, Larry Smyrlakis was a tolerant and understanding host who was willing to hold a tab if someone was temporarily short or would cash a check for regulars who called the place their evening home.

When he saw Sharon Faye Young take a stool at his bar, Smyrlakis was not pleased. He recognized her from two earlier occasions when she had visited his place, usually in the company of several tough-looking dikes wearing heavy leather gear, dressed for war. Looking for trouble.

He had heard her pull her "T.C." gag and remembered that the shrillness of her laughter had made him uneasy. It wasn't happy laughter. It was more like an angry scream.

It was still early. The bar was not yet crowded. Smyrlakis quietly hoped that the woman would become bored and move on before she caused any trouble at Patches Café. He was prepared to order her out of the place if he had to, but Smyrlakis took such measures only as a last resort. Scenes were always embarrassing, and with them came the chance that the police might have to be summoned, something any gay bar tried to avoid whenever possible.

The crowd drifting into Patches Café had started to build. The owner was pleased. The warm weather was making people want to get out. Orders for drinks were brisk. At several points, Smyrlakis opened the nickel-plated cash register and counted out and bundled some of the currency that had begun to accumulate. He reached beneath the bar and placed the cash inside a small gray money box. His hand brushed several times across the cold metal of a snub-nosed Smith & Wesson .38 that lay only inches away from the box. Larry Smyrlakis knew how to use the pistol he had bought for protection some months ago. But he never dreamed it would ever be fired in anger.

Sharon Young watched from the corner of her eye as the bar owner made the money transfers from the register to the box. She was careful not to let on that she saw them taking place or that she had also seen the dull black sheen of the .38 nestled nearby. But she had seen it all and begun to form a plan that would take care of buying dinner for her friends that night, and maybe for a few other nights too.

Sharon gave a noisy whoop of welcome when her roommates and another friend came through the door of Patches Café looking for her. Sharon bellowed loudly enough to frighten away several other customers from the bar so that her friends could all take stools next to hers.

Sharon ordered drinks for everyone—doubles. She was certain that by the time the tab arrived she would have the cash she needed to pick it up.

The jukebox was loud, and while the air conditioners groaned to handle the smoke and the lingering heat of the unseasonably warm June night, Sharon felt the liquor starting to hit her hard again.

Her laughter was almost hysterical and it was shrill, constant, and starting to make the other customers in the bar nervous. Larry Smyrlakis stared angrily in Sharon's direction several times. Her friends, who were still sober, managed to shush Sharon a bit and exchanged glances with Smyrlakis, indicating they would keep their friend in control. Smyrlakis doubted it, but hoped for the best.

In a short while, Sharon was creating a disturbance again. She had begun to heckle several homosexuals. Her taunts were explicitly vulgar, and people around Sharon and her friends had gotten up and left to find more congenial corners of the bar to drink.

When Sharon asked to use a telephone behind the bar to call a taxi, the young bartender who helped out Smyrlakis gave his approval.

"Thank Christ," he said to himself. "This crazy dyke is getting out of here."

But that wasn't really what Sharon Faye Young had in mind. She had carefully memorized the position of the gray cash box and the revolver. While pretending to use the telephone, she managed to lift the weapon up and conceal it by placing it at the back of her waist, beneath the overlap of her jacket. She fumbled desperately to lift the lid of the money box in the next motion, but cursed to herself when she found it locked.

While the bartender, occupied with serving drinks, did not notice Sharon's theft, another customer at the bar had seen what took place. He left his stool, walked quietly over to Larry Smyrlakis at the other end of the bar, and told him what Sharon Faye Young had done.

Now Smyrlakis was angry. Putting up with the noisy woman's crudeness was one thing, but having her steal from him was something else. Smyrlakis advanced angrily on Sharon Young. He shoved her out from behind the bar, quickly checked the cash box, happy to find it still locked, but a desperate search for the snub-nosed Smith & Wesson revealed it to be gone from its hiding place.

Smyrlakis now ordered Sharon Young to stand still as he came out from around the bar himself. "Hand me over that gun or there is going to be a hell of a lot of trouble," he demanded.

Sharon Young threw together a string of curses by way of reply. Smyrlakis seized her and patted her down police style while Sharon struggled to release herself from his grasp.

She accused him of trying to molest her sexually under the pretext of looking for some supposed missing gun. The scene was getting very tense, and very ugly.

Sharon's friends were making menacing noises now, backing up her claim that the elderly man was trying to take sexual liberties with their companion.

Larry Smyrlakis considered calling the police to prove his point, but what if he had been mistaken about the gun's being there? Suppose he had forgotten it in the trunk of his car, or back on the bedroom dresser of his home in Clifton. Yes, he was almost one hundred percent certain he had brought the weapon to the bar that day, but what if he were wrong?

Smyrlakis took the other option open to him. He ordered Sharon Young to leave the bar and forcefully escorted her to the door.

"Don't ever come back here if you know what's good for you," he said.

Sharon Faye Young was furious. Not only had she not managed to pilfer the money from the cash box, she had been humiliated in front of her friends by an old man. The son of a bitch had actually put his hands on her. It was like the way someone else had put their hands on her when she was little. She couldn't do anything about it then, but by Christ, she could do something about it now. Her hand reached toward her lower back. She felt the icy comfort of the .38 pressing against her spine.

"He's got to come out of there sometime tonight," she muttered incoherently to herself. "When he does, he is a dead Greek son of a bitch."

The parking lot where Sharon Young now found herself standing was hardly lit at all. In a far corner of the lot, Sharon spotted the 1979 Mercury she knew belonged to the elderly bar owner. She found the concealment of some flowering shrubs right nearby and sat down to wait.

Hamilton County Sheriff's investigators theorized it may have been nearly 3:30 in the morning when Larry Smyrlakis finally finished cleaning up inside Patches Café and wearily made his way out to the now deserted parking lot to enter his car for the drive to his home.

Sharon may have dozed once or twice as she waited, but when she heard the approach of his footsteps, she was fully alert. She rose to greet the startled bartender with the business end of the .38 snub-nose pointing in his direction.

The driver of the big *Cincinnati Enquirer* newspaper delivery truck braked sharply just after sunrise that morning after he had pointed his van loaded with Sunday editions down to Elstun Road, a remote throughway in Anderson Township on Cincinnati's east side. He was almost certain the form he had seen just seconds earlier was a human, lying facedown at the edge of the road. The dead man was Larry Smyrlakis. He had been shot once in the back of the head, in what appeared to be execution style. Deputies who arrived on the scene were convinced they had found another victim of Cincinnati's Homicidal Hitchhiker, who had already claimed three victims in little over a month. They did not know that Smyrlakis had suffered a run-in only hours ago with Sharon Faye Young.

While law enforcement agencies threw out an intensified

net for the killer hitchhiker, several anxious members of the city's gay community already knew that Casey Young was in some kind of trouble with the law. She had been seen in the very early morning hours driving around the neighborhood in Smyrlakis' auto. At one point she drunkenly waved a pistol at several lesbians she'd had nasty exchanges with before. And now a wild story was circulating that she was searching for the woman lover who had sent her the Dear Jane letter so she could kill her, only to discover that all the cartridges in the gun were spent.

Sharon had chatted briefly with several other neighborhood acquaintances. She bragged that she now had some money and a car. She was off for a short visit to Columbus, Ohio.

It took only a few hours for investigators familiar with the pattern of the homicidal hitchhiker to advise crime-scene detectives that the death of Larry Smyrlakis had not been at the hands of the deadly traveler. The M.O. was not the same. Detectives quickly turned the focus of their probe toward Patches Café, and when sleepy employees and patrons had been rounded up for a reconstruction of the events of the night before, police immediately began looking for Sharon Faye Young.

Her arrest in Columbus was an anticlimax. The car was spotted near the apartment of friends she had contacted a few hours before. Sharon was behind the wheel. Under the front seat of the car was the revolver that had been taken from beneath the bar. On the drive back to Cincinnati, Sharon tearfully admitted that she had shot Larry Smyrlakis.

"He was trying to rape me," she said. "He had been giving me free drinks all night. He said he heard I was bisexual and that all I needed was a real man once.

"He said to stick around, that he would give me a ride home and that we would have some fun together. He said he was a real man," Sharon told sheriff's investigators.

"He pulled a gun on me and made me drive down this

dark road. He was tearing at my clothes and I was fighting him when the gun went off."

By now, police questioning Sharon had received preliminary coroner reports. They knew that Casey Young was lying. The death of Larry Smyrlakis could not have happened the way she described. They told her they didn't believe her.

"She took back her first version then," Detective Lantry recalls.

"She told us she had shot him after robbing him.

"She still wasn't telling us all the truth, but she was coming closer," he added.

When Sharon Faye Young faced a judge and jury a few months later, defense attorneys fought desperately to prevent her taped confession from being entered as evidence.

Defense lawyers Thomas Conlon and James Rueger charged that Sharon had not been mentally capable of understanding the gravity of her situation. She had not eaten for nearly forty-eight hours and had hardly slept at all, and even though police had properly read her rights to her, she was unable to make a competent decision.

To bolster their contention, the defense called Sharon to the stand to describe how the taped confession was obtained.

"When I talked to the cops at first, they didn't tell me that he was dead. I knew he had been shot, but I didn't know how serious it was. I didn't know how serious the charges were they were going to bring against me."

Sharon also said from the witness chair that the detectives who first interviewed her had used guile to get her to confess.

"They were real nice. I thought they were there to help me. They said it was in my best interest to talk," Sharon told the judge.

"They didn't tell me what I was charged with until the end."

Sharon admitted under cross-examination that she had

lied when she told police that Smyrlakis was attempting to rape her when the gun was fired.

"I don't know why I lied. I just did," Sharon wept. "I knew I was in trouble. Big trouble."

Hamilton County Common Pleas Judge Fred Cartolano was not moved by the defense motion to quash the confession.

In his ruling permitting the jury to hear the confession, Judge Cartolano noted that Sharon Young was a high school graduate and was competent to understand the police procedures. The fact that she had been arrested before and put through the same procedures added to the judge's belief that the suspect had been granted her rights.

Judge Cartolano said he believed it would have been wrong if the officers had intimidated or brutalized Sharon Young in any way during their interrogation, but that the friendly demeanor displayed by the officers did not constitute a violation of her rights.

"I can't agree that being nice and getting a confession is wrong," he said.

When it became clear the jury would be allowed to hear Sharon Young confess to the murder of her victim, the defense gamely put forward another line of reasoning on her behalf.

"We're not disputing that she shot him or that she intended to rob him," attorney Rueger told the jury.

"But the state cannot prove it was intentional. She is not guilty as far as aggravated murder is concerned," he argued.

The defense continued to insist that Larry Smyrlakis had set the stage for that robbery that cost him his life by trying to proposition Casey Young on the night she was in his bar.

"There was sexual banter. He gave her drinks. He asked her if she was bisexual, because he wanted to go to bed with her," Rueger insisted.

"It was clear what he had on his mind. He offered to give her a ride home. On the way she decided to rob him."

Rueger also conceded that his client had stolen the gun from beneath the bar, but claimed she had no intention of using it as a murder weapon.

"That gun represented thirty or forty dollars to her. It was something she took to sell in order to get money," Rueger told the court.

When a hushed jury of six men and six women heard the tape of Sharon's confessions to police, newsmen covering the case were certain her fate had been sealed.

They listened as Sharon first told the story of the bartender's rape attempt. They heard the voice of a detective reacting to that first version:

"If that's the story you're going to stick with, you're not going to help yourself," the detective's taped voice echoed in the courtroom.

After a brief pause, the tape rolled on and Sharon Young told a different story.

"I didn't mean to shoot him. All I was going to do was take his money. It was all over before I knew what happened."

She admitted she had the bartender's gun. She pointed it at him and ordered him to drive down the deserted road. Then she ordered him out of the vehicle and demanded his money.

"He threw the wallet on the seat of the car. When I reached for it, he made a grab for me. That's when I shot him.

"I didn't mean to kill nobody. I ripped people off for their money, but I never hurt nobody," Sharon's voice said as the tape continued to play.

But the prosecution presented a grimmer portrait of how Larry Smyrlakis had lost his life that night.

"She took his money. It was probably less then three hundred dollars. She forced him to the ground, we believe in a kneeling position, and then calmly blew his brains out with the gun," said assistant county prosecutor Patrick Dinkleacker.

"It was an execution."

The county medical examiner agreed. The bullet that tore the top of the victim's head off was fired from behind, and even though he reluctantly testified to not taking hair burn tests to rule out any other possibility, the examiner offered his conclusion that the bartender had met death by execution.

Assistant prosecutor Claude Crowe put before the jury a theory the prosecution had formulated with the help of psychiatrists who had examined Casey Young.

"She was a woman trying to be a man," he told the court.

"For her a gun was a source of power and manhood."

Spectators in the courtroom would later believe the defense team made a regrettable error when they called several of Sharon's lesbian friends to the stand to beef up her story about the bartender's sexual advances.

"The prosecution was not trying to make a big deal out of her being a lesbian. They were confident enough that they had a guilty verdict on the facts surrounding the murder alone," one of those spectators remembers.

"But her lesbian friends really drilled it into the jury's head that this woman was something else. They showed up with one of them wearing a torn T-shirt and dressed up like real dykes. Their language was terrible and their impression on the jury was devastating."

As one of the witnesses stepped down, she looked at her friend Casey and blurted out, "I don't care what you did. I still love you."

Another, called as a witness by the prosecution, stared deeply into Casey's eyes at the conclusion of her damaging testimony and said, "Sorry, babe."

Not many who watched the trial were surprised when a verdict of guilty was returned against Sharon Faye Young. It remained now to determine only if the jury would recommend to the judge that the death penalty be imposed.

A new round of desperate courtroom drama unfolded.

Sharon's lawyers produced Cincinnati psychiatrist Dr. Glenn Weaver, who testified that "psychologically, Sharon is not a strong person." But Weaver did not tell the jury that Sharon was out of her mind at the time of the slaying. He found her to be sane.

The defense argued that Sharon's troubled life had brought her to where she was that day. She was an alcoholic. A mother who would never see her child. A victim of sex abuse as a youngster. A woman whose gentle heart produced sweet poetry. A full volume of it was placed into the court's record.

Attorney Rueger's pleas were impassioned. He argued that she be given a lengthy term in prison. "Do not take her life. Give her the benefit of the doubt. It may not be much of a life, in prison for thirty or forty years, but it is at least life. Give her that," he said.

Now Sharon took the stand to plead for her own life. There was a softness in her eyes the jury had not seen before. She was dressed prettily. She was a big woman, as they could see, but somehow her sorrow seemed to wash away some of the hardness from her face.

"I wish I could take it all back, but I can't," she tearfully told the jury. "I was so drunk.

"I feel the shame. I didn't mean to hurt anybody, but I did.

"I want to live. Maybe, somewhere down the road, twenty or thirty years from now I might wish I'd taken the other verdict, but right now I want to live."

The jury retired on a Saturday afternoon to weigh their recommendation about life or death for Sharon Faye Young. By Sunday morning they informed the judge they had again reached a verdict.

Jury foreman Wyatt Smith, Jr., handed up to Judge Cartolano the jury's unanimous conclusion: Sharon Faye Young should be sentenced to death.

Her life now rested solely in the hands of Judge

Cartolano. He asked Casey Young if she had anything to say before he passed sentence.

"Please don't kill me," Sharon Faye Young said as she stood before the stern face of Judge Cartolano. "Nobody could be sorrier for what happened than me.

"There's so many things during the trial that I've learned, that possibly if it wasn't for a tragedy like this I'd never have known. Things like that I was worth something to people. I'm worth something to me.

"All I can say is God's forgiven me. I know. I did not mean to kill that man and nobody, believe me, is suffering more because of that than me."

Judge Cartolano seemed moved by the young woman's plea. But his sentence was grim, and the tone in which he read it was a voice from the tomb.

"You will be delivered to the Southern Ohio Correctional Facility where the warden will cause a current of electricity of sufficient intensity to cause death to pass through your body. Application of such current shall continue until you are dead," he said.

The judge took into account in rendering his verdict that, at some juncture, Ohio's death penalty law might be struck down as unconstitutional, even though states with similar statutes have passed the examination of the U.S. Supreme Court. Should her death sentence be set aside, the judge ordered that her penalty be life imprisonment, with no chance of parole until serving thirty years of that term. He also sentenced her to a term of from seven to twenty-five years for aggravated robbery of her victim and an additional three years for use of a firearm in commission of a felony.

On the day following her sentencing, Sharon Faye Young spoke with reporters. She said that hearing the judge sentence her to death by electrocution was the most terrifying thing that had ever happened in her life.

She says that she still dreams each night about the death of Larry Smyrlakis, but can't explain how it was that he was shot in the back of the head.

"Mostly what I see is a flash of light and I hear a gun go off. I can still see him look up at me, and then I wake up. I still can't explain why he was shot in the back of the head. For my sake, I wish I could remember exactly how that came about.

"Sometimes when I have these dreams, I wish I was as cold as they say I was. Then it wouldn't bother me so much."

Casey Young is no longer the loud, brawling, and feisty young woman she once was. She has turned to God in her time of trouble, and she believes He will not let her die in the electric chair.

"I have to have faith. With God being the only other person there that night, I have to believe I won't ever die in the electric chair," she says.

Friends who have visited her briefly say Casey Young really has changed. And although she believes she will spend many years in prison while appeals work their way through the courts, it is only in her nightmares that she is escorted down a long corridor that leads to the death chamber.

"It bothered her terribly that in the dream they cut her hair before putting her into the electric chair," one of her friends says.

"That would be awful to her. As bad as the dying."

For now, Sharon Faye Young says she continues to write her poems. They are about beautiful things. Fields of daisies, puppies, friendship and love, stones skipping across the quiet waters of a pond.

There is no death row as such for women in the Ohio correctional system and so Sharon Young is presently confined at Marysville, an institution in which secured cottages take the place of prison cells. At present there are twelve men on death row in the state facility for men at Lucasville, and Sharon has been assigned her death row number—13—on that basis.

The state of Ohio has taken the lives of only three

women in the electric chair's grim history there. Not since June 1954, when black woman Betty Butler was killed by the current, has Ohio's death chamber claimed the life of a woman. Dovie Dean, a farm wife from Batavia who killed her husband, also died in early 1954 for the murder of her mate. The first woman to ever die by electrocution in Ohio was Anna Marie Hahn, who was executed in 1938 for the murders of several elderly suitors.

Chapter 6
Karla Windsor

RICHARD HARRIS REMEMBERS it today as one of the most difficult decisions he's ever had to make in his life. It has robbed him of sleep. It has forced him to rethink beliefs and feelings he's never had to examine so closely before.

When the reporter from the *Idaho Press-Tribune* braced Harris in the hallway of the Canyon County Courthouse and asked him again, for the hundredth time, what he planned to do, his answer was brusque:

"I don't know yet. I'm still thinking about it."

"Good God, Dick," the exasperated reporter sighed, "what's the big mystery? You're either going to ask the judge to give her the death sentence or you aren't."

"It isn't that damn simple," Harris snapped back, feeling his anger beginning to mount. "We've never executed a woman in Idaho, or didn't you know that?"

Dick Harris shouldered his way past the unhappy newsman and made his way to his own office, located on a different floor of the Canyon County government complex.

His greetings to members of his staff were perfunctory. He went straight to his private sanctum, with the sign on the door that identified him as Canyon County Prosecutor. He shut it, sat down behind his desk, and once more picked up the tattered file marked Karla Yvonne Windsor.

He had pored over the file dozens of times in the past few weeks, reading and rereading the statements the woman had made when she and her male accomplice had been arrested for the murder of Sterling Grammer.

What was he looking for now? Harris agonized to himself. Some possible sign that Karla Windsor has shown even the smallest pang of remorse for her role in the brutal killing? Some faint whisper in the endless blur of reports that might convince him the tough-looking twenty-six-year-old deserved a more merciful fate than death for the crime in which she had taken part?

Harris had sought the same clues as he intently watched the young woman in court each day while the murder case he prosecuted against her progressed.

He asked himself again if he had ever caught the slightest flicker of sorrow in her eyes as the cruel details of her crime were described to the jury now weighing the degree of her guilt.

His honest answer was that he had not. Karla Windsor didn't seem to care that she and her boyfriend Donald Fetterly had snuffed out a life for a hill of beans. It was as though she had no feelings at all. Maybe that was how he should feel about her now, Harris mused to himself. Maybe her life was worth no more consideration than she had given to the life of her victim.

You just don't think of women as being that way. Not in rural Caldwell, Idaho, at least. The women Dick Harris knew in that pleasant farming town of 17,000 were all someone's wife, someone's daughter, someone's mother. Gentle creatures, nurturing kinds. Women content in the happiness of their families, their kids, and all the good things that came to them under the perfect blue Idaho skies.

Richard Harris felt his resolve finally form. There could be no special consideration for Karla Windsor based on his feelings that women could not really have it in their hearts to kill in cold blood. Karla Windsor, the troubled California drifter, had convinced Dick Harris that some women could be pitiless killers and never give their savage crimes much of a second thought.

Harris knew now what he would do. If the jury brought in a verdict of guilty against Karla Windsor, he would ask the judge to sentence her to death by lethal injection. There was a taut grimness in that decision that Harris could not escape. He knew what the jury's verdict was going to be. It was an open and shut case. Karla Windsor was guilty as hell.

It had been almost nine months earlier that Karla Windsor had first seen the rich farm country that surrounded Caldwell. Karla had a painter's eye, and the raw beauty of the hills and valleys of Canyon County took her breath away.

Maybe this time things would be different, she let herself hope against hope. Maybe this really was a place where a person could start a life over. It seemed as though she couldn't get her eyes filled enough with the majesty of the summer Idaho landscape. She made quick pencil sketches of the scenery that cried out to be put on canvas. Then she would show them to Don Fetterly. He thought they were wonderful. But then, Don Fetterly thought just about everything Karla did was touched with magic.

It was funny how they had met. Donald Fetterly had just finished up a stretch in an Idaho prison for bad checks and decided to head out to California for a new start himself.

Karla Windsor had just had about as much of California as she could take. She was dealing dope and was badly strung out from the amounts she was using. She was a hooker, when she could get herself up for it, and a petty thief when she couldn't.

She couldn't remember a time when life had been very good. She had been only twelve, but maturing rapidly the way California girls sometimes do, when her stepfather developed a decidedly unfatherlike interest in her. She drew pitiful pictures that might have warned someone what was happening between her stepfather and herself if anyone had taken the trouble to look, and to care. But no one ever did.

Karla wasn't yet thirteen when she began running away from home. Each time she was returned she stayed no longer than the time it took her to plan what she hoped would be a more permanent escape.

Within a year, Karla found herself in the care of a Christian children's shelter. It would be her home until she reached eighteen, except for the repeated times she ran away from there too.

She had a tough life. There wasn't any question about that in the minds of the correctional authorities who handled her case dozens of times as she grew up near San Francisco.

By her own admission, Karla Windsor was a street-wise little hooker by the time she was in her early teens. There were two crazy marriages that she only half remembered. They had seemed right at the time.

When she and Don Fetterly met shortly after his arrival in California, there was an almost instant bond between them. Fetterly was twenty-seven. He looked like a guy who could handle himself, even though Karla didn't take some of his boasting too seriously. He was, after all, a self-proclaimed scam man who hadn't been too brilliantly successful. He'd been doing time, on and off since he was a kid, much of it for pathetically bush league stuff like stealing from his own relatives and neighbors.

He liked to brag that he'd been out in the world on his own since her was only twelve years old, but Karla knew what that really meant. She'd been inside more than her share of institutions too. There was a lot of hayseed behind Don Fetterly's bluster. A lot of small-town Idaho. But when Don talked to Karla about Caldwell, near which he'd been born and raised, he managed to make it sound like a beautiful place. Inside Karla's imaginative mind, Idaho began to take on a lure that glowed brighter with each tough day they spent together in California.

A set of stolen credit cards, taken from a man Karla had hustled, crystallized their dreams about heading out for Idaho together.

Donald Fetterly told Karla he could probably find work as a cowhand once they arrived, and she could paint pictures and sell them at one of the craft shops in Caldwell and Nampa, and maybe even Boise.

They had not been in Caldwell more than a few months when their dreams started falling apart. There wasn't, of course, any ranch-hand job waiting for Fetterly, or any other kind of job that he seemed willing to work at either. Finding drugs in upright Caldwell was like looking for bourbon in Iran. Not that they had the money to buy any even if the good stuff had been flowing freely. Once in a while they would manage to score a little grass, and on those rare occasions when they found themselves invited to someone's home, they'd pilfer whatever prescription drugs they might find in a bathroom medicine chest. But not many people opened their doors to Karla and Don. He was too well-known as a punk and petty thief in the town. They'd only been there a matter of weeks before the sheriff's unit in Caldwell was aware of their presence, and keeping a leery eye out for the pair.

Karla began to feel the walls closing in again. At least in Frisco she could head for the streets and turn a trick when finances became shaky, but in Caldwell, Idaho, the only johns around were probably guys whose name really was John. It was no place for a hooker to ply her trade.

By early September 1983, Don Fetterly and Karla Windsor were facing total disaster. Winter was coming on. Their rent was overdue, and the landlord wasn't listening to any more B.S. about the check being in the mail.

They made their way out to the home of Don's step-mother one chilly afternoon, hoping to borrow a few dollars for food until something turned up.

Sterling Grammer had driven up to the same home earlier that day to visit Don's stepmother. They had known each other for a while and had become friends.

Don wondered who the new pickup truck in front of his stepmother's house belonged to as he and Karla made their way up the lane. He had never met the forty-five-year-old Grammer before. But then, Don hadn't been around home much in the last few years.

Grammer was obviously pleased by the fuss Don and

Karla made over his brawny new pickup truck. It was loaded with off-road gear because of Grammer's passion for hunting and fishing and, yes, he replied, it had cost one hell of a pretty penny.

Karla was more than chatty. She hung with riveting attention on every word Grammer had to say, giggled charmingly at each small country witticism he offered, blushed with practiced coyness when he eyed her appraisingly, and gushed on and on, to his clear delight, on how much she had always been fascinated by men who followed the rugged outdoor life.

Karla was playing a game she had played many times before, and even Don Fetterly, rube that he was, had the smarts to see what she was doing. He joined in the friendly flattery Karla was smarming on their newfound friend.

Don jaw-boned Grammer about the possibility of work over at the small mobile-home plant where Grammer was employed as a skilled and well-paid welder. Grammer said he'd ask his boss.

Karla clucked sympathetically to hear that Grammer was separated from his wife and that he only got to see their three-year-old boy on the weekends. She knew just how he felt, Karla lied, she had a child she never got to see either.

They settled down on the front porch of the stepmother's house and happily tore the tops off a number of chilled cans of Coors. Their friendship warmed. Sterling Grammer was a wide-open kind of guy. Everything he was telegraphed out from his friendly eyes and easygoing manner. He was the best kind of Idaho. No tricks and no big-city crap. Most people were okay, he knew, give them half a chance. Sterling Grammer liked the outdoors. He liked cold beer, and he liked women who knew what they had on their mind. No, he wasn't a pillar of the community, but he was the bedrock on which it prospered. He knew Don Fetterly wasn't any model citizen, but, what the hell, he was still a kid and he'd had some tough breaks. He took a shine to Karla too. She was a bit of a pisscutter, the way he pegged her, but that too was okay with him. She had an easy laugh, and he was intrigued by the notion that she was an artist. He'd never met anyone who was an artist. Maybe she would paint his picture someday and he'd put it away for his son when he grew up. You bet your life she would, Karla answered with a wide grin. Maybe she'd make him take his clothes off and she'd paint him that way so everyone could see what a real Idaho mountain man looked like. It was the beer, maybe, but they all found that an uproarious idea.

As the day wore on, Don made a clumsy and drunken attempt to put the bite on Grammer for a few dollars. Karla kicked him savagely to warn him off. She had taken a good measure of Sterling Grammer, and her plans for him went far beyond a small handout. She reasoned shrewdly that such a two-bit hustle would offend Grammer. Sure, embarrassed, he would hand them a ten or a twenty, but that would be the very end of it. Karla dragged Don away from that pleasant first meeting before anything else stupid could happen. She gave Sterling Grammer an affectionate hug as they parted and held it just long enough to give him a small hint of what that might mean.

The next day Karla and Don took some desperate steps. The stolen credit cards from California were now hotter than the hubs of hell, but Don took them out and used them anyway. He picked up a little cash, but in almost no time a squad car pulled up and took him into custody. Karla had gone to a store to try her hand at a skill she had acquired as a kid. It had been awhile since she had tried shoplifting, and it showed. She was in the county jail for boosting almost as quickly as Don had gotten there.

The charges were misdemeanors and the bail was low. They used the last few dollars they had hoarded as an absolute last-ditch emergency fund to make their bail. An unhappy city prosecutor had tried to convince a municipal judge to set bond for Fetterly at $10,000 and for Windsor at $5,000. The judge found the request wildly excessive, given the petty nature of the charges, and swept the prosecutor's request aside.

Now there was no doubt they were in desperate trouble. Karla was waiting for a small amount of money owed her by a friend, but a quick reckoning of their finances showed they were literally down to their last dollar.

Karla brooded through the afternoon. She had been a fool to come to Idaho. She had been crazy to listen to a two-for-a-nickel loser like Donald Fetterly. Here she was again, stuck with a bozo. A good lover, a nice enough guy, but nobody really home upstairs.

She found herself thinking of Sterling Grammer again. Karla had only seen him once since that time they had met at the old lady's house. She and Don had made their way up to his doorstep over on East Elgin Street, toting along a six-pack, trying not to let on that they couldn't go back to their apartment that night because the landlord had been prowling around looking for them.

Grammer seemed happy to see the young couple. Had they had dinner? Then just sit still. You brought the suds, I'll take care of the chow. As the night wore on and the pair seemed reluctant to leave, Grammer calculated they needed a place to hang out for the night and invited them to bed down without prying any further. Both Don and Karla had surveyed Grammer's possessions with a practiced appraiser's eye, mentally tallying up what the stuff might be worth if a ripoff could be pulled.

Some money had dropped in their lap the next day and Don and Karla hadn't needed to do Grammer in. It was just as well, Karla thought. She was now starting to think of the lanky welder as an ace in the hole of sorts, something to put by for a really rainy day.

As she brooded that afternoon with Fetterly asleep on the couch, Karla concluded that the rainy day was here. She shook Fetterly to life and lit one of the few remaining joints they had put by.

"I've been thinking about the mountain man," Karla began. "I think it's time we cashed him in."

What they would do was this, Karla said: Sterling Grammer seemed to her like a guy who would go along with a gag. They would go over to his place and tell him straight out they were in a jam. He'd see why neither one of them could show up for the court dates they had been assigned for the credit card bit and the shoplifting fiasco. Karla would put some moves on Grammer and tell him how they needed money and some wheels to get the hell out of Canyon County and get a fresh start somewhere. She would tell him they wanted to do a scam in which no one got hurt and everyone got a little something for their trouble. Grammer would let Karla and Don tie him up, not too tightly of course, but enough to make it convincing that he had come home and surprised some burglars in his house. Don and Karla would take some of his stuff that was the easiest to peddle to a fence—the TV and stereo and some of his guns—and load it all up in the pickup and haul ass for parts unknown. Grammer would let as much time as possible pass before reporting the crime, and by that time they would be well on their way. With a police report to back up his claim, Grammer could file with his insurance company and collect the full replacement value of all the things that had been stolen. He'd be money ahead and have brand new goods for his trouble, and he'd be helping out a couple of kids who really needed a break right now.

It all sounded good to Donald Fetterly as he deeply inhaled the sweet savor of the joint before passing it back to Karla. Her eyes were dreamy now, but still glittered with the perfect logic of her plan.

"Wouldn't you know it?" Don Fetterly sighed as the pair walked up to the door of Grammer's darkened home. "The son of a bitch isn't here."

Karla felt tears of frustration form in her eyes.

"Well, fuck it then," she spit out angrily. "We'll bust in and wait for him until he does come home." They found an unlocked window, opened it, and boosted and pulled each other inside.

Sterling Grammer had spent the night with a lady. Ever since his separation, Grammer had been rediscovering the joy of being an attractive male out on the prowl. He was a little tired that morning as he pulled up in front of his house on Elgin, but he felt wildly alive too. It was a hell of a good feeling.

He was startled to find several empty beer bottles scattered around the house as he entered. He knew they hadn't been there when he left the previous night. He cautiously began a check of the house. He was not happy when he found Karla Windsor and Don Fetterly sound asleep on his bed. His mood didn't improve when he sternly awoke them and Karla started to put some crazy hustle on him about getting himself tied up and letting them steal everything out of his house, not to mention the truck he'd spent a young fortune on.

He asked Fetterly pretty straight if they were out of their minds, or if they thought he was.

"I don't even have the stuff in this house insured," he shouted angrily. "And I wouldn't let you take that truck around the block. You gotta be kidding."

"It looks like we're going to have to do this the hard way, Sterling," Don Fetterly said. "I wish the hell you'd think it over."

The first blow that struck Grammer on the side of the head put him down. Karla handed Don the wide rolls of grey duct tape she had found while rummaging through Grammer's house the night before. They taped his hands behind his back first, then taped his legs securely with wide swaths of the grey tape. Sterling Grammer's eyes burned accusingly at them as they wound loops of the tape around his mouth. Karla was doing the taping now, and like some demented Egyptian embalmer, she continued to wind the tape around all of Grammer's head. Now his eyes were covered. Now his nose. His head looked like a mummy's.

Grammer had been docile enough until the tape shut off all his senses. Now he began to struggle fiercely. He was making loud gasps. He couldn't breathe. Karla didn't seem to give a damn. She wound on more of the tape around his face, pulling to make it even tighter. Sterling Grammer made a terrific lunge forward. The top of his head smacked sharply into Don's face.

"For Christ sake, Sterling, calm down," Fetterly hissed. "We're not going to hurt you."

Grammer lunged forward again.

"Son of a bitch," Fetterly growled. He grabbed the short-bladed buck knife they had been using to cut measured pieces of the tape. He plunged it into Sterling Grammer's chest. He stabbed again, and then again and again. Sterling Grammer fell back dead.

"Oh, my God," Fetterly moaned. "What have I done?"

"You did what you didn't want to do, but now it's too late," Karla said.

"They really weren't up for this kind of work," Canyon County Sheriff's Department Chief Deputy Richard Appleton recalls today.

"They were a pair of small-timers and suddenly they were way over their head."

It had been shortly before 8 A.M. when Grammer had returned home to find his uninvited guests. The bloody work of his death was over a little before nine. Don and Karla removed the keys to the pickup from the dead man's pocket. They left his body in the house and set out, looking to find someone who might buy the vehicle from them.

They tried an acquaintance named Zeke Palacious, an ex-con they hoped would make them an offer on the truck. When Palacious heard them say the former owner wouldn't be needing it anymore, he took a pass on the deal.

The killers waited until almost eleven that night before returning to the house to deal with the problem of Grammer's corpse.

They wrapped it, weighted it down with stones, and

traveled by moonlight to a bend in the Snake River near Nampa where they gave the once-avid fisherman an unceremonious toss into the water.

"They were confident it would be days before anyone found the victim's body, so they planned to take their time about trying to sell the items from his home," Deputy Appleton says.

But like most of the plans the pair had set in motion since they teamed up, this one also went badly awry. Early the next morning two fishermen found the body of Sterling Grammer floating near a cement retaining wall at the Snake River's edge, barely more than a few yards from where the killers had dumped him.

Fate had another trick to play too. The same morning the fishermen were discovering the body, Grammer's estranged wife spotted Karla and Don driving slowly up a street in Caldwell.

She waved them down and asked the pair where her husband was. Don and Karla said he was at work but had been kind enough to lend them the truck. Grammer's wife said nothing, but within the next few moments she was on her way to the police department.

"Sterling wouldn't even let me drive that truck when we were happily married. He sure didn't lend it to that pair of weirdos," she told keenly interested sheriff's dupties.

They asked her to describe her husband. She did, adding in detail a description of the tattoos he bore on his arms.

"I'm afraid we have some bad news for you," the desk sergeant, who had taken her information, said. "We just pulled a man matching that description out of the water this morning up on Snake River."

Karla and Don were in custody within hours. They were still driving Grammer's spiffy truck when they were pulled over and apprehended without incident. Some of the items taken from the victim's home were in the truck. Others, already sold, were quickly traced.

Deputy Richard Appleton didn't mince words with the pair now lodged in Canyon County jail.

"You're in a heap of trouble. Somebody had better start telling the truth real pronto," he said.

"We separated them and started telling them what we already knew. By that time it was plenty.

"Karla started talking first," Appleton recalls. "She admitted she planned the robbery, but said she had no part in stabbing Grammer to death."

Before long, the investigators had tape-recorded an hour-long confession by Don Fetterly and Karla Windsor. There weren't many other loose ends.

But when the police file and the coroner's report reached the desk of prosecutor Dick Harris, an ugly subplot within the fairly ordinary robbery-murder showed its head. Dr. Tom Donndelinger, a Nampa pathologist who examined Grammer's body as it was taken from the water and who later performed the autopsy, reached a grisly conclusion. Even if Don Fetterly hadn't plunged the buck knife into the victim's body nine times, there was a strong possibility Grammer would have died of suffocation because of the horrifying way Karla Windsor had cruelly wrapped his face in the duct tape, making it nearly impossible for him to breathe.

Now Karla Windsor wasn't a simple accessory to a botched burglary job that ended with her boyfriend stabbing the victim to death. She had set in motion a chain of events that greatly increased her guilt in the minds of investigators putting together the final portrait of Grammer's tragic murder.

Who had really been to blame for what happened that night to Sterling Grammer? Richard Harris began to ask himself. There was no doubt that Don Fetterly was guilty of murder, but whose plan had it been that took them there in the first place, whose idea was it to go ahead when Grammer told them to shove off with their crazy insurance-fraud scheme? And who was it that found the duct tape, handed it to Don Fetterly, and then wound it so tightly around the victim's face that he stood a good chance of dying anyway, even if the knife had never been plunged into Grammer's heart?

Dick Harris knew the answer to that. It was Karla Windsor.

Fetterly was the first to go on trial for the murder. It was not a lengthy case, and Dick Harris says he didn't have the slightest doubt the jury would return a verdict of guilty against Fetterly.

"It was an open and shut case, and he was found guilty and later sentenced to death," Harris recalls.

Now the focus of attention turned to Karla Windsor. Her trial opened in early February 1984. Karla was represented by Renae Hoff, a smart young attorney from Caldwell who knew that her client faced a tough battle if she was going to escape with her own life. While the prosecutor was reserving judgment on whether he would seek the death penalty in her client's case, Renae Hoff felt certain Richard Harris would ultimately go for the maximum penalty. But Hoff also felt Karla would enter the courtroom with at least one hopeful factor on her side. The state of Idaho, as far as records went back, had never executed a woman for a capital crime. There was something else that might work in Karla's favor too. Within the past year, four particularly horrendous murder cases had been tried in Canyon County, a peaceful spot of the earth where that many cases hadn't been tried in the previous fifty years. In two of the cases, little girls had been the victims of sex criminals, and jurors wasted no time in finding them guilty and judges showed no sympathy in sentencing them to death.

By comparison, Karla Windsor would look like a minor saint to murder-weary prospective jurors in the county, Renae Hoff reasoned. A picture of Karla's troubled past, sketched sympathetically for the jury, the fact that she was an artist of some promise, might both be argued convincingly as reasons to spare the young woman's life in the event the prosecutor demanded that she pay for Grammer's death with her own. Members of her family would testify that Karla Windsor had never been a violent person. Guards who had observed her in custody would be called to describe her as a prisoner who offered them no problems. There was little doubt that Karla would draw a heavy prison term for her part in the murder, but Renae Hoff had good reason to think she might be able to save her client's life.

Hoff was hard put to conceal her concern when Richard Harris announced he would ask that Karla Windsor be sentenced to death by lethal injection.

"I became certain of several things as the trial of Karla Windsor moved forward," Dick Harris remembers.

"The more I considered the matter, the more unlikely it seemed to me that Donald Fetterly would ever have found himself in a position to take a life if it hadn't been for Karla Windsor.

"Fetterly had never shown any signs of being a kind who wanted to graduate to murder. There had been a few assault raps in his past, but they had been the kinds of situation you could understand, barroom brawls and that sort of thing.

"The more I studied Windsor, the clearer it became that she was the instigator. She had devised the plan. She had taken Donald Fetterly along. Sure, he did what he did, and what he did was murder, and I was determined to get him the death penalty for that, but Donald Fetterly wasn't a calculated killer. Karla Windsor didn't wield the knife, but she stabbed him just as surely as Fetterly did. She wanted him dead as much, and maybe even more," Harris said.

"Karla Windsor deserved the death penalty as much as Donald Fetterly when you weighed all the evidence. Maybe even more.

"I had to ask myself if a woman could really be that cold and vicious. Whether she was capable of wanting a man dead to cover her tracks so she could steal what amounted to a hill of beans.

"She had no concern at all for the life of Sterling

Grammer. She only had her own selfish concerns, her own hardened outlook about the life of a man as opposed to a small amount of gain.

"I watched her through the trial to see some show of regret on her part. Some inkling that showed she felt remorse. I never saw one, and I came to the conclusion she deserved no different consideration than the law would give to a man in the same position.

"Donald Fetterly had deserved to die, and Karla Windsor deserved it every bit as much. Probably more," Harris said.

Renae Hoff scrapped valiantly to exclude the taped confessions given to the deputies who had taken the pair in charge, but the judge ruled they had been properly obtained and were admissible.

Hoff fought hard against the theory put forward by Dr. Donndelinger about the effect of the duct tape Karla had wound strenuously about the victim's face. After that testimony had been elicited, Hoff read the expressions on the jurors' faces and moved for a mistrial on the grounds the doctor's speculations had inflamed the jury. All the doctor could accurately testify to was the official cause of death, Hoff argued adamantly, and that had been determined to be the stab wounds to the heart inflicted by Fetterly, not Karla Windsor.

Judge Edward Lodge denied the motion, and once again few were surprised when the jury returned a verdict of guilty against Karla Windsor.

Under Idaho law it was now that the life or death fate of Karla would be considered. There was no death penalty recommendation from the jury provided by the statute. The matter was now in the hands of Judge Lodge.

The testimony offered before sentencing was not, in Harris' opinion, as dramatic as he had anticipated it might be.

There was the reading of a psychologist's report that upon examination he had observed Karla Windsor to be a woman without a normally developed conscience. She was of average intelligence, the report observed, but showed evidence of a psychopathic personality. Her outlook on life was antisocial. She did not seem to have much concern for questions of right or wrong.

Renae Hoff presented a passionate plea for the life of her client. She said that Fetterly was to blame for Karla's involvement in the murder. Yes, Karla had been there in the act of a crime, but she had never intended any harm to Sterling Grammer.

Hoff entered as exhibits dozens of Karla Windsor's sketches and paintings. They were pleasing to the eye. They captured the rugged flavor of the western landscape that edged so closely to the courtroom. There were cowboys and Indians and working ranch horses and sunrises and sunsets along the spectacular hills.

Karla Windsor's life was worth saving, she entreated Judge Lodge. She was an artist who in the years of life he had the power to grant could develop even further as a first-rate talent.

It had been the same Judge Lodge who had considered pleas for mercy in the case of Karla's accomplice, Fetterly. Those appeals had not moved Lodge. In tones of wrathful indignation, Lodge had sentenced Donald Fetterly to death.

"In the nineteen years I have been a judge, I've never experienced such a senseless killing, one so void of any compassion or feeling for a fellow man," the judge told Fetterly as he handed down the decision. Recounting the night Sterling Grammer had cooked a meal for the hungry pair and without any questions gave them a place to spend the night, the judge's disgust showed through.

"You didn't kill someone you didn't know, you killed your friend. You killed him for a sordid motive."

Karla Windsor fared no better when she faced Judge Lodge on the morning of the sentencing.

"You are equally responsible for the death of a decent man," the judge told Karla. "To render any sentence other than that of death would create a disparity that could not be reconciled."

Karla Windsor showed no emotion when the death knell rang for her in Judge Lodge's courtroom. She had not begged for her life before a jury and she was not ready to beg for her life now.

"She was calm when the judge read the sentence," Dick Harris remembers. "In fact, she was as cool as ice."

The tough little street girl to the bitter end? Well, maybe.

Maybe she was just slammer-wise enough to know that a good number of years now stood between the judge's grave words and the faraway day that any such sentence might actually be carried out.

There is an automatic appeals procedure of any death sentence under Idaho law, and more than five years has already passed for several male prisoners on the state's death row.

"I would like to say that I have a great deal of confidence that Karla Windsor's death sentence will someday be carried out, but I can't say that I really do," prosecutor Harris acknowledges today.

"If the convictions that have been brought down against men in Idaho are an example, it would appear that Karla Windsor has little to worry about in the foreseeable future.

"We're a funny society," Harris opines. "We say we want the death penalty in place, but we seem to do everything in the world to see that it doesn't actually get carried out.

"I think Karla Windsor deserves to die for what she did, but I would not bet you hard-earned money that she ever will."

After Karla Windsor had heard her sentence of death, she was given over to the custody of Warden Dennis Bodily, superintendent of the new women's prison at Orofino. Workmen had hastily created a new death row area to accommodate Karla, and now she is confined there in isolation, as prescribed by state law.

"I would call her cell area pleasant," Bodily says, "even though you could hardly call the circumstances the same.

"She has not been a difficult prisoner. I would guess that her biggest problems are the loneliness and the depression."

She has a television set she bought for herself with money from the sale of some of her paintings. She reads a great deal and continues to paint, having done numerous renderings of a pleasant little hill she can see from a window in her cell on death row.

"She has mail privileges and does a lot of letter writing. She receives a good deal of mail too," Bodily says.

Yes, she and Donald Fetterly have exchanged letters from their cells on separate death rows, but Bodily says he does not know what feelings they may have shared.

"Karla has become a born-again Christian since she's been on the row," Bodily said. "It seems to be helping her. She meets with one of our volunteer chaplains, and it seems to give her a sense of peace." Is it a typical jailhouse conversion? "I don't think anyone can answer that," Bodily replied.

Because the prison is adjacent to a state mental hospital, Karla has had access to counseling. "She has asked to see them a few times," the warden recounted.

The warden says he talks to Karla every two weeks or so, just to see how she's doing. There was a small scare in early autumn when Karla was taken to a medical center in Boise for what appeared to be a malignant growth. "It wasn't cancer," Bodily said. "She appeared to be quite relieved."

And has the warden seen any sign of what Richard Harris had searched for before making up his mind to demand the death penalty?

"She has not expressed anything you'd call remorse to me. I think she's sad to be here, but she's never really indicated to me that she feels any anguish over what took place.

"She's lonely, more than anything else, I guess," the

warden added. "But she is a young woman who's had a lot of that in her life, it seems."

Today Renae Hoff is involved in the mountains of briefs and motions that will constitute the appeal for the young client she believes did not deserve the death penalty for her role in the murder of Sterling Grammer.

"I have to have optimism that she will be given a new trial, or at the least that her death sentence will be overturned," Renae Hoff says.

The death penalty will be automatically reviewed under the Idaho system to compare the imposition of capital punishment in her case with death sentences handed out to other persons convicted of murder in that state.

"Measured against the crimes which some of the persons sentenced to death in Idaho committed, Karla's sentence of death will have to stand out as greatly excessive," Renae Hoff believes.

"Karla Windsor was guilty of burglary, but not of murder. She expected to pay a price for what she did, but she does not deserve to die.

"She wasn't convicted of the same crime as Donald Fetterly. I think the jury was trying to give her a break. There was a major difference in the roles each played in the crime.

"The cause of the victim's death was stab wounds to the heart, and Donald Fetterly inflicted those wounds," Renae Hoff maintains.

The thirty-three-year-old attorney is still bitter about the way in which Prosecutor Richard Harris suddenly decided to seek the death sentence in her client's case.

"He wanted Karla to enter a guilty plea after the conviction of Fetterly. If she had, he would not have sought the death sentence.

"I don't think his decision was as much a question of conscience as it was of anger when Karla would not plead guilty to the murder count."

Renae Hoff says she has become almost a friend to Karla Windsor as a result of the trial and the appeals.

"She has been a victim of men all her life," the lawyer said. "And what happened in that courtroom was more of the same."

"When the judge passed sentence, I thought I was going to scream. It was just one more time in her life when Karla got the blame."

Renae Hoff visits Karla at Orofino as often as she can. Both of the women are mildly embarrassed by the elaborate security precautions in force when they meet.

"Because I know her, it seems so strange to me," Renae Hoff says. "I don't need to be protected against Karla Windsor."

"I always ask her how she's doing," Renae Hoff says.

"Her answer is always the same. She grins and says, 'I'm still alive.'"

What would have been justice for Karla Windsor?

"I think there should be the hope that one day she could rejoin society," Renae Hoff says.

"I think she could do it. I believe she should be given that chance."

Chapter 7

Velma Barfield

HER EYES WERE RED-RIMMED and her body shook with
quaking sobs that seemed to come from somewhere very
deep inside the plump and dowdy woman's sorely grieved
soul. But when the reedy old organ pumped itself up for the
first resurrection-promising notes of "Rock of Ages," her
clear Piedmont voice rose up toward the rafters of the tiny
white clapboard church with a certainty that put to flight any
notion that the dear departed was not bound for a much
better place.

Margie Velma Barfield knew how to mourn the dead.
She'd wept and sung more than her share of them through
those final rites of passage down in Robeson County, North
Carolina. She'd also killed at least four of them herself—
and maybe more.

If she seemed just about the most unlikely person you'd
ever think capable of committing a murder, you'd need to
understand that while folks who knew her say they live in
the kinds of small towns where everyone knows everything
there is to know about everyone else, they really don't.
There was a Margie Barfield not one of them knew, living in
a secret world not one of them could have imagined.

The woman they thought they knew was a Bible-quoting,
sympathetic angel of mercy who cared for elderly people
she worked for with a kind of Christian devotion that made
your heart glad you still lived in the rural South. She taught
Sunday school classes, loved her little grandchildren, and

just couldn't do enough when she heard that a neighbor was feeling poorly.

The woman they didn't know at all was a prescription drug junkie who had taken eleven separate doses of drugs on the day she was arrested for the poisoning death of her on-and-off fiancé, choosing from more than fifty separate vials of mind-altering substances police found in her house. To feed her incredible habit, she'd forged checks on elderly patients in her care, impersonated her own mother to obtain a fraudulent loan, and sent four people to their graves because they had discovered what she was doing.

When later she would sit in the witness box and hear herself described as a woman without a heart by a prosecutor who finally understood who she was and what she had done, there would still be those in Robeson County who couldn't believe how completely the devil had won the soul of the angel in the choir robes they thought they knew.

"She enjoyed the funerals. She enjoyed the grieving. She enjoyed the murders too. She enjoyed the whole scene," Prosecutor Joe Freeman Britt would say. And Britt was a man who knew about persons convicted of murder. He is America's deadliest prosecutor, with twenty-three notches on his briefcase.

It was the untimely death of her fifty-six-year-old fiancé, Stuart Taylor, that finally exposed Margie Velma Barfield for what she was, by her own admission—a low-budget Lucrezia Borgia who used cruel poisons to murder people who placed their trust in her.

"Hell, she probably poisoned half the county, but we don't have the resources to exhume all the bodies for autopsies," Prosecutor Britt says today. The ones they had exhumed proved sufficient to make their case.

Margie Velma Bullard was born October 23, 1932, in Cumberland County, North Carolina. She was the second of eight children born to a cotton mill worker and his wife.

There is some question about her life as a youngster. She

claimed it was a cruel, abusive childhood. She called it "permissible slavery."

But her brother, Jimmy Bullard, a forty-four-year-old Parkton, North Carolina, Baptist minister and part-time maintenance man, once exclaimed, "That's not true! We had a good childhood."

And Velma claimed her father, who died in 1972, raped her when she was thirteen. Two of her brothers said that was a lie.

She finished the tenth grade of high school but dropped out of the eleventh. When she turned seventeen, she ran away with Thomas Burke, who worked in a textile plant. Burke soon changed jobs. He went to work driving a Pepsi-Cola truck.

For the next fifteen years, the Burkes led a seemingly blissful life. They had two children—Kim and Ron. They moved to Parkton, a town of five hundred near Lumberton, where they made a down payment on a small house.

"We were an all-American family," her daughter recalled. "Everybody was happy. We'd go to the lake and have picnics. We'd go to the beach on weekends. We'd go to the mountains on vacation. We loved each other."

Then marital bliss ended and family problems began.

Burke lost his job. Then he was involved in an auto-mobile accident and suffered head injuries. He started drinking heavily. He soon found he had to hide his booze from his religious wife. Velma would empty it down the toilet when she found a bottle. He became an abusive alcoholic. Life, according to Velma, soon became unbearable. A doctor prescribed tranquilizers for her.

Velma went to work for Burlington Mills to try to hold the family together. She was soon able to get a job at the Belk department store in Fayetteville.

Finally, her husband's excessive drinking became such a problem that she had him committed to Dorothea Dix Hospital in Raleigh.

"He was so embarrassed when he got back that I don't

ever remember a kind word passing between them till the day he died," their son, Ronnie Burke, recalled.

His death came in 1969 when Thomas Burke met a particularly horrible end. He burned to death in bed. At the time it was thought he had been smoking in bed. Only the mattress burned. The cause of death was listed as smoke inhalation.

Britt believes Velma murdered him. In fact, her daughter said, "It's always been a question in the back of my mind whether Mama had anything to do with Daddy's death too, but I never asked her."

Velma denied murdering Thomas Burke.

She also denied murdering her second husband, Jennings Barfield. She married Barfield in 1971. When he died six months later, his death was attributed to natural causes. But when his body was exhumed in 1978, an autopsy found it contained a deadly dose of arsenic.

During the following years, according to her family, Velma Barfield became heavily dependent on prescription drugs—antidepressants, tranquilizers, and painkillers. She got multiple prescriptions by developing a "bullpen" of physicians. She routinely mixed drugs and doubled or tripled dosages of everything from Valium to Tylenol III with codeine. On four occasions, she was hospitalized with drug overdoses.

"She started taking the pills when I was fourteen," her daughter, Kim Norton, recalled. "She was like an alcoholic, staggering. When we'd come home from school, we didn't know whether she would be passed out on the floor or injured or what. I must have seen Mama passed out on those pills hundreds of times when we were growing up.

"It got so bad, Ronnie and I used to hunt up her pill bottles and throw them down the toilet, just like she used to do with Daddy's alcohol.

"She'd be furious. She'd yell at us. Sometimes she'd just cry. Then she started hiding them from us.

"She'd hide those pill bottles in the washer, in rolls of

toilet paper, in her bra, out in the yard. Once she even hid some in her hair rollers. She was walking around, and you could hear all these pills rattling around on her head.

"We could tell she had a really serious problem," Ronnie Burke remembered. "She'd sit at the table and be talking to us, and she'd all but fall asleep. Her speech started slurring real bad. We'd get her into bed for the rest of the day."

But despite her drug addiction, Velma Barfield was a very devout Christian. The short, dumpy, bespectacled woman who resembled actress Jean Stapleton, who played Edith Bunker in the TV series *All in the Family*, insisted on going to church one morning a week for volunteer work in the church office and attending services every Wednesday night and twice on Sunday.

At the First Pentecostal Holiness Church, Velma Barfield taught Sunday school for the small children in the congregation.

By 1974 Velma's drug dependency was so great that she could not handle the cost. She wrote worthless checks to cover the expense. She ended up in court, but the sentences were never very serious. Finally, in desperation she went to the local office of the Commercial Credit Corporation and applied for a $1,000 loan. The name she signed was Lillie McMillan Bullard.

Velma knew her sixty-four-year-old mother was going to find out that she had impersonated her and forged her name on the note. She feared her mother would turn her in to the police. She went to the drugstore and bought a bottle of Ant Terro, an arsenic-based ant killer.

At dinnertime, Velma Barfield poured Ant Terro into her mother's soup. And, just to be on the safe side, poured some in her Coca-Cola too.

That night Lillie McMillan Bullard died.

There was no reason to suspect poisoning, and the autopsy at that time failed to uncover the real cause of death.

Velma Barfield had discovered the perfect murder weapon—odorless, tasteless arsenic poison.

Two years later, Velma Barfield was hired by Mrs. Dollie Taylor Edwards, an eighty-five-year-old woman, as a $2.65 an hour live-in maid.

She impressed everyone who had a chance to visit.

"She appeared to be a very careful person," Alice Storms, Mrs. Edwards' great-niece, recalled. "The house was always clean. She was very neat. I was very impressed with her."

She also impressed Stuart Taylor, Mrs. Edwards' nephew and Mrs. Storms' father. Taylor was a tobacco farmer in nearby Saint Pauls in northern Robeson County. Pretty soon Stuart Taylor came courting the widow woman who was caring so well for his aunt.

Stuart Taylor was a married man, but he was getting a divorce from Emma Sibbett Taylor of Lumberton. And everyone was impressed with the way this sweet woman with her deep religious faith had changed Taylor.

J. Yates Allen, a Saint Paul farmer whose family had farmed tobacco for two generations with Taylor's family, observed:

"Stuart, in all his life, he wouldn't go to church. This one got him going two or three times a week! She about got him stopped from so much of his drinking. That's the amazing thing to me."

In February 1977, Velma Barfield mixed some Singletary Rat Killer in Mrs. Edwards' cereal. And she spiked her coffee with it too. Three days later, Dollie Edwards died. The cause of death was listed as acute gastroenteritis.

Velma went to the funeral with Mrs. Edwards' family. She cried throughout the services. Her body shook with grief as the body of the woman was lowered to its final resting place.

Mrs. Margie Lee Pittman was looking for a live-in housekeeper for her elderly parents, John Henry Lee, an eighty-year-old farmer, and his ailing wife, Record Lee, who was seventy-six.

The pastor of her church, who knew Velma Barfield was now looking for work, recommended the very Christian lady to Mrs. Pittman.

Mrs. Pittman's sister, Sylvia Andrews, had heard Velma Barfield testify in church. They hired her for $75 a week.

"We thought she was a very fine, a very Christian person. Velma joined in the Scriptures and prayer reading.

"You couldn't ask for a better lady," Mrs. Andrews said. "She could cook great meals. We were so happy with her."

A month after she started working for the Lees, Velma found a blank check while housecleaning. Unable to resist, she forged Mrs. Lee's name on a $50 check.

She soon became fearful that Mr. Lee might discover her forgery and turn her in. Her reputation in the community would be ruined. I can't let him do that, she thought. Maybe I can just make him a little sick until I can get the money to repay the $50.

She bought some more Ant Terro. Every day, when Velma Barfield served tea or beer to John Henry Lee, it was spiked with ant poison.

It was late April 1977. Lee became violently ill. For nearly four weeks, he suffered from severe diarrhea. His body was racked with pain. He vomited. He went into convulsions. His weight dropped from 165 to less than 100 pounds in one month.

Then on June 4, John Henry Lee died. Acute gastroenteritis was listed as the cause of death.

Velma Barfield helped John Henry Lee's ailing widow to the funeral. She embraced the weeping widow and cried right along with her. A stranger would have believed she was a member of the family.

She returned to the house with the widow and continued to care for her. She even put a little Ant Terro in her tea. But not enough to kill her.

Then, in October 1977, she quit.

I need more time for myself, Velma said. After all, I am going to be marrying Stuart Taylor as soon as his divorce becomes final. Meanwhile, Mrs. Hubbard wants me to work at the Lumberton United Care Rest Home.

So Velma went to work at the rest home.

"She was my best help out here," Mrs. Rae Hubbard, night supervisor, said. "She was a real good worker, kind and gentle and good to all the patients."

But the romance with Stuart Taylor was running hot and cold for Velma—mainly because of her thieving ways. Twice Taylor found she had written checks on his bank account and cashed them. And when he found out about it, he forgave her but admonished:

"Don't you ever do that again! If you ever forge any more checks on my account, I'm going to turn you in to the police!"

Velma cried and promised it would never happen again.

But on January 31, 1978, Velma forged another check on Taylor's account. Afterward she thought, He's going to find out about it and turn me in, and I'm going to be charged with forgery.

About that time, Taylor learned that Velma had been arrested on worthless check charges in the past. He confronted her, and she denied it.

"Don't lie to me!" he said scornfully. "I can forgive you for making a mistake, but I can't forgive you for looking me in the face and lying about it. There's not going to be any marriage!"

Several weeks later, Velma called Taylor.

"Can you give me a ride to the doctor?" she asked. Taylor, who wasn't doing anything in particular, replied, "Sure, when do you want me to pick you up?"

"Rex Humbard is having a revival meeting over in Fayetteville tonight. I sure would like to go. Could we go there after I see the doctor?"

Why not? Taylor thought.

On the way back from the gospel meeting, Velma asked

Taylor to stop at a drugstore so she could fill the prescription for tranquilizers that she had picked up from the doctor. At the drugstore, while Taylor looked at fishing gear, she bought a bottle of Ant Terro.

Then they dropped by the home of Taylor's daughter, Mrs. Alice Storms, to see her young baby.

That night, at Taylor's home, Velma Barfield poured Ant Terro into his beer. A few hours later, she called Alice Storms.

"Your daddy got sick after we got to the house," she told his daughter. "Don't worry, I'll stay here and nurse him."

"Maybe I should come over," Mrs. Storms told her.

"There's no need for you to do that," Velma protested. "I'm sure he'll be all right."

During the next three days, Velma poured more Ant Terro into the once robust farmer. He tossed and turned in agony. He was unable to lie still because of the pain.

Several times a day, she called his daughter to assure her that her father was doing well and resting.

Velma even took him to the hospital once where the medics, seeing flulike symptoms of diarrhea and vomiting, told him he had gastritis and sent him home.

On the fourth day, Stuart Taylor was taken to the hospital in an ambulance. As he was being wheeled into the emergency room, he tossed his head back and let out a loud scream. And then he died.

The hospital said the cause of death was acute gastroenteritis. But the family, who couldn't understand how Taylor could be healthy one day and dead four days later, wouldn't accept it. They demanded a more detailed autopsy.

Six weeks later, after special heavy-metal testing, the hospital pathologists came out with the real cause of death—massive arsenic poisoning.

The finger of guilt pointed at Margie Velma Barfield, the one person who had been with Stuart Taylor during his final days.

But District Attorney Joe Freeman Britt was unprepared for what he heard when he called Velma in for questioning.

Not only did she admit poisoning Taylor, she also admitted killing her mother, Lillie Bullard, Dollie Edwards, and John Henry Lee. In each case, she told Britt, she laced her victim's food and drink with Ant Terro or Singletary Rat Killer.

The confession shocked the residents of rural tobacco-growing Robeson County. Most people knew Velma Barfield, that devout grandmotherly lady who taught Sunday School and couldn't do too much to help others.

"The Mrs. Barfield I knew couldn't have done that," Mrs. Hubbard at the rest home where she worked said. "I never saw her do or say anything like she has been accused of.

"I just don't believe she could have done it."

Joe Britt Freeman didn't get the title of the world's deadliest prosecutor by sitting on his hands. He immediately moved into action.

He went into court and got an order to exhume the bodies of not only John Henry Lee, Dollie Edwards, and Lillie Bullard, but also Jennings Barfield, Velma's second husband. He ordered more detailed autopsies to be performed on the bodies. In each body, pathologists found lethal doses of arsenic.

Now Britt had a problem. For which murder should Velma Barfield stand trial?

"We had a death penalty statute in North Carolina but in 1975 it was declared unconstitutional," Britt explained. "We got a new capital punishment statute in 1977.

"The last one she killed—her boyfriend, Stuart Taylor—fell just within the new capital punishment law by a short period of time. All of the others fell under the period when the law was unconstitutional. So to try her for those would have only meant life imprisonment.

"As a result, what I did was put her on trial for the last murder. Then we had a law that wasn't well-known that we dug up that allowed me to prove the other killings by way of showing motive—intent—on the last killing. We ended up proving five murders, but she was only being tried for the last murder."

At the arraignment in the Robeson County courthouse, Velma Barfield wore a bright summer dress. She smiled at everyone. You might have thought she was sitting in the front pew at church.

She pleaded guilty by reason of insanity.

Then Superior Court Judge Hamilton Hobgood granted a motion for a change of venue. The murders had touched too many families in the close-knit society of Robeson County.

Velma Barfield went on trial in Bladen County, North Carolina, charged with the first-degree murder of Stuart Taylor.

She admitted poisoning Taylor and Dollie Edwards and John Henry Lee and her mother. But she denied killing either of her husbands—Thomas Burke or Jennings Barfield.

"I didn't intend to kill any of them," she insisted. "I only wanted to make them sick to give me enough time to cover up the money I took from them."

But she didn't steal from Dollie Edwards, Britt said. Why did she kill her?

"I can't explain it," she replied. "I put some in her cereal and coffee, but there was nothing really between her and I. I can't explain . . . there was no reason."

But, she confessed, "I figured it would kill her when I gave it to her."

She really hadn't meant to kill Stuart Taylor, she swore.

"I had forged some checks on Stuart and he found out about it. He said if I forged any more checks that he was going to turn them in."

After she had forged a check on January 31, 1978, she said, "It bothered me because he was going to find out about it. I was afraid he was going to turn it in and I would have been charged with forgery."

So she bought some ant poison and put it in his tea and beer.

Mrs. Storms recalled the night Velma and her father stopped by to see her baby.

"She came into my home with the poison in her pocketbook, knowing that as I sat there and talked to my dad, it would be the last time in my life I'd see him alive. I'm sorry, that's a cold-blooded person. It's a person who has no feelings.

"She kept me from even going over to his house by calling me several times a day, so concerned and thoughtful, telling me that everything was fine, that Daddy was resting.

"The night before Daddy died, she even called to ask if I thought it would be all right to give Daddy an aspirin.

"I think she's a serial killer—a killer that sits there and watches them suffer and enjoys every agonizing minute of it."

Prosecutor Britt told the jury, "Stuart Taylor lies out there in the cold, damp sod, wrapped in his shroud because of the callous, indifferent, malicious acts of this woman."

Velma Barfield's court-appointed attorney, Robert Jacobson, had never tried a capital case before. And while he invoked a plea of insanity, even defense witnesses said they didn't think Velma Barfield was insane.

But what was worse, Velma Barfield refused to show remorse on the stand, despite all of his efforts. Instead, she argued with Britt and even, after his summation to the jury, sarcastically applauded.

"I begged her to get up there and cry," Jacobson revealed. "Women can turn on the tears when they want to, and she sure needed them then.

"Instead, she did just what he wanted her to do. She tried to fight back. I hate to say it but it's all a big game and she just couldn't or wouldn't play it."

It took the jury less than sixty minutes to reach a decision in the case of *North Carolina* v. *Margie Velma Barfield*. The verdict: guilty of first-degree murder. The sentence: death.

During the trial, John Henry Lee's family approached Prosecutor Britt.

"They came to me and said that after Granddad died, they were worried about Grandma because she was vomiting," Britt said. "We clipped a lock of her hair and sent it to a lab in Atlanta and she was chock full of the stuff too. That was in the middle of the trial, and I couldn't use it because I didn't have time to get my witnesses."

Mrs. Andrews, John Henry Lee's daughter, commented, "She murdered three people in a year's time. There would have been a fourth if she'd stayed around for Mama."

Her mother died of a stroke in 1979.

Six years of imprisonment and exhausted legal appeal would pass until Velma Barfield faced the somber sentence of death handed down to her in 1978. Under North Carolina law, Velma was afforded an ironic choice. She would be permitted to decide whether she wished to die by poisonous gas in the state's death chamber or to relinquish her life through the administering of a lethal injection of drugs. In either case, she would die by poison. Velma chose the drugs. After making her choice she asked that her lawyers make no further appeals. Velma said she was ready to die. She met with ministers and planned her funeral. She chose to wear a pretty pink pair of pajamas as she lay atop the steel hospital gurney that would be her deathbed. At 2:15 A.M. November 2, 1984, in a windowless room at Central State Prison in Raleigh, doctors declared that she had died from the massive amounts of procuronium bromide that had been pumped through her veins reaching her heart and rendering it unable to beat. She was the first woman to die by execution in the nation in more than twenty-two years.

Chapter 8

Attina Marie Cannaday

"DAMN YA'LL!" SHRIEKED seventeen-year-old Attina Marie Cannaday, her heavy southern drawl cutting through the startled, crowded Harrison County courtroom like a knife slicing through soft butter. Her shoulders hunched, she stared at the six men and six women on the jury. Tears ran down her cheeks.

A matron came over, snapped handcuffs on her small wrists, and led the sobbing girl from the Gulfport, Mississippi, courtroom back to her jail cell.

Circuit Court Judge J. Ruble Griffin had just sentenced her to die in Mississippi's gas chamber. It had taken the jury only an hour to find her guilty in the stabbing death of her former lover, Air Force Sergeant Ronald Wojcik. Then it took the jury only another fifty-five minutes to recommend the death penalty.

At 10:15 P.M. on September 23, 1982, Tina Cannaday, a frightened little girl without a friend in the world, had just become the youngest person in Mississippi history ever to receive the death penalty.

Her court-appointed attorneys—Shannon Waller, Jr., and Evelyn Floyd—stood stunned. They were totally surprised by the sentence of death. How could the jury deliberate for less than an hour and come back with a penalty of death? thought Waller.

The poor girl, Mrs. Floyd thought. She has been like a little cur dog, trying to survive the best way she knew how.

"The poor girl never had a chance," Waller told

reporters. "She is the product of her heredity and a product of her environment."

Life was tough for Tina Cannaday. Her mother was a striptease dancer in Mobile, Alabama, and her father—Tina hated her father.

She loved her daddy until that night when she was nine years old. She hadn't even started to blossom as a woman when her father raped her.

Her mother divorced her father and remarried. Then, when she was thirteen, her stepfather looked at the budding, beautiful stepdaughter, and he also raped her.

Tina had to get away from Mobile and her sordid family life. Anyway, she hated school. Why should she keep going to classes when she didn't understand what the teacher was talking about. They said she was borderline retarded with her IQ of 71. She had the mind of a nine-year-old, they said.

Her chance came when she turned fourteen. She got married and fled to the Mississippi coast with her new husband. Eight months later, he divorced her. She was on her own wth nothing to sell—except herself.

It didn't take Tina long to find a "home." She discovered it was easy to find a man to live with. In the next two years, she found nine different men who took her into their beds.

But a girl needs money, so the fourteen-year-old put on makeup to make herself look older and went to Biloxi's Strip. She had decided to try to get a job as a stripper—just like her mother.

At the Gringo's Room, she talked to Dewey D'Angelo, the bar's owner.

"Do you need a dancer?" she asked.

"How old are you, kid?" he queried.

"Nineteen," she lied.

She got the job.

Tina soon learned there was another way for a pretty little girl to make some extra money. With the encouragement of Dewey, she started taking "dates." She became a prostitute.

There was no shortage of tricks in the bar. If men wanted sex so much, let them pay for it, she decided. Tina was learning how to get her way with people.

She soon lost her job, however.

"Me and Dewey had our ups and downs about things," she told those who asked her what happened.

The real reason? One of her customers told Dewey that she was only fourteen.

Tina moved down the street and went to work for another bar. Two years later, in an unrelated incident, D'Angelo was dead, the victim of a murder.

In the following two years, Tina worked as a stripper in four different bars.

Tina Cannaday was becoming wise beyond her years— street-wise. She learned how to fight and to get what she wanted.

She developed a strong feeling of defensiveness. If something went wrong, it was always somebody else's fault. But her street smarts—her alleycat personality— always came through in her relationships with others. She never became close friends with anyone. Her associations were always superficial.

Eventually, after a parade of boyfriends, Tina met a part-time bartender at the Sports Page lounge. She was now sixteen years old. He was a twenty-nine-year-old sergeant in the Air Force stationed at Keesler Air Force Base in Biloxi—Ronald Wojcik.

Ronald Wojcik had wanted to be in the Air Force as long as he could remember. While he was going to school in Newbury Park, California, he couldn't wait until he turned eighteen and could enlist in the service.

In 1971 he turned eighteen.

He had been in the Air Force for nine years when he was transferred to Keesler Air Force Base as an instructor with the 3410 Technical Training Group. That was in 1980.

This was the life, Ron felt. He even got married, but it

ended in a divorce. The only things he missed about married life were his two kids, who were four and six.

But he now had a part-time job as a bartender and there was always a lot of young stuff with hot pants around the bar. He had a nice pad at the Beachview Apartments on Beach Boulevard and he never had to worry about sleeping alone. And every once in a while, his kids even came to the beach to visit him.

It was love at first sight when Tina met Ron. "I love him better than I do my own ass," she said later.

When she told the airman that she needed a place to stay, he was more than happy to have her move into his apartment.

Ron was overjoyed. Man, he told his Air Force buddies, I've got a sixteen-year-old chick living with me.

But his boasting soon reached the ears of his commanding officer, and he was called on the carpet.

"We can't tell you who to live with, but we can tell you who you cannot live with," the officer asserted. "You cannot live with a juvenile."

Sergeant Wojcik shrugged his shoulders, saluted, and went to the bar. He told Tina she would have to move out. Orders are orders.

Besides, he thought, there is this barmaid. . . .

Tina was furious. She was still a child who had never grown up. She always expected to get her own way. But now she had to move out of Ron's place and she didn't like it.

But then she caught him sleeping with twenty-one-year-old Sandra Sowash, a barmaid where he worked. That was too much. Jealousy pierced her brain. Revenge became foremost in her childlike mind.

She went to the Biloxi bar where Ron was bartending. Sandra was there.

"You better be good to him, because if you don't I'll kill you because I love him better than I do my own ass," she shouted at the startled barmaid.

The feelings of rejection became stronger. Her heart ached. Maybe he told me the story about his commanding officer ordering him to kick me out just so he could get her to move in, she thought.

She went drinking. It was May 22. In a Gulfport bar, she ran into John R. Cooper, who used to be a neighbor of Wojcik.

"I caught him with that whore," she fumed to Cooper. "If I catch him in bed again with that whore, I'm going to kill them both."

She moped for days. She called Gina Picou. She had been a roommate of Gina's on one of those rare occasions when she wasn't living with a man. It was June 1.

"I want to get back at them," she told Gina. "I want to kill both of them."

David Gray was a twenty-eight-year-old drifter from Ellisville, Mississippi, about one hundred miles north of Gulfport. Since getting out of prison, if he wasn't stoned on drugs, he was gassed on booze.

A month earlier he came to Biloxi. He didn't have any place to live, so an abandoned, wrecked car on the service road along the beach became his home.

Then he met this young chick—Tina Cannaday. They got along fine. There was no hanky-panky. He started calling her "sister." She called him "brother." He liked that. He became very protective of her.

It was a warm, humid night and Gray decided to go over to the Red Garter Lounge and drink. It was June 2, 1982. A little later that evening, Tina came into the bar. Another girl came over. The new girl was young and chubby. They started calling her the "Fat Girl." Her name was Dawn Bushart, she was fifteen, and she was a runaway from Tuscaloosa, Alabama.

Tina and Gray danced and they drank. Tina couldn't get Ron and Sandra off her mind.

"My old boyfriend really hurt me," she told the drifter. "Will you beat him up for me?"

"Sure," he replied.

"What I'd really like to do is kill him," she pressed. "Will you kill him?"

"I don't want to go that far," Gray, remembering his days in prison, told the woman scorned.

It was now after midnight, June 3, 1982.

"Let's go over to Ron's apartment and give him a good scare," Tina told Gray. "I've got a key to the place."

"Sure," said Gray.

"Have you got a gun?" she asked Gray. "I'd sure like to shake him up."

"I ain't got a gun, but I got some knives back at the car," he replied.

"You want to come?" Tina asked the Fat Girl. "Sure," she replied.

The trio left the bar. It was a quiet night. The waves lightly lapped Biloxi's broad beach as they walked to the car along the beachfront.

At the car, Gray unlocked one of the doors, reached inside, and brought back a handful of knives. Four of them.

Then they started hitchhiking toward Ron's apartment, which was about five miles away.

At the apartment, Ron and Sandra had gone to bed. Ron's two kids were visiting. They were asleep in the other bedroom.

Tina, Gray, and the Fat Girl arrived at the apartment.

"You stay here," Gray told the Fat Girl on the porch.

Then, using Tina's key, they opened the front door and entered the darkened apartment.

The lights went on in the bedroom. Tina and Gray were standing by the bed. They had expected to find Wojcik alone. Seeing Sandra in the same bed in her nightgown surprised them.

Tina cursed wrathfully when she found her former

soldier-lover in bed with the new, hated rival. Anything she could pick up, she threw.

Gray was mad too.

"That son of a bitch has hurt my sister and now he's going to be hurt," he told Sandra.

At knifepoint, they forced the two to get out of bed. Sandra wanted to put on some clothes. "No," scowled Tina.

Ron slipped into some jeans and pulled on a sweater.

"I think it's time to go for a ride because you've hurt my sister," Gray snarled, pointing a knife at the airman.

"Gimme the keys to your van and your wallet," Tina demanded. Ron handed them to her. They then pushed the dazed couple to the van. The Fat Girl followed.

Meanwhile, Ron's children slept blissfully in the other bedroom.

Tina got in the driver's seat of the 1974 Ford van. Gray sat in the front passenger seat. Fat Girl was in the back with Ron and Sandra.

Screeching tires pierced the night air as Tina careened the van down U.S. 90. She drove like a madwoman along the empty street.

Wojcik knew they were in trouble. He had seen Tina's temper flare on other occasions but nothing like this. He leaned over to Sandra and whispered, "If this van stops, I'm going to push you out. Don't look back. Just run."

Tina heard him.

"You switch seats with Dave," Tina ordered the sergeant. The two men changed seats.

Tina's heart pounded. Her hatred was running rampant. She had the man who had betrayed her and his no-good girlfriend under her power.

Her foot pressed on the accelerator. The road made a sharp turn and she almost turned the van over going around the corner.

The road was running alongside a railroad track. And there was a train coming.

Tina stomped down on the accelerator again, trying to beat the train to the crossing. Wojcik grabbed the wheel and the van narrowly averted hitting the train.

"Cut him if he moves again!" Tina shouted to Dawn Bushart.

"We're going to kill both of you!" Tina yelled.

Finally Tina began to calm down a little as she continued to drive aimlessly.

"Dave," she told Gray, "why don't you see what Ron sees in her?"

Then, as the van rolled along and everyone in the van watched, Gray raped Sandra.

It was on a dirt road by a dark, secluded wooded area off Three Rivers Road in Harrison County just north of Gulfport where Tina finally stopped the van.

Gray pulled Wojcik from the van. Sandra got out with the Fat Girl's knife pressing against her side.

"You'd better say good-bye to him," Tina told the trembling girl. "You'll never see him alive again."

As Gray dragged him into the woods, he turned to Sandra and said, "I love you."

It was just a short time later that Gray called from the woods. He had fought and beaten Wojcik. Ron laid unconscious on the ground.

"Bring Sandra back here," he shouted. "It's her turn."

Sandra started toward the woods with Tina holding a knife at her back when Tina changed her mind.

"Get in the van," she growled. "I'm going to waste you there."

This may be my only chance, Sandra felt. She broke and ran. Furious, Tina threw the knife with all her strength. The blunt end stung Sandra between the shoulders. She kept running.

"I ran as fast as I probably ever ran in my life," she later told police officers.

As Sandra ran, she heard the enraged Tina screaming to Gray, "Kill him! Kill him! Kill him!"

Sandra reached a farmhouse about two hundred yards away. Frantically, the shivering, frightened nightgown-clad woman pounded on the door, but no one answered.

Spotting a trailer, she crawled underneath.

Infuriated, Tina ran into the woods where Gray was standing over the unconscious body of her former lover. She tore the knife from Gray's hand.

"I want to talk to him," she snarled. Gray knew what was coming. He wheeled and walked to the van.

Then Tina, her rage soaring to its peak, stabbed the unconscious Wojcik again and again and again.

She stabbed him in the back, in the chest, in the face. Sixteen times she stabbed him.

Then she cut his throat.

Again and again she tried to sever the head of the dying soldier from his shoulders. The blood of her ex-lover was on her hands. The jumpsuit she was wearing turned red.

Finally, her anger vented, she walked slowly toward the van. There was a faint smile on her face.

Sandra, frozen like a rabbit under the trailer, heard the van turn around and drive off.

She crawled out. Again she pounded at the door of the farmhouse. Finally, a light came on and a sleepy-eyed farmer came to the door. Sobbing, she told the man what had happened. He called the Harrison County Sheriff's office. It was 4:40 A.M.

Sandra told her harrowing experiences to the deputies. They took her to the Gulf Coast Community Hospital. A short while later, she left.

Deputy Sheriff Charles Purvis was the first officer to arrive on the scene where Sandra Sowash had told them they would find Wojcik. It was still dark. Purvis searched for nearly an hour, but he could find nothing. Investigator John Nix from the sheriff's office joined him. Then, just at the crack of dawn, they found Sergeant Wojcik's body lying about thirty yards from the road.

The body was so mutilated by the nineteen stab wounds

and slashes that Harrison County Coroner Edgar Little, Jr., could not determine the wound that killed him. A gaping neck wound had nearly decapitated the body.

"We cannot indicate the specific wound that killed him," Little later told the jury. "When the throat was cut, the carotid artery was severed; both the internal and external jugular veins and the esophageal airway were severed."

Wojcik had also been stabbed through the heart, Little testified. Any of eleven of the wounds could have been fatal, he explained.

The officers went to Sergeant Wojcik's apartment to continue their investigation.

Meanwhile, Tina was driving toward Slidell, Louisiana. She knew Timothy Page there. They could stay at his house.

As they were entering Slidell, Tina could see by the early light of dawn that she had blood all over her jumpsuit. She looked in the wallet she had taken from Wojcik, took out the money, and threw the billfold out the window as they passed a cement plant.

In Slidell, she had the Fat Girl, who did not have blood on her, go into a store and buy her a T-shirt to put over her bloody clothing. Then the Fat Girl parted company with Tina and Gray. She started hitchhiking back to Biloxi.

Tina and Gray went on to Page's house and woke him up. Tina washed out her jumpsuit in the sink. The water turned red.

Then the sixteen-year-old killer went to sleep to dream her sweet dreams of revenge fulfilled.

It was 8:30 A.M. and the concrete-truck driver was going to the cement plant off I-10 in Slidell for his first load of the day. As he turned in to the plant, he saw what looked like a wallet on the side of the road. He stopped his truck, stepped down, and picked it up. He looked inside. No money, but there were some papers.

When he got to the cement plant, he turned in the wallet.

"Somebody must have lost it," he told them.

An office worker found Wojcik's name and telephone number in the wallet. He dialed the number. A deputy sheriff answered the phone.

Investigators Jimmy D. Johnson and Pete Martin drove to Slidell to pick up the wallet. Slidell police and the St. Tammany Parish Sheriff's office were alerted.

It was about noon and Gray was getting hungry. While Tina slept, he and Page got into Wojcik's van and went looking for something to eat. Page drove while Gray sat in the passenger seat.

The flashing lights and blaring siren of a police car pulled them over to the side of the road.

"Where's the girl?" they asked Gray. He led them back to the house, and Tina, sleeping like a baby, was arrested.

"Where's the Fat Girl?" they asked Tina.

"She's headed back to Biloxi," she told them. She gave the officers a description of the clothes she was wearing.

Dawn Bushart, hitchhiking back to Biloxi, had just crossed the city limits on U.S. 90. She was tired. It had been a night she would never forget.

How did I ever get involved? she thought.

Biloxi Detective Louis Atchison saw the teenager hitchhiking and stopped to talk to her.

"Where are you going?" he asked.

"I was taken to Louisiana and dropped off, and I caught a ride back to Biloxi in an eighteen-wheeler," she told the detective.

Satisfied, Atchison drove off. But within minutes a description of the girl and her clothing came over Atchison's police radio. He quickly wheeled the unmarked car around and sped back to the girl. He arrested her.

All three of them—Attina Cannaday, David Gray, and Dawn Bushart were indicted for capital murder. All pleaded innocent.

On August 12 Gray was convicted and sentenced to die in

the gas chamber. The death penalty came even though Gray testified that he had only agreed to rough up Wojcik but refused to kill him.

On September 20 Attina Cannaday went on trial for the murder of Ronald Wojcik.

"I'm going to show you it was strictly her scheme because she was so mad he was seeing another girl," District Attorney Albert Necaise told the six-man, six-woman jury. "She was the one that set it up, the one that started the wheels rolling."

Deputy Sheriff Ronald Mason, a jailer, told the jury that on June 14 Tina had laughed and told him that after Wojcik's throat had been cut, she had taken his head and tried to shake it loose from his body. She wanted to take his head with her, Mason said she had told him.

Sandra Sowash took the stand.

"Tina caused Ron's death all the way down the line," she asserted.

Then David Gray took the stand against Tina. In exchange for immunity from prosecution on the charge of raping Sandra Sowash, Gray had agreed to become a state witness. Gray was hopeful that, on appeal, his partial involvement in only one crime might win him a new trial, particularly if evidence in Attina's case established her as the real killer of Wojcik.

"The reason I'm here testifying today at Tina's trial is to try to get this mess straightened out because I'm innocent of what I'm charged for," the condemned man testified.

Shocked at Gray's decision to testify against her, Tina sobbed during his entire testimony.

Tina, he said, came into the woods and insisted that she be allowed to talk to Wojcik, who was alive but on the ground as the result of their fistfight. He left when Tina grabbed the knife from his hand, leaving the girl alone with the airman.

Necaise showed him pictures of Wojcik's mutilated body.

"From the looks of those pictures," Gray remarked from the witness stand, "those pictures tell what Tina done."

Tina Cannaday took the stand in her own behalf.

"We just went to the apartment to pick up a pair of my jeans that I had left there when I was living with Ron," Tina told the jury. "We picked up the four knives because we were hitchhiking and we needed them for protection in case we got a ride with a nut."

Gray, Tina said, went berserk when he saw Ron in bed with Sandra.

"David Gray got mad at Ron because he thought me and Ron was still going together," she continued.

It was Gray who forced the couple into the van, she said. Gray and Bushart had knives. The blade on her knife was closed, and she didn't force them into the van.

"I just drove," she insisted. "I didn't know what to do."

She swore she never entered the woods where Wojcik was killed. She said she and Dawn Bushart stayed at the van with Sandra.

"Why didn't you drive off?" Necaise asked.

"I don't know," she whined.

Didn't she wash the blood from her jumpsuit when they arrived at Timothy Page's house? Necaise asked.

Yes, she conceded.

Didn't the water turn red from blood?

Yes, Tina replied, but that was because she had just started her menstrual period.

Necaise walked over to the clerk's table, picked up the photographs of Wojcik's body which had been admitted into evidence, and sauntered over to the witness chair. He thrust the pictures in Tina's face. She recoiled, winced, and refused to look at them.

"Didn't you laugh and joke about the pictures with deputies at the jail?" the district attorney thundered.

"No!" Tina sobbed.

Necaise then called Larry Turner, a serologist with the Mississippi crime lab. Turner testified he had found trace amounts of blood on the front of the jumpsuit that Cannaday had worn on the night of the crime, but there were no traces of blood found in the crotch of the garment.

In her argument to the jury, Evelyn Floyd, Tina's court-appointed attorney, said:

"This girl had no idea that Gray, half-crazed with drugs and liquor, would go berserk and stab and nearly decapitate Wojcik.

"How could a sixteen-year-old with the mind of a nine-year-old mastermind a crime like this?

"Tina Cannaday was in love with Ronald Wojcik. She didn't want him dead."

On September 23 the jury returned its verdict: guilty as charged. Then, in the penalty phase of the trial, it recommended the death penalty.

Dawn Christina Bushart, fearful that she would also be given the death penalty, pleaded guilty to a reduced charge of manslaughter. She was sentenced to ten years in the state penitentiary. She had refused to answer questions about the crime when called to back up Tina's story.

"I think the jury reached the right verdict," District Attorney Necaise commented afterward. "I think it took courage for a jury to do this. We had a case that had overwhelming evidence. The jurors were willing to come in and take their responsibility seriously and conscientiously."

Mrs. Floyd was shocked by the death penalty.

"She grew up from a very sordid family life, and she just tried to survive the best way she could and ended up being a prostitute," the attorney said. "She didn't know how to do anything else and that's the way she continued.

"This fellow Gray kind of considered himself a knight in shining armor and Tina was a damsel in distress, and when he saw Wojcik there with a new girlfriend in bed, he just flipped out," she commented. "He has this notion of protectiveness toward Tina."

On December 17, 1982, from his death row cell, Gray

tried once more to become the knight in shining armor. He wrote a letter to Tina.

"Please forgive me for what I have done to you," he penned. "I don't blame you if you don't but when I went back to Gulfport I told my lawyer the whole truth. I told him that I was the one who took Ron's life, that you had no part in it."

A request for a new trial based on the letter was denied.

On May 16, 1984, the Mississippi State Supreme Court ruled that Tina Cannaday's rights had been violated when the remark made to Deputy Sheriff Ronald Mason about wanting to take Wojcik's head with her was admitted in evidence. She should have had a lawyer present when she made the remark, the high tribunal said. It called for a retrial on the penalty portion of the trial.

But Mississippi State Attorney General's Office disagreed. It has appealed to the U.S. Supreme Court to overturn the state court's ruling. In the meantime, the original sentence stands.

Chapter 9

Patricia Ann Thomas Jackson

PATRICIA JACKSON SAYS SHE can point straight to the day when her luck went bad. It was on New Year's Eve, 1947. The day she was born. And things haven't gotten much better since, she says.

Her parents were poor blacks in a run-down town in Alabama who never had gone anywhere and weren't going to. Praco was a little mining crossroad in rural Jefferson County, and if the horizons were bleak for any child born there, they were that much worse for a black child born into rude poverty, faced with the hopeless prospect of growing up in backwater Alabama in the early 1950s.

She was the firstborn. Two sisters would come along soon enough, and the tiny house without a real bedroom or proper plumbing would just provide more daily reminders that there weren't too many good things to look for in life.

Patricia Jackson was a tiny six-year-old when her tearful mother broke the news that their family's life had taken an even worse turn.

"Your daddy's dead, sugar. He won't be coming home again," Patricia's mom sobbed.

He was stabbed with a knife, the child would hear later from little playmates. He was killed in a fight over nothing, maybe just out of pent-up rage over being poor forever.

Patricia's mom did her best to keep the family going in the ramshackle house at the edge of Praco, but without a man around to bring in some hard cash, the vegetable plot and a handful of scraggly chickens weren't going to be enough to keep body and soul together.

Three years after her father had been laid to rest in a small colored cemetery, Patricia's mom bundled up the few things they owned, took her children in hand, and headed for the big town of Tuscaloosa. The University of Alabama was there and the mother hoped there might be girls at the school who needed washing and ironing done, or maybe there might even be work there as a cook or a maid in a fancy house. And there was something else too. A black child could go to a halfway decent school in a town like Tuscaloosa. The mother had given a lot of thought to her bitter life and knew that if there was any hope for her daughters at all, it waited for them in the pages of books. They'd get the chance she never had, the mother vowed.

Patricia liked going to school in Tuscaloosa. Learning didn't come all that easily, but she tried. She did try. She wanted her mom to be proud of her.

"I just couldn't put all those words down on paper," she explained.

Nevertheless, she finished the eighth grade.

But while she wasn't learning too much in school, she was learning the facts of life on the streets.

"I was so fast," she recalled.

She was so fast that before she could start back in the ninth grade, she found out that she couldn't go back to school. Not that year anyway. She was pregnant.

Alabama school authorities at that time required schoolgirls who got pregnant to stay out of school until their baby was at least one year old.

During that year, with Mama to take care of the baby, Patricia learned to live it up.

A year later she wasn't interested in going back to school.

"I was more interested in going out and playing cards and having fun."

It was a year later that she started carrying a knife—a

habit that has led her to the threshold of Alabama's electric chair.

Patricia knew what a knife could do. Hadn't her daddy been killed with one?

Still, she never thought of carrying one until a girlfriend got in an argument with her and the girl pulled a knife. When the fight was over, Patricia had a nasty four-inch cut on her right breast and another cut on her upper left arm.

Never again, she thought. Why should I be the only one without a knife?

"I said from then on nobody would ever cut me again."

She saved her money, and then she went out and bought a knife.

"It was a matter of survival," she insists. "Everybody needs a knife."

She proudly showed her new weapon to her sisters. They got all excited.

"Mama," they yelled, "Patricia's got a knife!"

The memory of how Patricia's father had died flashed through the mind of her mother.

"Gimme that knife, child!" she demanded. Patricia never saw the knife again.

But that didn't stop her.

"I bought another and hid it under the steps," she says now, smiling.

She didn't have trouble hiding things from her mother soon afterward. Her mother had cancer. She was sick a lot, but mostly she was drunk.

But, Patricia says now, "She loved us."

Patricia was seventeen years old in 1966. She was still a little girl—only five feet two inches tall and weighing only one hundred pounds.

Her boyfriend was Andrew Hughes. It was nice to have a boyfriend. With a baby daughter at home, maybe he will marry me someday, she dreamed.

But it was not to be.

"We got into an argument, and he started knocking me around," she remembered.

"I stabbed him with a Chinese razor."

He died.

Some sixteen years later, for the first time, she would say she acted in self-defense, that he came at her with a dagger. But there was never a mention of the dagger or what she considered to be a threat on her life at that time.

The confused teenager saw the inside of a jail for the first time. She cried when her mother didn't come to post bond to get her out.

"Mama didn't try to get me out on bond, as the boy's family had said they would kill me," she recalled.

She was charged with first-degree murder. That could mean the electric chair.

Tuscaloosa attorney Tom B. Ward represented her in court.

The bargaining began. The state, not especially eager to try the case, offered a deal.

"They are offering life," he told Patricia. Plead guilty and she would not go to the electric chair.

"No," she replied.

He went back to the prosecutors.

"They are offering twelve years," Ward told her when he came back this time. She cried, but she had to accept it.

She began serving her term at the Julia Tutwiler Prison for Women in Wetumpka.

"I had never been away from home before," Patricia said. "The hardest thing about prison was being away from Mama."

And she had to leave her baby daughter behind.

"Mama stopped her drinking and she really took care of my daughter while I was in prison."

In prison the small seventeen-year-old girl found out more about the facts of life.

"There is no way to describe prison to somebody who ain't been there.

"I'm not talking about going on vacation, but it was not all that bad."

In prison she found older women who were more than happy to take her under their "motherly" wings.

"By my being the youngest, everybody down there treated me like I was their daughter. I had two or three 'play' Mamas.

"They were my 'state mamas.'"

Four years later, Patricia Ann Thomas was paroled from prison.

Patricia came home to Tuscaloosa. She had to find work to support her little girl.

First, she went to work for Peco Foods. Then she got a job answering phones and dispatching taxicabs for a local company.

She got married in 1972 to a man from Bibb County by the name of Jackson. But three months later, he left her for another woman.

Her mother died when her daughter was eight. Patricia started drinking.

"I became an alcoholic," she admits now. She lost her job, but she found a boyfriend and discovered she didn't need to work. Anyway, it gave her more time to party and booze it up.

"My boyfriend took care of me. His check took care of the rent and we got food stamps."

She was constantly getting into trouble.

When she got drunk, she was mean—and she was drunk all the time. She was boisterous. She would break things. She always had problems when she drove a car because of her drinking.

In one incident, she was arrested and convicted for assaulting a police officer and resisting arrest.

Another time she was convicted for malicious destruction of property.

In one of her accidents, she was convicted for hit-and-run.

Seven different times she was arrested and convicted for disorderly conduct.

Patricia Ann Jackson became well-known to the Tuscaloosa Police Department.

In Alabama the black community has what is known as "shot houses." They are usually someone's home where an individual can buy liquor by the drink—unlicensed saloons.

This was a time of boozing and partying for Patricia.

"I would get up in the morning and start going to shot houses. I would drink and play cards."

If she had money, she would buy for her friends. But they weren't her friends, she learned later.

"Blacks don't have friends," she said. "They have associates when you live like I did. They are with you today as long as you are buying and with somebody else tomorrow."

She added, "When the money runs out, the friends run out."

It was just after 1 P.M. when Charlotte Archibald stopped her van in front of her cousin's duplex apartment at 3515 Twenty-first Street. It was February 28, 1981, a brisk, sunny day in Tuscaloosa, Alabama. Her cousin, Bonnie May Walker, made a living by running a shot house out of her apartment.

After visiting awhile with her fifty-year-old cousin, Ms. Archibald was about to leave when she heard the voice of a woman—an angry woman—coming from the adjoining alley.

"She was talking loud and cursing," she recalled. It was Patricia Ann Thomas Jackson.

Patricia walked onto the porch demanding a drink. She has already had enough, Ms. Archibald thought.

"No drink for you," Patricia was told.

Patricia left the porch, and Ms. Archibald said good-bye to her cousin, walked down to her van, opened the door, and got in and looked for her keys. She was getting ready to leave when she saw Patricia Jackson walk back onto the porch and approach her cousin.

Again, Patricia demanded a drink. The two women argued.

Pelma Smith lived in the other apartment of the duplex. He was sitting on the porch when Patricia returned.

"She pulled a knife out of her purse and stabbed Bonnie in the chest," he said.

It happened so fast, Charlotte Archibald didn't know what had happened.

"I saw her when Mrs. Jackson hit her," she remembered. "It looked like she gave her a shove. It looked like she hit her. I didn't see a knife in either woman's hands."

The knife went right through Bonnie May Walker's heart.

The mortally wounded woman staggered. With the last bit of strength in her rapidly dying body, she made her way to the kitchen, dripping a trail of blood.

In the kitchen, she rummaged through a drawer until she found a butcher knife. She wheeled and headed back toward the front door to face her assailant.

But when she reached the front door, she collapsed. Life was over for Bonnie May Walker.

Murder after conviction for second-degree murder within twenty years is a capital offense in Alabama.

Assistant District Attorney Jerry Hudson was going for the maximum—death in the electric chair.

"The evidence will show that on February 28, 1981, in Tuscaloosa County, Alabama, Patricia Ann Thomas arrived on the scene mad and came up on the porch of the duplex where Bonnie May Walker lived," he told the jury of ten women and two men."

"Testimony will show an argument ensued and Patricia Ann Thomas pulled a knife from her handbag and stabbed her in the chest in the heart once," he added.

He continued:

"I expect the evidence to show that after Bonnie May

Walker was stabbed, she turned, walked to the back of her house, got a knife from her kitchen, and walked back onto the porch where she died."

Tuscaloosa attorney Joel Sogol—Patricia's court-appointed lawyer—told the jury:

"The evidence will show that Bonnie May Walker operated a shot house and Mrs. Jackson and some friends were going there to buy some whiskey.

"The evidence will show that Mrs. Walker, at the time she was stabbed, was threatening Mrs. Jackson."

Hudson continually referred to the defendant as "Thomas." Sogol called her "Jackson."

The reasons became evident as the trial wore on. Sogol said there was no evidence that Patricia Ann Jackson and Patricia Ann Thomas were one and the same. He ultimately lost that argument.

Patricia Ann Thomas Jackson told the jury she went to Bonnie May Walker's house to buy some whiskey and got into an argument with her.

She claimed Charlotte Archibald pulled a gun and forced her to leave.

She came back and got into an argument with Bonnie. Bonnie had a knife, Patricia said. She claims she didn't have a weapon.

In the following scuffle, she told the jury, Bonnie dropped her knife and she picked it up and stabbed her.

The jury didn't believe her. It took them less than two hours to find her guilty of first-degree murder. They recommended the death penalty.

After the trial, Hudson said:

"This occurred on the front porch of the victim. The woman had no business being there. She was not in any kind of danger at the time.

"At worst, bad words were being spoken back and forth, and she pulled out a knife and stabbed this other woman. This is just about as bad as you can get."

First-degree murder requires premeditation. Was there premeditation on the part of Patricia Ann Jackson?

"For premeditation, she doesn't have to plan it for an hour and a half," Hudson explained. "All she has to do is to intend to do what she does."

Mrs. Jackson had been drinking, the prosecutor agreed, but "voluntary intoxication is not a defense to murder."

The murder of Bonnie May Walker by Patricia Ann Jackson came fifteen years after she had stabbed her boyfriend, Andrew Hughes, to death.

"Without the prior murder, this case would not have come under the death penalty," Hudson conceded.

If the incident had happened five years later, Patricia Ann Jackson wouldn't have found herself on death row in the shadow of the electric chair.

Still, it was Circuit Judge Joseph A. Colquitt's decision whether to accept the jury's recommendation of the death penalty.

On December 23, 1981, Judge Colquitt presided over a sentencing hearing. Neither side called witnesses.

But Lawrence Scott, a black minister, came to the hearing with a dozen women from his church. He stood up in the courtroom and asked Judge Colquitt for mercy for Patricia Ann Jackson.

As he spoke, the women started chanting, "Praise the Lord."

The judge had to remind them they were in a court of law.

Afterward, Scott identified himself as a cousin by marriage of Mrs. Jackson.

On December 28, 1981—three days before her thirty-fourth birthday—a weeping Patricia Ann Jackson was sentenced to die in Alabama's electric chair.

Joel Sogol, her attorney, knew it would be difficult to get the more recent murder verdict overturned, so he went after the first conviction.

If an error was found in the 1966 trial, he reasoned, it

would mean she could not be sentenced to death for committing two homicides within twenty years.

The judge who presided over the 1966 case—W. C. Warren—was now dead.

But, more important, the court reporter who took the transcript of the proceedings was also deceased and, incredibly, the state was unable to find a transcript of the case or any shorthand notes taken at the time.

Patricia was never informed of her right to appeal the original 1966 conviction, Sogol told the court. And her attorney at that time never told her that she could plead innocent by reason of self-defense.

"I never intended to plead guilty to any charge in that case," she told the judge.

Tom B. Ward, Jr., who represented her at that time, came to court and testified against her.

Yes, Ward said, he was aware of self-defense as a defense. But, he asserted, at the time she never told me that Hughes was armed with a knife.

Ward said he didn't recall whether Judge Warren informed her of her right to appeal.

But, Ward commented, "It would be the height of absurdity to appeal from an agreed-on settlement. I considered twelve years a good settlement.

"It was not a guilty plea, it was an agreed settlement."

Judge Colquitt refused to throw out the 1966 verdict. The death penalty, he said, stands.

Patricia Ann Jackson is now back at Julia Tutwiler Prison for Women. Only, this time there are no "state mamas." Instead, she spends twenty-four hours a day in a cubicle about thirteen feet long and seven and a half feet wide, and she spends most of the time crying.

"It's hell," she told a reporter for the *Tuscaloosa News*. "Pure-o-D hell."

Although she doesn't have contact with anyone and she's constantly under guard, she was completely stripped and searched each time she went outside.

The humiliating searching and probing after every thirty-minute exercise period were too much. She doesn't go outside anymore.

Patricia's only joy in life now is her daughter and grandson in Germany, and her two sisters and her nieces and nephews.

Her family has stuck by her, she says proudly.

"My daughter understands. All she says is, 'Regardless of what you do, you are my mama.'

"If they electrocute me, I know my daughter will cry, but I feel she will forgive me and, as the years go by, she will forget."

Prison is now a living hell for the little black woman from Praco, Alabama.

"It's not that they are bad to me," she weeps. "They are not. It's just the knowing."

Tears rolling down her black cheeks, she cries, "I'd rather be dead."

Then she shakes her head no.

"I don't mind dying. It's just that I don't know how to die. I don't want to know when."

Being poor and black has been against her all her life, Patricia believes.

"If I had money and hadn't been black, I wouldn't be on death row.

"I may be the first woman in years they electrocute just to get a point across. There are going to be killings until the world comes to an end. They are not going to stop it by electrocuting me."

Since returning to prison, Patricia has found God.

She has been saved, she says.

"I pray to God to let me love everyone," the condemned woman says.

Then, as the tears begin to roll again, she sobs, "They can take my life, but they can't take my soul."

Chapter 10

Annette Louise Stebbing

IT WAS THE CLASSIC TALE of the dim-witted oaf wanting to be loved, trying to please, suffering the taunts of friends and foes alike, finally rebelling and going a step too far.

In the case of Annette Louise Stebbing of Baltimore, Maryland, that extra step ended in murder.

Annette was an unplanned, unwanted child, the last of five children in the family.

Her father—Clifford Paul Wendricks, Jr.—is a retired Baltimore policeman who works as a maintenance foreman. Her mother was a waitress.

During the time her mother was pregnant with Annette, she neglected herself. She became sick and was forced to give birth to the baby two weeks early. When Annette was six weeks old, her mother went back to slinging hash eleven hours a day. Until she was two, Annette saw a constant succession of babysitters. Some of them abused her.

In the first grade of school, the teacher sensed that Annette wasn't like the other kids. Even her mother thought something was wrong about the way Annette would go for a whole week without speaking to her. Annette was taken to Johns Hopkins Hospital in Baltimore for evaluation. The findings: neurological dysfunctioning and social learning disorder.

The shy, easily frightened girl was put in special-education classes. But even there, the gawky, fat youngster stood out like a sore thumb. The other students teased her. They needled her and called her "dummy" and "stupid."

Home was not a happy place for Annette either. She shared a room with her sister, Mary Ann, but they disliked each other. She and her brother Tony hated each other. He would beat her up for no reason at all, she said. Her younger brother, John, always told their parents that Annette did it when he did something wrong. Clifford was the only sibling that she liked.

Her relationship with her parents was no better.

Her mother?

"I hated her," she said. She would have nightmares that her mother was beating her, and wake up black and blue with bruises she had inflicted on herself in her sleep. Those nightmares later turned into dreams of her beating her mother. In prison she has refused to see her mother.

Her father?

"Me and my father never did get along," Annette replied. "He never told me he loved me until I went to jail."

Though she was pliable and easily swayed by others and rarely protested injustices done to her, she would sometimes throw temper tantrums, screaming violently.

Her dog could take food from her plate and she wouldn't protest. Someone could take a toy from her and she wouldn't utter a word.

One day her brother Tony dragged her to a sewing machine, put her hand on top of it, and put the needle right through her finger. She didn't protest at all. She stayed stitched to the sewing machine until her mother found her there.

She was always looking for affection and attention from anybody who would offer it. Her overwhelming desire to please allowed others to easily exploit this awkward youngster.

When she was twelve, she fell off a monkey bar and broke her right arm. The pain didn't bother her. She was more concerned that her mother would beat her for breaking her arm.

Annette started stealing liquor from the house when she was thirteen. She would go out in the woods and drink it.

When her family moved from Baltimore to Edgewood, Maryland, Annette was taken out of special-education classes and put into a regular tenth grade. She couldn't handle it.

This was an extremely trying time for the young girl. She soon found she needed to drink all of the time. She would take liquor to school in her pocketbook, slip off to the girls' restroom, and drink it. She began to cut classes at school.

Despite her young age, the big-boned teenager had no trouble buying booze at local liquor stores with her school lunch money.

She began running away from home. At fourteen she had her first sexual experience.

Before she was seventeen, she would have run away at least ten times. Sometimes she ran away from home after an argument with her mother, fearful that her nightmares of her beating her mother would come true.

One time, after she was brought back home drunk, her ex-cop father handcuffed her to her bed in an effort to keep her from running away again.

Her mother found her when she ran away one time. She brought her home, sat her down at a table, and took a gallon of whiskey from the closet. Then she kept pouring the whiskey down Annette's throat until she gasped for air.

On another occasion, she ran away again and went to the home of a neighbor. The woman called her mother. Her mother picked her up and took her home. Then she marched her into the kitchen and tied her to a chair while she went into the bedroom to get her father's off-duty revolver. She untied Annette and told her that she had better shoot her mother or she was going to shoot Annette. Her father came home from work at that time and grabbed the gun. It was a traumatic experience for the youngster.

Her parents felt she was associating with the wrong people. They ordered her to stop seeing them and then picked others that they felt would be a better influence on her. Ironically, the youngsters that her parents chose for her got her involved with drugs.

Another time, Annette got into a physical confrontation with her mother, and her mother ended up sitting on top of the girl on the floor.

Frantically, Annette's mind went blank, and she pushed, shoved, and flailed at her mother. Her mother ended up unconscious on the floor.

Her brother Tony found them. He took his mother to a neighbor when she regained consciousness. Then he beat Annette.

Tony was constantly beating up Annette. When she ran away from home and he found her, he would beat her up. If she was with a boy, he would beat them both up. If he didn't like the way she looked at him, he would beat her up.

By the time she was fifteen, Annette was smoking marijuana, snorting coke, taking downers. By now she was drinking a pint of whiskey a day along with beer.

Annette dropped out of school in the tenth grade. She was beginning to mature into a large-boned, overweight woman. Her long brown curly hair framed her white, fleshy face.

She ran away from home with two other girls and broke into a closed motel in Edgewood. They were arrested. She was referred to a juvenile counselor.

That didn't stop her. She and three friends broke into a vacant apartment and were sitting on the living room floor smoking pot when the police came and arrested them. This time she and another girl had to pay for the broken glass.

She stole a gun from a man she had been living with. Only, this time she didn't get off easily because of her age. She was sentenced to eighteen months in prison for grand larceny. After two months, the judge placed her on probation.

She took a part-time clerical job at Harford Community College for about a year while trying to pass her high school equivalency test. But she never did pass the test. Later, she

worked for a brief time as a security guard at the Baltimore
Gas and Electric Company warehouse, but they fired her for
incompetence. She joined the ranks of the chronically
unemployed.

Then, in February 1979, she met Bernard Lee Stebbing.
She learned he had been married twice—his first wife had
died and his second wife had divorced him because of his
drinking. On August 24, 1979, Annette married Stebbing.
She was eighteen. He was thirty-four.

Marrying Lee Stebbing was the only successful thing
Annette had ever done in her short lifetime. A failure in
everything she had ever undertaken, this was the first time
she had ever received any kind of recognition. In her eyes,
it was the first time that she had amounted to anything.

The fact that Lee was almost twice her age was seen as a
triumph by Annette even though her mother told her that she
didn't care for him. "He looks sneaky to me, greasy, not a
reliable sort," her mother said.

Lee Stebbing was an alcoholic, Annette learned. A
hypersexed alcoholic. He worked as a carpet installer for
Art Crafts, Inc., but he could never earn enough money for
a place of his own. They lived in the living room of Lee's
mother's place. Lee slept on the couch while Annette slept
on the floor.

Within one week, the marriage started going downhill.
Lee verbally and physically abused her. He beat her. He
sexually abused her. He punched her in the face, and one
time he even knocked her out. It made no difference
whether he was drunk or sober. She was the target of his
violence. Bruises always covered her body.

Although she outweighed her husband by ten pounds, he
was four inches taller and always managed to have his way.

Annette, no stranger to abuse, tolerated the brutality of
her new husband becaue she thought he loved her.

Meanwhile, her drinking increased. She was downing a
pint of Jack Daniel's or Lord Calvert a day. Every day she
and her husband would drink a case of beer—Pabst in

bottles. At one time, she even joined Alcoholics Anonymous.

In her presence, Lee would make comments about other women, that he wanted to have sex with them. She ignored his remarks because he said them all the time.

Stebbing had been in trouble because of his sex drive. He had been arrested for sexually molesting two juveniles.

On April 5, 1980, the Saturday before Easter, Lee and Annette Stebbing went to the home of Edna Stebbing, Lee's sister-in-law, in Essex, a blue-collar community east of Baltimore. Mrs. Stebbing—her friends call her Sam—was there with two of her daughters, Dena Polis and Vickie Lawback. Lee had a sword that Mrs. Stebbing thought she could sell for him.

Lee boasted to Annette that he had slept with Dena and her mother before he had married Annette.

As the couple were arriving, Dena remarked to her sister, "Oh, God, here he comes again."

In the house, Lee grabbed at his niece's breast.

"Don't you ever touch me like that again!" shrieked Dena as she hit Lee and kicked him in the shins. She dug her long fingernails into his shoulders.

"I want to screw her," Lee told his wife later. "I want to have sex with her."

When Edna Stebbing arrived home about 5 P.M. on April 9, the following Wednesday, she found Dena there with her brother-in-law, Lee Stebbing, and his wife, Annette. She had sold the sword for $20. They split the money.

Dena was planning to visit her boyfriend, Brian Taylor, in nearby Glen Burnie, and the Stebbings offered to give her a ride in their van to Light and Pratt streets in downtown Baltimore where she could catch a bus. "I'm going to screw her tonight," Stebbing whispered to his wife.

The three got into the van. Lee was driving, Dena sat in the passenger seat, Annette knelt on the floor between them. Dena was wearing jeans, a flowered shirt, a white sweater, and a sapphire ring. She had $1.80 in her pockets.

Instead of going to downtown Baltimore, the scheming Stebbing drove in the other direction—to neighboring Harford County.

"Dena, do you mind us going up to Harford County for me to check this job out?" Lee asked his niece.

Dena, who had several hours to kill before meeting her boyfriend, agreed. Lee stopped and bought a case of Pabst beer. They each opened a bottle.

About eight miles out, Lee pulled the van onto the side of the road.

"My oil is low," Lee explained. He got out of the Ford van, went around to the front, and pulled up the hood. He opened a can of oil and poured it into the truck. Then he shouted to Annette, "Do it, do it."

Annette, who was standing behind Dena, put her arm around the girl's neck, dragged her out of the passenger seat, and pulled her into the back of the van.

As Lee bolted into the van, the frantic Dena yelled, "Lee, stop her!"

The large Annette had pinned down the smaller girl. She was sitting on her chest with her legs over her arms. As his niece repeatedly called to him for help, Lee Stebbing grabbed her jeans and underpants and ripped them off. Then he began raping her.

Dena started screaming. Annette put her hands on her throat. Her powerful fingers tightened on the soft, yielding neck of the girl.

"Turn her over," Lee ordered his wife. "I want to fuck her up the ass."

With Lee's help, Annette turned the struggling girl over. She still had a stranglehold on her. Then Stebbing sodomized his niece. Over a period of thirty minutes, he experienced two orgasms.

"Please don't kill me," Dena gasped to Annette. "I have too much to live for."

Annette squeezed harder until blood gushed from Dena's

nose. Then the girl stopped breathing. Annette looked at the clock on the van's dashboard. It was seven o'clock.

When Dena Polis failed to show up in Glen Burnie by 6:30 P.M. to meet Brian Taylor, the boyfriend called Edna Stebbing. Her daughter had left Essex, she told him. He called several times during the next twelve hours to tell her that Dena had not arrived. The next day a missing person report was filed.

Edna called Lee and Annette.

"Do you know where Dena is?" she queried.

"We left her at the corner of Light and Pratt streets last night," Lee replied. "I'll go down there and see if anybody has seen her," he offered.

At 7 A.M. on April 11, the seminude body of Dena Polis was found in a sewer in Fells Point in Baltimore. It was clad only in blue booties, a pink thermal underwear T-shirt with embroidered flowers, a multicolored blouse, and a white bra that had been pulled up to expose the breasts. Her sapphire ring was missing. A buttonhole on the shirt was torn and a button missing. In her hand was a brown button.

An autopsy showed that death was caused by strangulation some thirty-six hours prior to discovery of the body. Sperm was found in the vagina and the anal canal.

Baltimore City Detective James Ozazewski was assigned to the case. He called Dena's brother, George Jones, and a neighbor to identify the body.

"Sodomy had been performed on Dena, but don't tell anyone in the family because they have been through enough," he told them.

He called the Stebbings and asked them to come over to Edna's house. He just wanted to talk to them about Dena, he explained.

"We left Dena on the corner of Pratt and Light streets at six o'clock on April ninth," Lee and Annette swore.

After the interview, Annette went to the neighbor who had identified the body.

"Did they find her clothes?" she asked. "Can the police

tell who she did it with from the sperm found in her body? Do they know who did it? Have they found her ring?"

Then Annette asked, "I know Dena was screwed up the ass, but can they tell whether a man did it with his finger or his dick?"

The neighbor told Detective Ozazewski about Annette's questions.

At 12:20 P.M., April 19, at the request of Detective Ozazewski, Lee and Annette Stebbing drove to the Baltimore City Police Department for another interview. He asked their permission to search their van. Lee agreed. He accompanied the officer to the van.

While he was looking in the van, Ozazewski noticed a brown button was missing from the yellow shirt that Lee was wearing. The buttons on the shirt looked like the button found in Dena's clinched fist.

He immediately took Lee to an interview room and advised him of his constitutional rights. Stebbing refused to give him a statement.

Meanwhile, Detective John Hess took Annette into another interview room. She sat down on the hard wooden chair.

"Lee is wearing the same shirt that he was wearing the night that Dena Polis was murdered," he told Annette.

Annette bolted from the chair.

"He didn't kill her, I did!" the frightened girl exclaimed.

After a brief time, the officer, taken aback by the suddenness of the confession, asked, "How did it happen?"

Still standing, Annette stretched her arms out and held her hands in a vise position.

"I was sitting on her chest and my hands felt like magnetic vises when they closed around her throat. And I was squeezing until blood came from her nose," she told the detective.

In the struggle for her life, Dena had scratched Annette on the left hand. The fresh scratches could still be seen.

"I strangled her until there was no life in her," she confessed.

Annette's confession continued, "We drove around for a long period of time and then we went home and I went in the house and got something to eat. Lee stayed in the van with Dena. I don't know why he stayed in the van, because Dena was dead.

"After I got done eating, we drove around trying to think what to do with the body."

Then, while Annette sat in the front passenger seat getting drunk on what was left of the case of beer they had bought earlier, Lee went to sleep in the back of the van next to the body of his dead niece.

"We kept her in the van for two days and took her to work with us. The second night after I strangled her, we got off work early. We drove around the waterfront. When it got dark, we drove to Washington and Aliceanna. We stopped at a manhole and checked to see if any cars or persons were around.

"Lee took a large screwdriver to get the top off.

"Then we stuck her down the sewer hole and Lee put the cover back on.

"We took the van to Wilson Point and parked by the creek and got buckets of water and washed it inside and out.

"On Thursday during the day, her pocketbook and shoes we threw in the dumpster at Arts Crafts, Incorporated. Her dungarees, white sweater, and her panties we threw in the dumpster at the Seven-Eleven on Eastern Avenue across from the Edgewater Apartments. The blanket Dena was lying on that had blood on it, we threw in the dumpster at Seven-Eleven."

Annette took the officers to the scene of the murder. On Old Philadelphia Road in Harford County, she pointed out an oil can and a Pabst beer bottle that Lee had discarded.

At Wilson Point, where they cleaned the van, officers found a white button that matched the missing button from

Dena's blouse. There was a piece of sandpaper that matched sandpaper recovered from the van.

On April 23 Annette saw Lee for the first time since she confessed to strangling Dena Polis.

"I had to do it when they told me what they knew from you," she whined to her husband.

"You didn't have to tell them anything," her irate husband snarled. "A wife doesn't have to testify against her husband."

On April 25, armed with a search warrant, officers went to the house where the Stebbings had been living. In a closet, they found Dena's sapphire ring inside a ceramic candleholder.

The court ordered psychiatric tests of Annette Stebbing.

One examination revealed an IQ of 76 with mental retardation "of unspecified type and severity." Another test showed her with an IQ of 83, reflecting dull normal intellectual functioning. But they found she was not insane.

Before her trial, Annette changed her story repeatedly.

On July 14 she said she left the van to relieve herself and returned to find Lee and Dena engaged in sexual intercourse. She said she got angry when Dena asked Lee "for more" in her presence, and then attacked and strangled her in a rage.

On August 8 she said her husband held a gun to her head and ordered her to kill Dena.

In court she told still another story.

She had lied to police, she told the jury, because she knew she was going to jail and "Lee was going with me."

Here's what she said "really happened":

As they drove to Harford County, Lee told Dena, "I'd like to have a piece of ass."

Annette said, "I didn't take it as serious. I thought he was messing around. That's all I took it as.

"Dena just looked at him."

Shortly afterward, she said, Dena asked her to comb her

hair for her, and Annette shifted behind her and started doing it.

Lee, she said, put his hand on Dena's thigh.

"I told him to get his hand off of her lap. Then I got back in between Dena and Lee.

"He didn't say nothing. He gave me a dirty look, like he was going to hit me. That's all."

At this point, she and Lee had consumed about twelve beers between them. Dena, in this version, did not drink anything.

Annette asked Lee to stop at a filling station so she could go to the bathroom. Instead, he pulled over to the side of the road. She grabbed a roll of toilet paper from the truck. She told Dena she could come with her if she was afraid to stay alone with Lee. Dena declined.

She was in the woods for only three or four minutes when she heard a noise.

"It sounded between a moan and a scream. I started walking up to the van and it seemed to get louder and louder. So I opened the door. It was Dena. Dena was making the noise because Lee was screwing her.

"I said, 'What in the hell are you doing?' And then he jumped, and replied, 'I didn't expect you to come back this soon.'

"You'll know what will happen to you for raping her," I told him.

"Then Lee replied, 'It's not rape.' And then Dena said, 'He is not raping me.'

"I was angry. I was so mad I started shaking and I didn't know what to do.

"She called me a pussy. Then I said, 'You no good bitching whore, you would lay with anybody.'

"And she replied to me that I'm a whore. And I said, 'I'm married. If I'm a whore, I guess that's what I am.'

"From there, I said, 'You and no one else is going to mess with my husband. He is my husband and if he wants sex, he can come to me.'

"She said, 'If I want him and his dick, I will get it.'

"I said, 'You or no one else will get him or his dick.'"

During this entire exchange, Dena had remained on the floor of the van stripped from the waist down while Lee put his clothes on, Annette said.

At that point, Annette said, she got up, went over to Dena, and raised her fist.

"I'm going to beat the shit right out of you," she recalled saying.

"And she said, 'If you're big enough, beat my ass.'

"From there, I held back because if I would have hit her, I would have hurt her bad. Then I told her, 'One time too many you're going to mess with somebody else's husband, and you're going to get hurt.'"

"And then she says she can mess with anybody she wants. From there, I said, 'You're just a complete whore.'

"She called me a whore and a pussy and a no-good bitch.

"At that time, my mind . . . I felt like I didn't have nothing in my head. Then I realized I had my hands around Dena's neck choking her.

"Lee was behind me. When I realized I was choking Dena, Lee went to grab me, to pull me from Dena. He just couldn't pull me from Dena.

"After that, I let go and I checked her pulse and her heart to see if she was still alive. I figured she was because I didn't choke her that hard.

"But when I said, 'We should take her over to the hospital,' he goes, 'No, she's dead.'

"I was scared and sorry. I didn't realize that I killed her.

"I sat there and I started crying and shaking. I couldn't believe that that happened.

"I kept saying to Lee, 'What are we going to do?' And then he said, 'Bonnie and Clyde.'"

Psychiatrists testified at the trial that, because of her intellectual and memory impairments and the stress of the situation, Annette was unable to accurately recall the events of the crime.

The differing statements, they said, were consistent with her memory deficiencies and her history of fantasizing in stressful situations, and the statements reflected her vacillation between a desire to punish her husband and a desire to protect him.

On January 13, 1981, a jury found Annette Louise Stebbing innocent of a charge of premeditated murder, but they found her guilty of first-degree felony murder, first-degree rape, first-degree sexual offense, and robbery.

In an appeal for leniency, Annette told Harford County Circuit Court Judge Albert P. Close:

"I am very sorry for taking Miss Polis' life. It wasn't meant to be. It was accidentally. I please ask you to let me live instead of . . . of sitting me in a gas chamber."

On April 28, 1981, Judge Close sentenced her to death on the murder charge. No sentences were imposed for the other crimes.

Bernard Lee Stebbing was found guilty of first-degree felony murder and sentenced to life in prison. He escaped the death penalty because, under Maryland law, only the person who actually takes another person's life can be sentenced to death.

Chapter 11
Lois Nadine Smith

THE TWO MEN WERE UP early on that Fourth of July, 1982, working horses out at the barn. It was Sunday as well as a holiday, and the sun was already inching its way up in the Oklahoma sky. It sure looked like it was going to be a hot day.

Charles Smith, superintendent of the rural Gans, Oklahoma, school district, and Larry Ringgold, a teacher at the Gans school, closed the barn door and started a leisurely walk over to the home of James "Hork" Smith. Hork's car had gotten a flat tire the previous night, and Ringgold had loaned Hork his car. They were going over to retrieve it.

In the driveway along with Ringgold's car was a copper-colored Cadillac.

At the door of the modest one-story brick rancher, they were met by Gregory Smith, Hork's eighteen-year-old son, wiping his hands with a towel. It surprised the school superintendent. Gregory was the son of Hork and his former wife, Nadine. He lived with his mother over in Tahlequah.

They could hear what sounded like a nasty argument going on in the house. Ringgold recognized Nadine's voice.

"Don't come in here," Greg told the two men. "Dad isn't home, but he'll be back in about thirty minutes."

Then a woman's scream pierced the hot morning air. It came from the house.

Ringgold walked over to his car, opened the door on the driver's side, and got behind the wheel. Charles Smith went to the other side of the car and got into the vehicle.

Ringgold turned on the ignition and started backing out of the driveway. As they turned to drive away, the men saw someone waving frantically from the front window.

In Sequoyah County, in the northwestern corner of the state, they have a name for Lois Nadine Smith—Mean Nadine. They call her the meanest woman in Oklahoma.

She has been a hard-drinking, hard-looking woman for many of her forty-three years. She talks tough and her short reddish hair helps to give her a mean look. In addition to drinking, Nadine has also been a pill-popping drug user.

Her son, Greg, was a Xerox copy of his mother, only taller and thinner. And he acted and talked just like his foul-mouthed mother.

Nadine and Greg had been out boozing it up all Saturday night.

They were mad. They had heard that Cindy Baillie, one of Greg's old girlfriends, was planning to tell police about their drug trafficking.

At 5 A.M. July 4, Nadine called twenty-year-old Teresa Baker at her home in Tahlequah. Teresa was Greg's current girlfriend.

"Let's go boogie," a seemingly happy Nadine told the sleepy woman.

"Who is this?" she asked.

"Nadine," came the reply.

"Let me talk to Greg."

When Greg got on the phone, Teresa asked, "What's your mother high on?"

"She's just been drinking," Greg asserted.

Cynthia Lee Baillie was spending the night in a cabin in a tourist court between Tenkiller Lake and the tiny town of Gore in adjoining Cherokee County.

The twenty-year-old was awakened from a deep sleep by someone pounding on the door early that morning.

It was Nadine Smith, the mother of her old boyfriend.

"Hey, Cindy, you want to go party with us?" Nadine roared.

"Sure," she replied. "What's happening?"

She slipped quickly into her yellow print dress, the one she wore off the shoulders.

As she walked out to the Cadillac, she saw Greg and Teresa. Teresa sidled up to her.

"I don't think it's a good idea for you to get in the car," Teresa, who had heard Nadine and Greg venting their anger in the ride over, whispered to Cindy.

"I can take care of myself," she replied, crawling into the back seat of the car. Nadine got in beside her. Greg got behind the wheel and Teresa sat next to him.

Greg drove out of Gore and turned east on interstate 64 heading toward Gans.

As they got on the interstate, Nadine turned to Cindy.

"You told the police on us, didn't you?" she asked menacingly. "You've been trying to set us up."

"I don't know what you're talking about," Cindy retorted, beginning to feel some concern for her safety.

Nadine grabbed Cindy's purse and tossed it over the front seat to Greg. Then she opened her own purse and took out a pair of black gloves. Slowly she pulled the gloves on.

Then, as the Cadillac rolled over the county line into Sequoyah County, Nadine reached over and grabbed Cindy by the throat.

"You'll never see Cherokee County alive again," she vowed.

As the car continued toward Gans, Greg started rummaging through Cindy's purse. He found a paring knife.

"Look, Ma," he said, holding the knife up over his shoulder, "she was going to hurt you with this."

Nadine snatched the knife from her son's hand.

"Were you going to hurt me with this?" she snarled at the frightened Cindy. Before the girl could answer, she plunged the blade into Cindy's neck and twisted it. Then she slowly pulled it out.

Cindy cried in pain as blood spurted from the nasty wound and ran down her dress.

An hour later, the car pulled into the driveway of the Gans home of Hork Smith.

Greg took a .22-caliber revolver from the glove compartment as the foursome got out of the car and went to the front door. It was still early and there was no activity in the neighborhood. Everyone was apparently sleeping late today.

When Hork came to the door, Nadine pushed her way into the home of her ex-husband. Robin Smith, Hork's wife, came out to see what the commotion was all about. She gasped at the sight of the bleeding Cindy.

"Please help me!" Cindy begged the couple.

"You can say anything you want to them or me," Nadine told the shaking girl. "It won't do you any good. It's gone too far."

"We got to kill her," Nadine told the Smiths, "or else Greg will be killed."

Turning to Cindy, Nadine said, "The girl is going to have to die slow."

"I want to die fast," Cindy pleaded. "I'm going to have a baby. You're going to kill the baby too."

Then, threatening her ex-husband's new wife, Nadine said, "Get out of here. It's been nice not seeing you. I haven't been down here. You haven't seen me. Tell anybody anything and I'll kill you."

Robin turned on her heel and raced out the front door. I'll go to the Ringgolds, she thought.

Nadine ordered Cindy to take a shower to wash some of the blood off.

When Cindy came out of the bathroom, Nadine turned to her ex-husband.

"Get in the bathroom and don't come out," she ordered. Hork Smith obeyed.

Nadine took the revolver from her son and started teasing

Cindy. Horrified, the girl shrank into a recliner in the living room.

"Stop her, Greg," Cindy pleaded. She was nearly hysterical now. "Don't let her kill me."

Greg, smiling, tossed her a pillow. Frantically, Cindy feebly held the pillow between herself and the muzzle of the gun.

Nadine laughed. She began to tease the girl. When Cindy moved the pillow up to her face, Nadine would move the gun down to her stomach.

It wasn't funny to Teresa. She got up to leave the room. As soon as her back was turned, she heard the gun go off. She looked at Cindy. The bullet had exploded into the recliner.

Hearing the shot, Hork rushed in from the bathroom.

"Get your ass back in the bathroom!" Nadine snapped, waving the gun at him. "Stay out of this."

"Greg, don't do it," Hork told his son. "You'll never get away with it."

Greg stopped smiling. Maybe he's right, he thought.

Then Teresa said, "We've got to go ahead and do it because it's my ass too."

Nadine resumed her deadly game as she towered over the cowering Cindy. Suddenly the gun belched again—and again. Blood spurted from Cindy, splattering Nadine's blouse. The girl's head jerked. Her body lunged forward out of the recliner and onto the floor. Nadine stood over the whimpering girl whose limbs flayed the air as life began to leave her. Then she handed the gun to Greg to reload it.

While Greg reloaded the revolver, Nadine viciously stomped on the squirming girl's neck, bouncing up and down.

Greg handed the reloaded .22 back to his mother.

"Go ahead and empty the gun in her," he urged.

Nadine got behind the dying girl. She fired two shots into the back of her head. Then she fired four more shots into her body.

Hork Smith burst out of the bathroom and saw the dead girl on the floor of his living room.

"If you had to do it, why did you do it here?" he asked his ex-wife.

At that moment, Gans's only police officer—Vernon Barnes—pulled up in front of the house.

Charles Smith and Larry Ringgold thought something was very fishy at Hork Smith's house. When Greg told them to leave and come back later, they drove to Ringgold's house.

Robin Smith was in the kitchen with Ringgold's wife, Bonnie.

"What's happening down at your house?" the superintendent demanded.

Robin Smith didn't respond.

"What's happening?" he insisted.

"Nadine is down there and she's going to kill a girl they brought with them," Robin sobbed. "Nadine told me if I told, she'd kill me."

"Nadine's not going to kill anyone," Smith commented. She's just overreacting, he thought.

"She's already stabbed her!" Robin cried. The school superintendent picked up the phone. He tried to reach the Sequoyah County Sheriff's office. There was no answer that holiday morning. Then he called the nearby Muldrow Police Department and asked if they could investigate.

Then he and Ringgold drove over to Vernon Barnes's home.

Vernon Barnes had worked late the night before. Things can get pretty rowdy on a Saturday night. He was determined to sleep in today. But all of a sudden he was awakened from a sound sleep by someone desperately banging on his front door.

He pulled himself out of bed, slipped into a pair of pants, and went to the door. It was the school superintendent and one of the teachers.

"There's something funny going on over at Hork's," they told the officer. He quickly put on his uniform and got into his police car.

"We'll be over at my house," Charles Smith, the superintendent, told the officer. "Let us know what happens."

Barnes drove the few blocks to the Hork Smith residence. As he arrived, he saw Hork just leaving.

"Hey, Hork," he hailed Smith. "What's going on?"

Hork, who had just seen the murdered girl in his living room, nervously replied, "Not a thing. Just a family argument. Everything will be fine as soon as I leave."

Barnes accepted his explanation. Everything seemed in order except for the copper-colored Cadillac in the driveway. Just some of the family in town for the holiday, he thought.

He got back into his police car. He returned and told Charles Smith and Larry Ringgold that it was just a family squabble. Then he went home and went back to bed.

After he left his house, Hork walked to Charles Smith's home.

He told Smith and Ringgold, "Nadine's just roughing that girl up."

Nadine and Greg were trying to figure out what to do with Cindy's body. Greg went into the kitchen and returned with two large plastic trash bags. They tried to stuff the body into the bags but it wouldn't fit.

"She won't fit in the car," Nadine said. "We'll leave her here. Hork can get rid of the body."

Nadine, her white and orange tank-top blouse splattered with blood, dragged the corpse into the master bedroom. Then she took the revolver and placed it in the dead girl's hand.

"That will make it look like a suicide," Nadine told the others. "Pull down the window shades," she ordered.

She turned to Teresa. "If you tell anybody about this,

you'll be the next one to die," she threatened. The trio locked all the doors to the house as they left.

Hork and Robin Smith stayed at the Ringgolds all morning. They wanted to give Nadine time to clear out of their house and take the body with her.

It was two hours later when Hork and Ringgold went to Hork's house to pick up a grill for the barbecue they were going to have that afternoon. Hork noticed that Nadine's car was gone. Thank goodness, he thought.

Hork, who wasn't accustomed to locking his house, was surprised to find the shades drawn and the front door locked. The two men went around to the back door. It was locked too. Hork didn't have a key.

Ringgold took the screen off a window and Hork helped him climb inside. Once inside, Ringgold went to the back door and opened it for Hork. Then they walked down the hallway. At the doorway of the master bedroom, they saw Cindy's body, her pretty face twisted grotesquely in death.

Blood had dried to a crust on her dress. A crimson smear of blood formed a necklace around her throat. Her chest was perforated with small, bloody bullet holes. There were dark bruises on her face.

"Get out of the house!" Ringgold shouted at Hork. But Hork had already seen the body.

As he reached the carport, Hork's emotions gave way. Suddenly he became violently ill, vomiting and sobbing.

The two men rushed back to the Ringgold house and told Charles Smith what they had seen. The school superintendent got in his car and sped to Vernon Barnes's home.

Pounding on the police officer's door, Smith shouted, "Vernon, you have to come right now. Hork and Larry have found a dead girl in Hork's house!"

"What?" Barnes demanded.

"A dead girl," he repeated. "It looks like she shot herself."

The officer rushed back to Hork Smith's house. He walked down the hallway to the master bedroom. There, lying on her back with her arms spread out, was the dead girl. In her right hand was a black pearl-handled .22-caliber revolver.

Barnes leaned over to look at the body. He found two gunshot wounds in the back of her right ear. The wound on her neck was not caused by a gunshot, he realized.

"This is no suicide," Barnes said. "This is murder."

The officer saw dried bloodstains on the carpet leading to the bedroom.

"She was dragged in here," he said.

The officer turned to Hork. The man had assured him just two hours ago that everything was all right at his house.

"I didn't do this," Hork protested.

"Who is she?" Barnes asked.

"Her name is Cynthia Baillie," Hork responded. "They call her Cindy. She lives in Tahlequah. She came here this morning with Nadine and my boy, Greg. They were here when you came before but she was alive then."

Barnes knew he was going to need help. He called the Sequoyah County Sheriff's office and the Oklahoma State Bureau of Investigation.

Sheriff San Lockhart was the first to appear on the scene. Then came OSBI Agents Perry Proctor and Kevin Ottwell and Assistant District Attorney Michael Daffin.

The sheriff immediately corralled all of the witnesses. He took them down to the sheriff's office in Sallisaw for questioning. Proctor and Ottwell began the crime scene investigation.

"There's a bloodstain on the living room floor," an officer found. "It looks like someone tried to clean it up."

In the living room, the officer found a single bullet hole in the recliner.

Outside the back door, the detectives found a plastic trash bag stuffed inside another bag. Also in the bag was a bloody towel. The towel obviously had been used to clean up the blood in the living room.

In the bedroom, the officers found a woman's white and

orange striped tank-top blouse smeared with blood. Whoever wore the blouse was obviously standing very near the victim when she was shot.

Dr. Mohammed Merchant, the state forensic pathologist, found that Cindy had been shot eight times—once in the back, twice in the head, and five times in the left breast. He also found a stablike wound in the throat that had been thrust upward and exited in the mouth, cutting the tongue.

At the sheriff's office, Superintendent Smith and Ringgold were telling their story to the sheriff.

Relating the experience of their first trip to Hork Smith's house, the superintendent said, "Greg Smith was over there this morning. We heard quarreling, and one of the voices belonged to Nadine Smith."

Bonnie Ringgold told the authorities, "Robin Smith came over about nine or nine-thirty, and she was upset. She said, 'Nadine is at the house and they're going to kill that girl.'"

At 1:30 P.M., a statewide all-points bulletin was put out for the three people in the copper-colored Cadillac—Nadine Smith, her son, Greg, and Teresa Baker.

Assistant D.A. Daffin knew Nadine Smith. She wasn't the type to stay out of trouble very long. At the Tahlequah Police Department, they agreed.

"I've never in my life seen so many grown men afraid of one woman," Daffin commented.

Then at 3 P.M., just a few blocks from the campus of Northeastern State University in Tahlequah, Officer Albert Penson spotted the Cadillac in front of a rundown house that was the residence of Nadine Smith. He called for backup, and Oklahoma Highway Patrol troopers Loy Lee and K. H. Buchanan responded immediately. Then they surprised Nadine and Greg Smith inside. They offered no resistance.

"What's going on here?" Nadine, who obviously had been drinking, asked belligerently.

Told they were being taken to the sheriff's office in Sallisaw for questioning about the death of Cindy Baillie in

Gans that morning, she retorted, "We don't know what you're talking about. We haven't even been in Gans."

At the sheriff's office, Nadine and Greg were arrogant. They were abusive to Daffin, Sheriff Lockhart, and Agent Ottwell. But Teresa Baker seemed frightened. She didn't utter a word.

The authorities cut off questioning the Smiths. They took them back into holding cells at the county jail. Then they turned to Teresa. Within minutes the girl was in tears. And she told them the horrifying story of what had happened that Fourth of July—a holiday that she would never forget.

Teresa Baker agreed to turn state's witness in exchange for immunity from prosecution. She would get on the witness stand and tell the whole grisly story. The Sequoyah County Grand Jury indicted Nadine and Greg Smith for the first-degree murder of Cynthia Lee Baillie.

The Smiths were innocent until proven guilty, and Nadine decided their best chance was to shift the blame to Teresa, the state's star witness. She wrote a note to her son spelling out the plan. The authorities intercepted it.

"Read this over and over till you learn what to say," she told her son. "Don't let anyone see you with it. Flush down stool when finished. Throw away.

"Teresa put gun in Cindi's hand. Me and you never touched gun. Teresa pulled Cindi in bedroom. I did not step on her throat. Teresa did if we are asked.

"You have got to say that me and you heard two or three shots, ran out in the hall. Cindi was in her chair holding knife. Teresa was standing beside her with gun.

"We did not help clean up blood. Don't know where gun came from. I did not once have gun.

"Teresa and Cindi were fussing. Teresa had been taking pills and drinking beer. I did not try to choke her coming from Gore.

"Teresa was very jealous of you. I was never fussing with no one. Teresa asked Cindi to go to Gans with us."

Daffin knew he had to produce enough evidence to

convince a jury that the Smiths' defense was all an act. The gun was a good place to start.

OSBI Agent Proctor started tracking down the ownership of the murder weapon. At a Tahlequah pawnshop, he was startled to learn that the victim had bought the gun a few weeks earlier.

But a friend of Cindy's told the officer that she had loaned the gun to Greg Smith in June and he had refused to return it to her.

Then the crime laboratory experts got to work.

First, they found that Cindy Baillie had died from gunshot wounds inflicted by the .22-caliber revolver found in her hand. Then they found hair specimens recovered from the body and the bloody orange and white blouse belonging to Nadine Smith.

OSBI chemist Kenneth Ead added the finishing touch. By using a series of elaborate experiments, he found that the bloodstains on the blouse matched the precise angles of the bullet wounds in the body. When a bullet hits a body, blood, flesh, and body fluid spurt from the point of impact toward the direction of the gun that fired the bullet.

"Nadine either killed Cindy or someone had to stand directly behind Nadine and reach around her to do the shooting," Daffin explained.

On December 18, 1982, Nadine Smith was convicted of first-degree murder in the death of Cynthia Lee Baillie. At a trial to determine the penalty, sobbing members of the Smith family flocked to the courthouse, concerned about what would happen to Nadine.

Daffin demanded the death penalty.

"Nadine Smith deserves no mercy," Daffin told the jury. "The murder for which she has been convicted was heinous, atrocious, and cruel. Nadine Smith showed no human compassion for the pleas of the frightened girl she tortured and then gunned down.

"There have been many tears shed during the trial," he continued, "but no one cries for Cindy."

The jury recommended the death penalty.

On December 29, 1982, Sequoyah County District Judge Bill Ed Rogers sentenced Lois Nadine Smith to die by lethal injection for the murder of Cynthia Lee Baillie.

On June 13, 1983, James Gregory Smith was convicted in the same death. Although Daffin again recommended the death penalty, the jury returned a sentence of life in prison.

James "Hork" Smith was charged with being an accessory to murder. By publication time, his case had yet to be brought to trial.

Chapter 12

Andrea "Felice" Hicks Jackson

IT WAS A COOL EVENING that night of May 16, 1983, in Jacksonville, Florida. Police Officer Gary Bevel was glad it was cool. The bulletproof vest that he had worn since joining the force could get awfully hot when it was warm.

And things were quiet in Jacksonville's Northwest Zone 1, where he was patrolling alone in his squad car. The area could get pretty rough. There were always reports that had to be investigated about unexplained gunshots in the middle of the night.

The Fraternal Order of Police Lodge was observing Police Memorial Day with special ceremonies tomorrow to recognize the thirty-three Jacksonville police officers who had died in the line of duty. Maybe I'll go, Bevel thought.

It was nearing midnight and all was quiet. That was good.

Jacksonville had been good to Gary Bevel since he and his family moved here from Darlington, South Carolina, in 1973.

Back then, Gary wanted to be a computer programmer. He enrolled in Massey Business College and got his degree in computer programming.

But office work wasn't for him. He was very athletic and he wanted something more physical. So on July 16, 1975, he went to work at the Duval County Jail as a corrections officer—the job they once called a jailer.

His supervisors liked him. He was conscientious about his work and he had a smile and a friendly hello for everyone. And he was the star of the corrections officers' softball team.

That was the time when Jacksonville was under tremendous pressure from the federal government to increase the number of minority officers on its police department.

Gary's supervisors asked him to make the switch to the streets. Not now, he told them.

They kept asking him to become a policeman.

Everyone wanted more black officers. Gary found it hard to keep turning people down.

Finally, after six years as a corrections officer, he decided to take them up on their offer.

In December 1981, Gary Bevel graduated from the Northeast Florida Criminal Justice Training and Education Center and became certified as a police officer.

A few days later, on December 30, 1981, Officer Eugene Simmons was shot and killed at his home by his girlfriend. Bevel was assigned to fill his job in Northwest Zone 1.

The young officer fitted in perfectly with the police department. It wasn't long before he had two commendations in his personnel record for excellent work in the arrests of felony suspects.

And he joined the sheriff's office's Magnum Force football team and instantly became its star tailback.

"He runs a legitimate 4.6-second forty-yard dash," his coach, Jacksonville attorney Fred Abbott, told friends. That's as fast as many pro football players.

"He is the best athlete on the team. He's the best thing that's happened to us," the smiling coach said.

Unfortunately, one of Abbott's cornerbacks—Tom Szafranski—had been killed in the line of duty three years earlier.

Football wasn't the only sport where Bevel excelled. He starred on the sheriff's basketball team too.

And he always found time to play with the kids at the Arlington apartment complex where he lived with his mother and younger brother. Kickball, Frisbee—you name it.

He worked during his off-duty hours as a security officer at the apartments.

Andrea "Felice" Hicks Jackson had moved into the four-unit tan stucco apartment building at 3521 Boulevard with her husband, Sheldon Jackson, and their two sons, Sheldon, Jr., five, and Michael, three, just two months earlier.

She had tried to make a better life for herself and her family. She had gone to Florida Junior College and received a certificate of applied science in industrial electronics. She had even enrolled in an adult basic education class. She had a good job as an electrical technician now at the junior college.

But things had started going wrong for the twenty-five-year-old woman about three years ago when she began having problems with her husband and financial worries. That's when she started drinking.

Over the previous three years, she had been convicted on eight counts of writing worthless checks. She also was convicted for disorderly intoxication, making threats to a witness, and trespassing.

On top of all of her problems, she had to pay numerous fines and eventually served forty-five days in jail.

Felice Jackson didn't like jail. She hated jail. She never wanted to go there again.

But her problems didn't stop her from always dressing well and seeing her friends. Just a few days earlier—on Saturday night—she had fifty friends over for a barbecue.

Mrs. Renee Gardner, who lived with her husband and four-year-old son in the apartment beneath the Jacksons, was getting accustomed to her neighbors.

Felice Jackson was friendly and talkative when she was sober, but she was violent when she had too much to drink, which was pretty often.

"There was a fight up there every other day," Mrs.

Gardner said. "It happened so often that I just stopped listening to it. She usually lost the fights and got beat up.

"When she was drunk, she hated white people," Mrs. Gardner, who is white, said. "She made nasty remarks about me."

On this particular night, Felice Jackson wasn't happy.

"She kept going in and out of her apartment and breaking things," Mrs. Gardner recalled.

She went into the street and tried to start her 1973 Buick. It wouldn't start.

Fuming, she smashed out the windshield and rear window.

Then, having second thoughts, she decided to call the police and tell them someone had vandalized her car. That way, the insurance company would have to pay for it.

Officer Bevel received a call on the police radio at 11 P.M. Go to Twenty-sixth Street and Boulevard and investigate a car that had been vandalized, the twenty-nine-year-old officer was told.

At last, a little something to break the boredom, he thought.

He pulled into Boulevard and spotted the car. He stopped and got out of his patrol car. As he approached the old car, a woman dressed in jeans and a striped blouse approached him.

"It's my car," Felice Jackson told the officer.

"Did you do this?" Bevel asked.

"Why would I do this to my own car?" she replied.

"Let me see your car registration," the officer told her.

"I've got it in my apartment. I'll go get it for you," she replied, and left for the apartment.

Anna Allen was visiting her parents at 447 West Twenty-sixth Street and she had seen the whole incident.

She was one of five persons who saw Felice Jackson try to start her car and then smash the windows while she cursed and yelled.

After the woman left to go to her apartment, Anna went out and told the officer what had really happened.

That does it, the officer thought. He got on his police radio and called for a wrecker. The wrecker arrived, hooked up the car, and left with it.

I'm going to have to arrest her, Bevel concluded. He didn't like this kind of situation. Police procedure called for you to make a pat search for weapons of prisoners, but it also prohibited officers from patting down suspects of the opposite sex.

I'll have to have a good reason to search her, and she could make things tough on me if she files a complaint, he thought.

Finally the woman returned with her car registration, saw the car gone, and charged, "I want to know where you sent my goddamn car."

"I'm placing you under arrest for making a false police report," Bevel responded.

That's when the woman lunged out at the officer.

"She struck him. She was hitting him in the chest," Ms. Allen recalled.

Bevel grabbed the woman and pushed her into the back seat on the driver's side of the patrol car.

"Why are you doing this?" she roared. "Why are you manhandling me?"

She was now in the car and his head and shoulders were in the car to make sure she would stay there.

"Wait a minute, you made me drop my damn keys," she said.

Bevel backed up, still leaning down to look for the keys.

Then there were shots. The woman had pulled a .22-caliber revolver from her jeans and shot him in the forehead. Then she shot him twice more in the face, once in the shoulder, and once in the back.

Gary Bevel's bulletproof vest couldn't save him.

"I knew the man was going to die," said Mrs. Gardner,

who saw the officer lying in the street, blood gushing from the bullet wounds.

"He was in agony. He was mumbling something.

"When the ambulance left, they didn't turn on the siren."

Neighbors called the police. It was 12:38 A.M., May 17, 1983—Police Memorial Day—and Officer Gary Bevel had become the thirty-fourth Jacksonville policeman killed in the line of duty.

Felice Jackson fled the scene. She went to the home of her friend, Shirley Ann Freeman, at 9620 Priory Avenue.

Shirley was shocked. Her friend was visibly upset and her clothes were soaked with blood.

"I shot a cop," Felice told her disbelieving friend.

"He was going to take me down to the jail. I'm not going back to jail."

Then she added, "I hate men. I don't like men to touch me, especially police officers. That's why I shot him."

She picked up the telephone and called the nearest hospital.

"There was a policeman shot near where I live. Could you tell me how he's doing?" she asked.

"He's dead," came the reply. She became even more shaken. She could feel the policeman's blood cool and clammy against her skin.

"He's dead," she was told. She became even more shaken.

"I need a drink," Felice told her friend. Shirley fixed vodka drinks for both of them.

"Let me wash the blood off your clothes," Shirley Ann Freeman told her. While the clothes were washed and dried, they had a few more drinks. Then at 4:30 A.M., Felice called a Checker Cab.

It's always dangerous driving a cab at night, twenty-seven-year-old Carl Lee, Jr., thought. It doesn't pay to take chances.

When he picked up the woman at 9620 Priory Avenue, she got in the front seat and asked to go to the south side.

But he had driven only a few blocks when she asked to be taken to the downtown Greyhound bus station.

"I don't think it would be in your best interest to go to the bus station at this hour," Lee told her. "It could be dangerous."

He couldn't change her mind.

As he got closer to downtown, he decided to try to convince her again but found she had fallen asleep.

Lee pulled the taxi off on the side of the road. He shook her twice and called her before she awakened.

She opened her eyes, reached her right hand into the front of her jeans, and pulled out the revolver.

Lee grabbed her right hand. They struggled. The gun fell to the floor.

Still holding her, the taxi driver reached for his two-way radio and called the dispatcher for help.

"You're going to have to pay the fare," he told the woman while waiting for help to arrive. She reached into her pocket and pulled out a $10 bill. He gave her $2 in change.

I've got to find that gun, he thought. If she finds it, she'll shoot me. He fumbled around on the floor. His fingers touched cold metal. Lee grabbed the gun and quickly threw it out the window.

Suddenly the woman broke from his grip. The right front door of the cab flew open and she darted out. Before Lee knew what had happened, the woman had dashed around the taxi, spotted the gun on the side of the road, and lunged for it.

The panic-stricken cabbie quickly turned on the ignition and stepped on the starter. He put the car into gear and started to drive away.

The woman had the gun now. She pointed it straight at him through the windshield and fired twice. The windshield shattered. The scared cabbie fled in terror. He couldn't believe it. The bullets from the small .22-caliber revolver had not penetrated the windshield. He had been lucky.

"I never had a gun fired at me before," Lee later told a

jury. "It's worse than a leaf on a tree. You just shake. I was convinced she wanted to kill me."

About twenty minutes later, Felice Jackson had returned home to 3521 Boulevard.

Shortly after the shooting, police arrived at the scene and started a house-to-house search for the killer.

Mrs. Gardner and her husband, Jerry, were ordered out of bed and ushered outside while police searched for Mrs. Jackson. Her sleeping four-year-old son, Brian, was allowed to sleep through the search.

A couple who lived in one of the apartments was not home. Another couple was allowed to stay in the apartment because the man was an invalid.

The police found no one in the Jackson apartment.

At dawn the police returned. Her husband, Sheldon, told police she was not back yet.

But the officers insisted on searching the apartment. They found the killer lying on the porch beside a clothes hamper.

As the police tried to arrest the woman, her husband started fighting with them. Both were arrested. He was charged with aiding an escapee and being an accessory after the fact to murder. She was charged with the first-degree murder of Officer Bevel and the attempted murder of Carl Lee, Jr.

Jacksonville was up in arms at the brutal killing of one of its eighty-two black policemen.

"Who will play kickball with the kids in the courtyard now that Gary is dead?" asked the neighbors of the slain officer.

"All the children around here loved him so much," Yvonne Creswell at the large Arlington apartment complex told a reporter for the *Jacksonville Journal*.

"He would let them play in his police car, talk on the loudspeaker. He'd play with them in the courtyard. Kickball, Frisbee, whatever they were playing, he'd be there with them."

Barbara Rosenkranz was the resident manager of the

Arlington apartment complex where the officer lived and worked on his off-duty hours.

"There was none finer than Gary in my book," she said. "He was part of our little family around here.

"He took the time to talk to the high school kids who drove through and gave us trouble. He knew who the problem tenants were and how to talk to them.

"He took an interest in the kids. He loved to play with the children. Having him here gave us security."

Gary had just talked to Mrs. Rosenkranz about getting a weekend off to visit his relatives in South Carolina. Now his relatives would be coming to Jacksonville instead.

Mrs. Rosenkranz told Gary's mother, Etta, that the relatives coming for the funeral could stay in the model apartment at the complex.

Mrs. Rosenkranz pondered, "I just can't understand why a fine young man like Gary has to lose his life because he can't protect himself by searching a woman."

Bevel's fellow officers felt frustrated—particularly about the policy on searching members of the opposite sex. Maybe, just maybe, a clearer policy would have saved the young officer's life.

"But I don't think Bevel even reached the search stage," police information officer Scott McLeod told a reporter.

"From what we have been able to reconstruct, he was trying to contain her when a scuffle ensued during the arrest and he pushed her in the back seat of the patrol car.

"Ideally, you would search someone prior to putting her in the back seat, but when things happen quickly like that, you do what you have to do," the police spokesman said.

At the police building, the entrance was draped in black bunting, the flag was at half mast, flowers lay at the base of the flagpole.

"The morale always goes down when something like this happens," Lieutenant D. B. Anderson reflected. He was the supervisor of the Northwest Zone 1 where Bevel met his death.

"But something like this you always have to be ready for."

Word had gotten around the other 892 officers on the force that one of their comrades was dead.

Officer Rick Lewis was on duty when word came over the radio that a fellow officer had been shot. He and Gary had worked together as corrections officers, played on the softball team together, and both made the switch to the streets.

"I just had the feeling it was Gary," Lewis said. "I can't explain it.

"He was a real easygoing guy. He always had a smile. Everybody who met him liked him. It bothers the hell out of me."

Officer William Kearney, class liaison officer at the academy, frowned and said, "Right now I feel rotten. I'm just sitting around feeling really terrible and wondering what it's all about."

On November 2, 1983, Andrea "Felice" Hicks Jackson went on trial for the attempted murder of Carl Lee, Jr. The trial for her murder of Officer Gary Bevel was set for November 29.

Assistant State Attorney Brad Stetson was frustrated. Under the law, he wasn't allowed to tell the jury that the incident had occurred after the woman had killed a police officer.

"We were trying the case in a vacuum," Stetson complained afterward.

William White, the chief assistant public defender, said the woman fired at the cabbie in self-defense.

She believed, White told the jury, that Lee was trying to attack her when he awakened her after she had fallen asleep in the taxicab. She had no intention of killing him when she fired two shots from the same revolver that had killed the officer only hours before, the public defender contended.

"In her own mind, she believed she was the victim," he

asserted. Felice Jackson did not take the stand to testify in her own behalf.

In the end, the jury believed her attorney. They found her not guilty of the attempted murder of Lee.

In his opening remarks to the jury, White said it was a "confused, frightened woman" who shot Bevel to death.

As Bevel's parents and relatives listened from the front row, the defense attorney told the twelve jurors, "She acted out of fear, out of frustration. It was hot- rather than cold-blooded. This was not a cold, calculated act.

"The bottom line is this is not murder in the first degree," the defense attorney contended.

Hogwash, thought State Attorney Ed Austin.

In front of the jurors, he charged, "She didn't have hot blood. She had an evil, diabolical state of mind. There wasn't anything passionate about her state of mind."

On December 1, after three days of testimony, the jury reached a verdict.

Felice Jackson was brought into the courtroom. She stood silently in front of Circuit Judge Donald Moran. She looked straight ahead, her face expressionless, her cold, sweating hands clasped.

In the front row where they had sat through the three days of the trial, the Bevel family leaned forward to hear the jury's verdict.

Then the verdict hit the courtroom like a shot out of the revolver that killed Officer Bevel. Guilty of murder in the first degree!

It had taken the jury less than two hours to reach its verdict.

Bevel's parents and relatives smiled and patted each other on the back.

"I'm a little bit more relieved," Jesse Bevel, the officer's father, said. "I don't have any hatred in my heart."

His twenty-five-year-old brother, Nathaniel Bevel, commented, "I'll be happy if she just gets put away for a while and doesn't get back out on the streets."

Assistant State Attorney Stetson, who had seen the woman go free for the attempted murder of Carl Lee, breathed a sigh of relief when the jury of five men and seven women brought in their guilty verdict.

"I think justice has been served—up to this point," he said. The next step, Stetson knew, was to demand the death penalty.

On December 7, in the second stage of the first-degree murder trial, the jury voted 9–3 for the death penalty.

"I think the jury showed by their verdict that they cared about the officer who was gunned down," Stetson commented. "She killed the point man of society. I think they naturally gave some weight to that."

He added, "She's just a bitch. We learned she got in a fight with another officer two years before and threatened to do him bodily harm. She doesn't have a lot of respect for law and order."

On February 10 Judge Moran sentenced Andrea Felice Hicks Jackson to die in Florida's electric chair.

Andrea Jackson is the seventh woman sentenced to die in Florida's electric chair since electrocution became the final punishment in the state in 1924. All of the other women had their death sentences commuted.

The last woman to be sentenced to death in Florida was Sonia Jacobs, who was thirty-five when she and her boyfriend, Jessie Tafero, shot and killed Florida Highway Patrol trooper Phillip Black and Donald Irwin, a Canadian constable in Florida on vacation in 1976.

The pair shot and killed the officers as they were making a routine check of a parked car on interstate 95 just north of Fort Lauderdale.

Both were sentenced to death.

Tafero is still on Florida's death row, but the Florida Supreme Court overturned Miss Jacobs' conviction on March 26, 1981. She is still serving time in the Broward Correctional Institution.

Another inmate at Broward is Marie Dean Arrington,

who escaped the electric chair when the U.S. Supreme
Court struck down the death penalty in 1972. Her sentence
was commuted to life in prison.

Mrs. Arrington, who was fifty when she was sentenced to
death on December 6, 1968, murdered June Ritter, secretary
of the Lake County public defender. She was out on an
appeal bond for her manslaughter conviction in the death of
her husband when she went seeking revenge against the
public defender who had unsuccessfully defended two of
her children on felony charges.

She became only the second woman ever named to the
FBI's Ten Most Wanted list since its inception and was
captured two years later.

One of the most famous cases involving the death penalty
of a woman in Florida took place in Live Oak in 1952.

Ruby McCollum, the wife of an alleged gambling
kingpin in Suwannee County, shot and killed Dr. C. L.
Adams, a newly elected state senator, in his office in a
squabble that was supposed to be over a medical bill.

But author William Bradford Huie wrote a sensational
book four years later which alleged that Dr. Adams had
fathered one of Ruby McCollum's children.

She spent two years in prison under sentence of death
before the Florida Supreme Court reversed the sentence.
She was then committed to the state mental hospital in
Chattahoochee before retrial and remained there for twenty
years before being released to her family and placed in a
home near Silver Springs. She is now seventy-four.

Irene Laverne Jackson, along with her son and another
man, was sentenced to death in Pasco County in 1962 for
murdering her husband, Johnnie, for insurance money. But
the courts reduced her sentence. She was paroled in 1972
and discharged from the supervision of the prison system in
1980.

BLOCKBUSTER FICTION FROM PINNACLE BOOKS!

THE FINAL VOYAGE OF THE S.S.N. SKATE   (17-157, $3.95)
by Stephen Cassell
The "leper" of the U.S. Pacific Fleet, SSN 578 nuclear attack sub
SKATE, has one final mission to perform — an impossible act of
piracy that will pit the underwater deathtrap and its inexperienced
crew against the combined might of the Soviet Navy's finest!

QUEENS GATE RECKONING   (17-164, $3.95)
by Lewis Purdue
Only a wounded CIA operative and a defecting Soviet ballerina
stand in the way of a vast consortium of treason that speeds toward the hour of mankind's ultimate reckoning! From the best-
selling author of THE LINZ TESTAMENT.

FAREWELL TO RUSSIA   (17-165, $4.50)
by Richard Hugo
A KGB agent must race against time to infiltrate the confines of
U.S. nuclear technology after a terrifying accident threatens to
unleash unmitigated devastation!

THE NICODEMUS CODE   (17-133, $3.95)
by Graham N. Smith and Donna Smith
A two-thousand-year-old parchment has been unearthed, un-
leashing a terrifying conspiracy unlike any the world has previ-
ously known, one that threatens the life of the Pope himself, and
the ultimate destruction of Christianity!

*Available wherever paperbacks are sold, or order direct from the
Publisher. Send cover price plus 50¢ per copy for mailing and
handling to Pinnacle Books, Dept.17-249, 475 Park Avenue
South, New York, N.Y. 10016. Residents of New York, New Jer-
sey and Pennsylvania must include sales tax. DO NOT SEND
CASH.*

THE BEST IN BONE CHILLING TERROR
FROM PINNACLE BOOKS!

Blood-curdling new blockbusters by horror's premier masters of the macabre! Heart-stopping tales of terror by the most exciting new names in fright fiction! Pinnacle's the place where sensational shivers live!